Spring in CRANBERRY Harbor

Book 2 in the Cranberry Harbor Series

CANDACE HAMMOND

Sea Crow Press

ALSO BY CANDACE HAMMOND

Christmas in Cranberry Harbor

Spring in Cranberry Harbor
Published 2025 by Sea Crow Press
Barnstable, MA

www.seacrowpress.com

First Edition

Paperback ISBN: 978-1961864269
Ebook ISBN: 978-1961864276
Library of Congress Control Number: 2024949888

www.seacrowpress.com

To my amazing, creative, eclectic, big, blended family. I love all of you so much. To Frank, for always lifting the heavy things, both metaphorical and real. And to my beloved Cape Cod community, the place that means home to me, and keeps on inspiring me in ever-surprising ways.

Spring in CRANBERRY Harbor

CHAPTER 1

IN THE YEAR since Lizzie had partnered with her father, becoming co-editor and co-owner of the Cranberry Harbor Gazette, the subscription base had tripled, and their followers on social media, which hadn't existed before she came on board, had hit 50,000 followers. Not bad for one year. However, getting followers on Facebook, X and Instagram was one thing, getting Peter Martin to actually post on them was another.

"Dad, you can reach so many people right at the moment when you're sitting at Town Meeting or while you're on-site at a new project, by sending out a tweet or posting a photo on Instagram, it's super easy!" was a daily refrain heard across their partner's desk.

"I know, I know," Peter would always say, "I just get caught up in the moment, taking my notes, and I don't think. I'm old school, yo," he joked. Lizzie shoots him a curious look. Yo? She shakes her head and laughs.

She could never get really upset with her dad; he was the most endearing and wonderful man in the world. She just wanted the paper, which thanks to their angel investors was on solid financial ground, to be all it could be. There was a lot happening in Cranberry Harbor these days, and the rest of the country, actually the world, was taking notice.

Lizzie yawns and stretches, "I'm supposed to meet Jack, Sean, and Ben at Sea Coast for a late afternoon tea, you good if I skip out a little early?" It was a question that didn't really require an answer, but out of respect, she wanted to ask.

"Of course not, honey, you go on ahead, I'm just tweaking a story about those two young women who took over the old five and dime with an artist's co-op," he says, a little distracted.

Lizzie laughs, "Dad, it hasn't been the 'five and dime' since before I was born, it was last an appliance store." She slips her coat on. It may be nearing spring, but the Cape is notorious for seducing you into thinking it's already here, then watch out - some heavy snow squalls knock any hope of spring right out of you. March was the cruelest of months. A total tease.

"Uh-huh," he says, distractedly, "whatever you say."

"I'll see you later. Everything is all set to go on my end, as soon as you send that in we're good for this week's edition." She's aware he's not really paying attention. "Snuffleupagus!" she calls, as she heads out the door, just to see if he is listening at all.

"Yup, you too!" he calls back, and Lizzie laughs as she heads out the door to the coffee shop.

The days were starting to get a little bit longer, but Lizzie pulled her coat around herself a little tighter, bracing herself against the stinging, damp cold, because... Cape Cod spring. There were small signs of hope; the witch hazel tree next to the gazebo, always the first to flower, was in full bloom, a wonderful harbinger of yellow blooms, but other than that, everything was still looking pretty... brown.

"There you are!" Jack jumps up and gives her a kiss. He helps her off with her coat and places it on the back of her chair. "Sean texted me that they are running late. Baby issues. What would you like, sweetie? Cocoa? Chai? Decaf?"

"I am still officially in my post-Christmas cocoa detox. I swear between the cookies and cocoa around here at Christmas it's like living at Santa's Workshop!" She looks over at the tea menu board, even though she sees it every day, and notices it's been newly updated and beautifully illustrated by one of the new baristas. "Hmm, maybe a decaf green tea with one squeeze of honey, please?" She smiles up at him, and he leans in and kisses her again.

"For you? Anything. Be right back."

Even after having been back together for a year, her heart still catches sometimes at how this almost didn't happen. There but for the grace of lots of circumstances, and some good old-fashioned Cranberry Harbor Christmas magic, they could have stayed apart forever. He could have stayed in California having his big tech career, and well, she's not sure where she would have gone. After having been laid off by the Boston Sentinel, chances are she'd be here, alone. She always made sure to never take the serendipity that brought them back together for granted because she knew things could have turned out very differently. Being back with Jack, and being back home were not where she'd seen herself ending up, but as she sits back, taking in for the millionth time, the coziness and warmth of this place, the familiar faces, the well-worn path to the counter, all the local art, she feels happy.

Just as Jack arrives at the table with Lizzie's tea, Sean and Ben, along with baby Ollie, come in, carrying enough baby paraphernalia to stay for a week. They place the car seat holding the sleeping baby on the floor between their seats, along with a red, hand-woven bag of toys, bottles, and diapers, and then they both collapse in their chairs. They both have circles under their eyes, and look completely exhausted.

Until a few months ago they had been fostering a brother and sister, who were three and five, throughout much of the last year, but they had recently gone back to live with their mother. They'd been in the beginning stages of adopting Mia and Matt and had been devastated when it fell through. They were of course happy the kids were reunited with their mom who had turned her life around, but they had truly loved them and had planned to be a forever family. They'd been scared to foster again not wanting that disappointment, but Ollie came along, and he was available for adoption, so they decided to take a leap of faith. Jack and Lizzie were his godparents and they adored him.

"Hey! The boys have arrived!" Jack says putting Lizzie's tea on the table. "What do you guys want - I'm up already, let me grab it."

"Coffee!" they both say at the same time. They all laugh. "We are so exhausted, just bring us the whole carafe," Ben says. Jack goes back to the counter to get their order.

"I'm so sorry, guys, short night?" Lizzie asks, looking at their tired faces and uncombed hair.

"We try to take shifts," Sean says, "but just the act of getting up, getting him out of his bassinet and everything wakes the other one up, so we're just all up through the night."

Lizzie knew nothing about babies really. She'd taken care of her niece, Sophie, here and there, but she'd been a baby when Lizzie was living in Boston, so she was pretty unfamiliar with being kept up all night by an infant.

Jack was back in no time, "Cream no sugar, for you, Ben, and milk with two sugars for you, Sean? I think I got that right."

"You can certainly tell we've spent a lot of time together here," Sean laughs. And then switches the coffees between the two of them.

"Ah! So close!" Jack laughs. "So, short night, huh?"

Ben yawns and leans back in his chair. "I don't think I've ever existed on so little sleep in my life. I thought our hours in the summer with the inn were crazy, but boy, this little guy," he looks down at Ollie in his fleece overalls, and green knit cap and smiles, "it's a whole other level of sleep deprivation, and yet somehow we don't really mind."

"I just keep wondering how we're going to do this in the summer season, that's what freaks me out," adds Sean.

"Can you hire a nanny for the summer?" asks Jack. "Someone who can live in and be flexible? I'm betting there's someone who'd love to get to live at the Marshview and work with you."

"Well, it just so happens that Sean's cousin is getting her Master's in early childhood education and we're talking to her about coming to Cranberry Harbor for the summer, so finger's crossed that works out," says Ben.

"I feel so lazy listening to you two," Lizzie says.

"What? You work all the time," Jack says, incredulous. "You almost never take a day off. You bring work home, work weekends..."

"Yeah, seriously, Lizzie, you are the hardest working person I know, well, except for that guy," Sean points to Jack. "Between the two of you, it is all work all the time. Do you ever get out and have fun? Could you, please? For us to live vicariously through you?" Sean teases.

"It has been a minute, that is for sure," Lizzie says. "My dad's been after me to take a vacation, or at least a weekend away. The last time we went to Boston was to pack up my apartment, so that wasn't exactly relaxing," she looks at Jack, "We definitely need to take a weekend away someplace."

"Okay, we will try to make that happen," he winces. "Though I do have three zoning board meetings to prepare for, meetings with the wastewater team and applications to get to for people applying for spots to live or farm in the neighborhood, which still does not have a name by the way." He rubs his forehead. "I don't want to be, but I'm really worried about the final approvals coming through. There are a couple of tough folks on the planning board that I'm worried could go either way."

"You haven't said that before," Lizzie says, concerned. "My dad's been going to all the meetings and he hasn't said anything."

"This is all under the radar, don't say anything," Jack says looking at everyone. "The idea for the project is really popular–an eco-friendly, off-the-grid community, a blending artists and farmers–so those who aren't for it are scared to say anything publicly, but there are a couple of hard-core, old-timers who don't ever want anything to change in Cranberry Harbor. Those who think, 'if it ain't broke don't fix it.'"

"But so much isn't working," interjects Ben. "Housing, jobs? How can they not see it? There's a lot that's broken."

"It will pass, Jack, you've gotten too far for it not to," Lizzie says, reassuringly putting her hand on Jack's arm. "And when it goes to the Town Meeting, everyone will vote for it." Even as she says this she's not one-hundred percent sure herself. She's heard the rumblings around town, she knows there are people who look at the town as a Norman Rockwell painting, not as a living and breathing community in need of changing and evolving with the times. "I think we should do another story the week before the Town Meeting about it, and have Stan interview you. Dad and I are too close to the story, but Stan would be able to be more objective. We'll get all the final approvals." She smiles that smile that Jack knows so well, the one that says, 'I've got this, don't worry,' and she's almost always right.

Jack feels himself choking up, so clears his throat and changes the subject. "So seriously, you all have to help me come up with a name for this community that has farmers and techies, animals and artists."

"Eco-Village at Cranberry Harbor?" Sean says, yawning. "Ack, no, that's sleep deprivation talking, that's a completely lame name."

"Well, I wasn't going to say anything, but yeah, rather than a farming and arts and tech community that sounds like a condo community, though 'Lame Name' has sort of a nice ring to it," Jack says, and they all laugh.

"I am so sorry, my creative brain is permanently gone I fear. Maybe when Ollie is in middle school it will come back. But then it will leave again when I am wracked with worry when he starts driving," Sean says.

"I think parenthood just forever changes your brain and how you think," Ben adds. "Seriously, I was in the grocery store in the oral care aisle a couple of days ago and found myself explaining to a young guy, just there buying toothpaste mind you, the importance of flossing. I do not know who I am."

Lizzie and Jack can't stop laughing. "You two are a cautionary tale for all we millennials," Jack says, through tears of laughter. "I used to consider you guys super cool, next up will be dad jeans and dad jokes."

"I think it's kind of a rule that when you become parents you are officially no longer cool," Lizzie teases, "but, and there is a but here, if anyone can undo that perception it's you two. Give yourselves a break, Ollie is still itty bitty and you're just getting settled in. No one can be at their best on as little sleep as you've been getting. You will rise from the depths of no sleep and will be once again the coolest guys in Cranberry Harbor."

Sean and Ben look at each other and laugh. "I think that bar is pretty low, Lizzie," Ben points to Jack.

"Hey!" Jack feigns offense. "I am totally cool!" Even he can't keep a straight face as he looks down at his brown sweater, khakis and brown loafers. "Fine, I will always be the nerdy tech guy I was in eleventh grade. But, nerds make the cool things cool people use, so that should count for something."

"Yes, without folks like you I would not have an app to remind me of how I haven't run in three weeks, thanks!" Ben jokes.

"I know you're tired and things are hard right now, but I am so grateful that we're all here, that we're all living in Cranberry Harbor again and," Lizzie shakes her head, embarrassed. "I know I'm gushing, but about once a day I still find myself shocked that this is my life. I never, ever wanted to come back here, and now I can't imagine being anywhere else, with anyone else," she takes Jack's hand. "I know, I'm such a sap!" She shakes her head, and sits back with her cup of tea. "Feel free to make fun of me, guys, I totally deserve it."

"I can't make fun of you because I cry at least once a day looking at this little guy," Ben says, pointing to Ollie, still sound asleep in his seat, his hat now jauntily tipped to the left. "I'm so grateful that you two came back, that we're friends, and I hope we have many, many years together making this town all it can be, and have lots of time hanging out like this."

"Hear! Hear!" Jack says, raising his cup. He looks over at Lizzie who is checking a text that just came in. "I am all in on making this a forever thing," he catches himself, thinking how that might land with Lizzie, "with *all* of us, I mean. To friendship, love and community," he says. They all touch cups, and Jack leans over and kisses Lizzie on the head. "Yeah," he says almost inaudibly, "forever has a nice ring to it.

"Huh?" Lizzie asks, distracted by a work issue. "Did you say something?"

"Nope," he says. "I'm just happy to be here with you, that's all."

She looks over at him and smiles, and goes back to work. Still smiling to herself.

CHAPTER 2

SINCE MOVING BACK to Cranberry Harbor Lizzie had found a group of a few good friends that made leaving Sarah back in Boston a little easier. It had been so hard at first to go from working right next to each other in their little newspaper cubicles to FaceTiming when they could, and texting at first daily, and now only a few times a week. Being so far from her best Boston friend, and giving up her apartment were the hardest things about moving back home. That, and the lack of pizza from the North End.

For now she was still living with her parents, which, once she got past the embarrassment of being in her thirties and living at home, was actually pretty sweet. Her parents were the chillest people around, and treated her like the adult she was. They all took turns making dinner or providing healthy take out, and Jack was over often as well. They were already very much family. Jack's parents had taken to traveling to warmer climes in the winter, so he often joined the Martin's for meals, sports events, they had even started a weekly movie night, and hosted a game night once a month. Things weren't exactly popping in Cranberry Harbor in the winter, so they made their own fun.

After leaving Sea Coast, Lizzie headed to yoga class at Lotus. She was now a regular, practicing at least three times a week, usually joined by Alexis and her sister-in-law Shannon, who was lucky enough to have Grabby, aka, Gabby, Lizzie and Matt's mom, to babysit Sophie. Sometimes Leah Alden, Sea Coast Coffee owner Hope's granddaughter came too. They were a group of young women who were committed to making changes in the community and were inspiring a whole new group of people to want to get involved with what was happening in Cranberry Harbor. And they were fun.

Lizzie and Alexis grabbed a space in the back corner of the class and rolled out their mats. Lizzie loved Tamara's classes because, well, for one thing she kept the temperature at a comfortable 71 degrees, and it was the perfect mix of flows, strength work and relaxation. She also diffused a very subtle blend of aromatic oils, and had sweet-smelling beeswax candles scattered throughout the room, so it felt tranquil and relaxing.

"I promise I will have my column for next week by the day after tomorrow," Alexis says, placing her props - two blocks, a strap and a bolster by her mat. "This is all still so new to me, I freak out every time there's one due," she places the bolster in the middle of her mat and sits down, crosses her legs and sighs. "And I know, for someone like you who has multiple stories in every issue that stressing over writing a single column once a month must seem ridiculous, but--"

Lizzie laughs, "Uh, do I get a say in how I feel about this, or should I just sit here and have you spell it out for me?" she smiles at her friend as she joins her, sitting down on her mat right next to hers. "'Cause I have no problem with you meeting your deadline, your content or anything really, but it seems you think I should. And we're supposed to be relaxing here, not stressing more about work! For the record? I love what you're doing and am grateful to have you in the Gazette. Stop beating yourself up. Not allowed!"

Alexis laughs, "Ugh, I know I sound crazy, right?" She shakes her head. "Yoga does not seem to be chilling me out too much, does it?" She laughs.

"Stop apologizing for your work," Lizzie says. "I love what you're doing and so do the readers. You are doing a great job helping build community with your column. Considering you had never written professionally until this, it's really remarkable. So stop making assumptions and just keep doing what you're doing, okay?" Lizzie puts her arm around her and gives her a hug.

Alexis takes a deep breath and lets it slowly out. "I will give it my very best, it's just you pay me well, and I want to do a good job." she says.

"And you are," Lizzie says, bending down to do some stretches and try to limber up.

Right before class is about to start Shannon and Leah come rushing in, and spying Lizzie and Alexis, quickly scoot over and roll out their mats next to them.

"Sorry I'm late - as usual," Shannon says, plopping down, looking pretty exhausted. "Sophie did not want me to go, which is so weird, she always loves being with your mom." She lies back on her mat and sighs. "Can I just lie here in savasana the whole time and you can jostle me when class is over?" she jokes to Lizzie, who laughs too.

"Hey, Tamara always says, 'do what feels good to you,' so yeah, go for it," Lizzie says.

The lights dim a little, and Tamara sits down on a bolster in the front of the room. She is one of those people who just exudes calm. Lizzie often wonders, was she born like that, or is it the yoga? If it's yoga, Lizzie wonders how many thousands of hours she will need to practice in order to achieve that Tamara-like chill.

"Everyone join me in a seat that is comfortable for you," she says in a voice that should be on a meditation app. "Let go of whatever you've brought to the mat today, and breathe it out." She closes her eyes and takes a deep breath in, and then lets it go. Lizzie does the same thing, but in her head she's thinking about the call she forgot to return to the goat cheese maker who wants to advertise in the Gazette, and then there's that story about the alpacas..."Stop!" she says quietly under her breath, but Alexis hears her and giggles a little.

After an hour of Vinyasa flows, downward facing dogs, childs' poses and planks, lying down in savasana, or corpse pose, feels well-earned. As she lies still on her mat, Lizzie finds herself thinking about Jack, the future, their future, and wonders if he thinks about it ever. After their broken engagement four years ago they've both been a little reluctant to talk about marriage yet. As she slows her breathing, feeling the warmth of the radiant floor heat, the scent of lavender wafting over from the diffuser, she feels calm and centered, which immediately makes her nervous. She smiles to herself. Only I can find a way to make feeling relaxed feel stressful, she thinks and then sighs.

"Oh my gosh, I needed that," Leah says as they all come back to reality. "I do not know what I would do without yoga in my life. And you three of course."

Leah was younger than all of them, just in her early 20s, but she was very mature, and having taken over more and more of the day to day responsibility of running Sea Coast, the family coffee shop from her grandmother, she was very much aligned with these three women who all had a good seven or eight years on her. Though they still liked to tease her about how young she was. On top of running Sea Coast, Lizzie had also tapped her as well to write a monthly column in the paper, this one centered on business. How local businesses could become more ecologically sustainable, use social media to build a year-round following, and what it is like being a Gen-Z'er living year-round on the Cape in a town where the median age was 65. She often lamented about the lack of dating opportunities, and Alexis assured her she wasn't alone. They often commiserate about how the year-round population was so small that when it came to the very small dating pool you'd either dated someone already or, if your family was historically old Cranberry Harbor, were related to them.

"Anyone want to go to Murphy's for some soup or something?" Leah asked the others as they all rolled up their mats and put back their yoga props.

"I can't," Lizzie said, feeling a bit guilty, "I promised my mom I'd help her with a project she's working on to get people out to vote for the high school improvement fund. I'm sorry." They walk out to the entry and Lizzie takes her coat off a hook and puts it on. "Rain check?" She pulls her hat on and braces herself for the cold.

"I have to hustle along too," says Shannon. "I need to have dinner with my family. It's been a crazy week and we've only had dinner together once." She puts her coat on too. "I feel like such a failure as a mom."

Lizzie looks over at her and Shannon looks like she's about to cry. "Oh my gosh, Shannon, you are one of the best moms I know!" Lizzie drops her mat and purse to the floor and hugs her. "You are doing an amazing job raising Sophie. She's confident, bright, curious and kind." She's hugging her and Shannon is sobbing a little. "And we know she did not get that way from my brother," she sensed a little levity might be helpful right then.

Shannon laughs, wipes her nose on her sleeve and nods. "Oh, yeah, that's all me!" She's smiling now, and looks at her friends. "Ugh, I am so sorry, guys, It's just sometimes it all gets to be a lot. I feel like a mombie." They all look at her quizzically. "A mom zombie," she quickly explains. "Since I'm now running all the children's programs at the library it's an awful lot."

"Don't you ever apologize for sharing your feelings with us, that's what friends are for! And none of us have kids, so you feel free to remind us of how easy our lives are, okay?" Alexis says. "And I am going to remember that word - I'm betting all mothers feel like Mombies at times."

Shannon nods. "Okay, I will be sure to do that." She takes a deep breath and lets it out slowly. "Okay, namaste ladies, I will see you next week." She looks at Lizzie, actually I'll see you in five minutes when I come pick up Sophie at your house."

"I'd love to go get something to eat, Leah," Alexis says, linking her arm through hers. "I think tonight is their awesome kale soup, and it's the perfect night for that."

As they spill out into the parking lot Lizzie can't help but think about what her own future holds. She's very glad to be out of the dating world, but wonders if and when she and Jack will take things to the next inevitable place, and if she will ever feel ready to become a mom. She watches Shannon and her brother Matt and cannot imagine balancing being co-editor of the Gazette and the senior reporter, with a baby. She gets in her car and starts it, fastens her seatbelt and sighs. She wasn't someone who just crossed a bridge before she got there, she was crossing it when she wasn't even in the county yet. For now she was just going to go home, help her mom make some signs or whatever she wanted her to do, and call her boyfriend when she was done to tell him she loved him, and that was enough for now.

CHAPTER 3

WHEN LIZZIE ARRIVED home Gabby was already hard at work making posters, sitting on the floor, surrounded by markers and poster board, while on a Zoom call with organizers across the Cape. Their regional school district was a sought-after system Cape-wide and the high school was in dire need of upgrading. It was actually the same campus where not just Lizzie, but also her parents had gone many years prior. Before moving home Lizzie would have made a donation and posted something nice and supportive on social media, but now that she was back home she felt more invested and wanted to really be of help.

Gabby puts her fingers to her lips to signal to Lizzie that she's not on mute, and she can see through to the living room that Sophie is asleep by the fireplace on the couch. She points to some soup simmering on the stove. Lizzie ladles herself a bowl of the yummy smelling lentil soup, tears off a piece of a whole wheat baguette, and sits down at the counter, out of camera view.

"Yes, I know we have to overcome that group of 'last ones over the bridge' people who don't want to pay for anything relating to kids because theirs are all grown up and why should they pay for schools they won't use?" Gabby says to the group, clearly irritated.

That was a phenomenon of the retiree community that the long-time year-round residents often had to contend with. The same when it came to affordable housing and jobs. What so many failed to see was that not everyone who lived in Cranberry Harbor could afford home prices inflated by lack of inventory and the abundance of desirability. The problem then became, how do you have a thriving community with no young adults, no children? And a place where the people a thriving community needs - police, firefighters, teachers, healthcare providers, and retail workers, can't afford to live? Lizzie had been writing about it practically weekly since moving back. She was a prime example - a young adult who grew up in Cranberry Harbor, had a fantastic education, even a Master's degree, who worked more than fulltime and could never afford to buy a house of her own in her hometown.

While Gabby is still on her call Shannon comes bustling in, and Lizzie quickly jumps up letting her know her daughter is sound asleep on the couch. Together they bundle her up in the blanket she's sleeping under, and Lizzie follows Shannon, carrying Sophie's coat and little backpack out to her car.

Lizzie is astonished that nothing is rousing her niece, not being carried into the cool night air, or being put in her car seat.

"I think this fatigue might explain her being upset with you leaving," Lizzie says, handing Shannon Sophie's belongings after she gently closes the backseat door.

Shannon opens her door and places the things inside. "Yeah, she woke up last night with a bad dream, hopefully tonight will be better." She gives Lizzie a hug. "Please tell your mom I said thank you." She gets in and closes the door, smiles and waves to Lizzie, who waves back, turning and heading back to the house.

Gabby's meeting has ended, and Lizzie sits down on the floor next to her. "Shannon said thank you, we got Sophie into the car - she never woke up, poor baby." She pauses and looks around at the pile of poster board and markers. "So, what do you need me to do? Do you need more 'Vote Yes!' signs or something else?" Her mom looks tired. "Have you taken a break since I saw you in town earlier? I think you need some soup and a glass of wine break."

Lizzie stands up and motions for her mom to do the same. Gabby groans a little as she gets up. "Dear lord, listen to me! I sound like an old lady!"

"Mom, you are hardly an old lady, and I would moan too if I'd been on that floor for hours." She points to a stool, "You, sit here."

She gets two wine glasses out of the cupboard and pours herself and her mom servings of a nice Merlot. "Start with this, and I'm getting you some of your delicious soup." Lizzie places the bowl of warm soup, a napkin and spoon in front of her. She brings over the bread and a little saucer of olive oil - the retired doctor's preference - no butter for her.

Gabby sighs. "Thank you, honey, I needed this." She takes a few spoonfuls and sits back with some bread. "I'm so worried this isn't going to pass. I just keep thinking of more people to call, to reach out to, I just can't."

"Mom, you can only do so much, you've done everything you can." She takes a sip of her wine. "There are a lot of us who want this town to be a place for everyone, and I think we're growing in numbers. Thanks to all the years of work you put in caring for everyone not just as the town doctor, but as its conscience as well." She smiles at her mom and raises her wine glass. "You have done an incredible job, you still are, but give yourself a break now and then and enjoy yourself, okay? You don't have to do it all," she gently clinks glasses with her mom. "There's more of us here than even a year ago, and I think the renovation is going to win," she laughs, "Okay, maybe only three or four of us have come back, but that's better than nothing!!"

Gabby, relaxing a bit, nods. "You're right. I can fight the fights I can, and then I have to let it go," she eats some more of the soup. "I did make an exceptional batch today if I do say so myself," she jokes. "So you really think we've got this?"

"I do. I wish I was as certain about Jack's project, but I'm pretty optimistic about that too," Lizzie says, finishing her wine.

"You are certainly your father's daughter," Gabby says, finishing her wine as well. "I love that."

"We're both good windmill tilters, that's for sure," she says smiling, and pouring them each a second glass. Lizzie is pensive as she sips her wine.

"Penny for your thoughts," her mom says, wondering where Lizzie has disappeared to. "Everything okay?"

"Yeah, sorry," she picks up a purple grape from a platter on the counter and pops it into her mouth. "Before yoga class I was with Jack, Ben and Sean, and baby Ollie of course, at Sea Coast," she says, "and Jack was so stressed out about what to name the project, and I've been wracking my brain, it's all about the ocean, and the land, and bringing them and people together, and nothing has sounded like anything more than a condo community. I want to help him and I feel frustrated."

"That is a hard one, when in doubt I go to the classics," Gabby says.

Lizzie laughs, "Like what, Jane Austen? I don't think calling it 'Pemberley' would work."

Gabby laughs too, "No silly, the *real* classics, Latin and Greek."

Lizzie pulls out her phone, "Oh my god, I think this could be it! You're a genius Mom!"

"What? How am I a genius, do tell? I have had a very un-genius day and could use that."

"Land and sea in Latin is 'Terra Marique,' I love the way that sounds!" Lizzie says, very enthused.

"How's that spelled? It's pronounced Marick, but I'm guessing it's not, i,c,k on the end, q,u,e?"

"You're so smart," Lizzie says. "Exactly."

"A product of all those years in medical school with lots of Latin," Gabby says, finishing up her bread. "I love it! It ties together the farming, the houses, and the ocean. You think Jack will go for it?"

"I think he's pretty desperate to have something to call it when he goes before the planning board, so yeah. I'll call him a little later," Lizzie says, looking around at the poster materials and files.. "So I have done absolutely nothing to help you here, and you have helped me potentially solve a very big issue. What do you want me to do?"

"You know, I think there's enough signs, you had three pieces running in the last two issues of the Gazette before the vote, and a bunch of letters to the editor from supporters. I think we may be good," Gabby says, digging into the fruit as well.

"Are you sure? You must need me to do something," Lizzie says, cleaning up the dishes and putting them in the dishwasher.

"There is one thing you could do," Gabby says, looking at her and grinning.

Lizzie puts her hands on her hips and cocks her head, "What, walk Daisy for you? Clean the downstairs bathroom? Anything you need, I'm here."

"There's a new show streaming, 'London Calling,' that I know your dad wouldn't like, it's about a young woman who moves to England all by herself and creates a new life in a new city, and-"

"She meets a guy she doesn't like at first but then they fall madly in love?" Lizzie teases.

"Yes! Have you seen it already?" Gabby asks, a little disappointed.

"No, I have not, but you just described almost every romantic comedy ever made, and I am definitely all in. You had me at 'a young woman moves to London,'" She starts the dishwasher. "Popcorn? We have to have popcorn, right?"

Gabby gets up and starts getting out the air popper and a bowl while Lizzie gets the jar of popcorn out of the cupboard. "Have I told you lately how much I love having you here? You have made life so much brighter."

Lizzie puts her finger to her lips and looks toward the ceiling. "Hmmm, I don't think you've said it since... yesterday? I was starting to wonder if the luster had faded, if I'd worn out my welcome," she laughs.

"Fine, so I tell you a lot how much I love having you here. I won't apologize for it!"

Lizzie walks over and hugs her mom as she's getting the popcorn all set up. "I love hearing it. Don't ever stop, okay? And for the record? I love it too."

"Well good," Gabby says, pouring the kernels into the popper and plugging it in. "Now let's hurry up, we should be able to get at least two episodes in before your dad gets home from his curling night. I don't want to hear him complain about what a silly show it is."

"Well, I think we can take with a grain of salt anything coming from a man who will have spent two hours at an ice rink chasing a stone around with a broom about how we're spending our evening."

"Good point," Gabby says, sprinkling a bit of parmesan and sea salt on the hot popcorn. "Let the romance commence!" she says as they head to the living room for a cozy night together.

CHAPTER 4

Lizzie and Gabby loved *London Calling*, and did manage to get two episodes in before Peter got home. They were all hanging out on the couch relaxing when Lizzie's phone rings.

"It's Jack, I'm going to run upstairs, night guys," she says as she answers her phone, "Hey, I was going to call you," she says, happy to hear from him.

"Well good thing I saved you all that effort," he teases. "How's your night going?"

"Tell him we say hi," Peter calls after her as she heads upstairs.

"Dad and Mom say hi," she says as she climbs the stairs.

She walks into her room and closes the door. "My night's been good, I ate soup and popcorn and watched a new show with Mom, I'm pretty much living the hermit dream," she says, getting cozy on her bed. "What about you?"

"Nothing too exciting, ate some ramen, and am honing and editing my presentation for tomorrow night. I can't believe how nervous I am!" he says.

"Oh! I almost forgot! I have an idea for a name," suddenly she feels nervous and wonders if it's any good. She sits up on her bed and clears her throat. "Okay, you ready?"

"Uh, yeah, I need a name like yesterday!"

"'Terra Marique,' it means 'land and sea' in Latin." She's quiet, waiting for a response. "You still there?"

"Yeah, I was just writing it down, It's m-a-r-i-q-u-e?" I love it! It might take people a bit to not call it Terra Marquee which would be a very different place, a land and theater situation," they both laugh. "But no, I love it, it has a certain gravitas to it that I like."

"It was my mom who suggested looking at some Latin words, and I loved the way it sounded," Lizzie says, relieved that Jack likes it. It may be his project, but she feels so invested as well. She has to maintain some distance given her role at the newspaper, but it's personal, not just because of Jack, but because of what it could mean to the town. "I'm so glad you like it!"

"It will be good to go in there with an actual name they can hang their hats on, like it's actually something, not just an idea." He lets out a huge sigh. "Thanks so much, sweetie, I really appreciate this."

"Hey, we're a team, remember? The Gazette might not even be here anymore if it wasn't for you bringing in your angel investors, so we help each other, right?" she says, feeling so lucky to have that partnership with him. She'd kissed a few frogs in her lifetime and was very happy to have found her way back to her swan. She never thought in terms of princes, but swans, who mate for life? She could get behind that.

"Are you coming to the meeting tomorrow night?" Jack asks, they hadn't actually firmed up that plan.

"I keep going back and forth, Stan's going to cover it, but I worry that it might muddy things up a bit for you if I was there. Would they be reminded of us being a couple and think we're biased because of that? That's partly why Dad asked Stan to cover it. Small town politics are so hard because everyone knows everyone, but this is a bit more than just knowing each other, we're…" she stumbles a little not really knowing what to call them, they're not married, not engaged… "Uh, since we're-"

"A couple?" Jack says, filling in the blank.

"Yeah, a couple" She shakes her head, feeling so silly. "Anyway, I don't want to do anything that might screw it up for you. And on the other hand, the non-professional part of me feels terrible about not being there for you for something so important. So I do want to come."

"Lizzie, I understand. And all those same thoughts went through my head too, it's okay. Whatever you and your Dad decide is cool."

"You sure? I feel like a jerky girlfriend being hesitant."

Jack laughs, "Hey you just named the place, you're not a jerky girlfriend. Don't worry about it. Though I know telling you not to worry about something is futile. Worrying is your superpower."

"Ugh, I know! Why couldn't I have gotten flying or invisibility?" She laughs knowing he's exactly right, and also comforted at how well he knows her, and accepts her, just as she is.

"Do you want to practice your presentation on me? We could FaceTime, or Zoom? Or you could come over?" Again, feeling like a jerk she's kind of hoping he'll say no because it's after 10 and she's really tired. But she'd rally if he needed her.

"No, thanks, I'm good. I think I'm going to head to bed pretty soon and try to get some sleep. We'll see how that goes."

"Rub some of that lavender cream I got you at the farmers market on your wrists, it's supposed to help you relax," Lizzie says knowing there is no way he's going to rub lavender on himself.

He laughs, "Yeah, I'll get right on that."

"Yeah, I had a feeling that was a ridiculous suggestion as soon as I said it. Maybe if you put some dirt in it too it will feel more manly?" she jokes.

"Hey, I'm not some Neanderthal kind of guy, I did those Korean face masks with you, I can do skincare and relaxing, I just don't really think some lotion is going to help me stop thinking about how I have the chance to either make everything I've been working for come together tomorrow, or it can all just, well, float out to sea. I'm feeling just a little bit of pressure and performance anxiety."

"Which is why I know I have to be there. I just decided. To hell with what anyone thinks. I'm a Cranberry Harbor resident as well as co-editor of the town paper." Lizzie says, now feeling like the lotion was a stupid suggestion when he's got so much on the line. "There are so many people who believe in this project, it's going to happen. And if there's any glitches or questions from the town, we will deal with them, but they have to know we need to do something now. The climate is changing, our shores are eroding, we're losing young people in droves, and average people can't afford to live here. If they push back I'd ask them, 'what's your plan then?'"

"I know you're right, we just have to hope that there is enough foresight on the board to see that this is not a drill, we're at DEFCON 3, headed quickly to 2, and not far from 1 if we don't act," Jack says.

"Use that! The older guys on the board will relate to that," Lizzie says. "And remind them that the beachfront property so many covet here will be in the ocean if we don't start taking climate change seriously."

"Let's change the subject, this isn't helping me relax, how was yoga?"

"Oh it was good, relaxing, and a good workout, a tough combo to find. I feel so grateful to have found friends to do things with. It's not easy here," Lizzie says, feeling grateful for her crew.

"Yeah, I'm feeling a little bit of a loss not having Ben and Sean to hang out with now that they're parents. I need to find some guys to go mountain biking with and stuff like that," Jack says, sounding a little lonely.

"I know Matt loves that stuff too, but between his solar business and his family, he's not free much either."

"I love your brother, but yeah, he's never free." They're quiet for a minute. "I'm probably crazy to even think about this because if this goes through I'm not going to have any free time, so it's pretty moot."

"I should let you get to bed, and I'm going to try to get to sleep myself." Another silence. "It's going to be okay, Jack, it really is, no matter what. I will be there silently backing you up."

"I know. I just keep going back to my past failed attempt here to do a start up and don't want to let anyone down again. I love this town and really want to help solve some of its problems. I know I can't fix decades worth of mistakes in zoning, climate and opportunities for locals, but I want to use my skill set to at least try."

Lizzie wishes he was there so she could hug him and reassure him. "I love that about you. It's actually one of the things I love most about you. How much you care. We're in this together. Sink or swim. Okay?"

'Okay. I love you too Elizabeth Jane Martin," he says. Making her smile as she's curled up in her bed.

"We'll talk in the morning, okay? Get some sleep. And don't discount the lavender lotion," she teases.

"I will not. Talk to you tomorrow, love you," he says.

"I love you too." Lizzie puts her phone down on the nightstand and stares up at the ceiling and quietly says a little prayer that it all works out for Jack, and for Cranberry Harbor.

CHAPTER 5

THE NEXT MORNING Lizzie woke up to see it had snowed a few inches overnight. She looked out her window and saw the back deck was covered in snow. Of course it hadn't been in the weather report the day before, it was the prerogative of March to be mysterious and keep surprising you.

She was the first one up which surprised her. Daisy, their little rescue pup almost always had Peter or Gabby up at the crack of dawn.

As she padded down to the kitchen she was thrilled to see that her mom had been organized enough to program the coffee maker and as the smell of just brewed coffee filled her nose.

"Thank you Gabby for being so on top of things," she quietly says to no one as she takes a cup off the shelf and pours herself a nice warm cup of the delicious locally roasted coffee. Yet another addition to the Sea Coast Coffee repertoire, that Leah was something else.

Lizzie sat down in a chair at the kitchen table, pulling her knees up to her chest, and looked out at the snow-covered deck and yard as she sipped her coffee. Her life had changed so much in the last year. It was almost hard to remember what her life had been like back in Boston. Certainly getting a thoughtful and peaceful start to her day was not on the menu back then. Working for a big city paper may have at one point had a certain cache, but no longer. It was endless days of grinding out stories with as few words as possible, there was rarely a local angle, and it didn't feel at all satisfying or fun.

She'd long gotten past feeling like she'd failed by returning to the Cape and joining her dad in the family business. The living at home part took a little time to not feel weird about, but she knew so many others on the Cape were doing the same thing that she'd ceased feeling awkward and just embraced it. And besides, getting to live in the beautiful old farmhouse she'd grown up in wasn't too shabby.

"Good morning sunshine," her dad's voice pierces the silence. "You're sure up early," he says as he pours himself some coffee, walking to the fridge to get out some Gabby-approved oatmilk to put in it. "You got a lot on your mind?"

She shrugs, "Yeah, I'm worried about the Town Meeting tonight," she says, getting up to pour herself some more coffee. "I've decided I'm going, by the way. I'm not going to let some small-minded group make me feel like I shouldn't be there. Jack is my boyfriend, partner, whatever...and I want to be there, and more than that," she's getting passionate about this as she walks back to the table, second cup of coffee and a bran muffin in hand, "I was born here, darn it, and I have every right to go and listen, and vote, right?"

Peter, not fully awake, is trying to keep up with her excitement. "I totally agree, you should go, and I will too." He drinks some more of his coffee, trying to keep up with Lizzie's energy.

"Oh good, I was hoping you'd agree. Both the school renovation and Terra Marique need all the votes they can get," she says, biting into her muffin.

"Terra what?" Peter asks, looking confused.

"Oh! Mom and I came up with the name, it means land and sea! What do you think?"

"I think it sounds great!" He says, "The Latin was your Mom's idea, right?" he smiles.

Lizzie laughs. "Oh you know your wife very well, sir."

"You live with someone this long and you get to know how their mind works," he says, taking a last sip of his coffee. "Mostly," he laughs,

"Mostly what?" Gabby says as she comes into the kitchen, trailed by Daisy.

"Mostly I know you and what you're going to do, but not always," Peter says, getting up and giving her a kiss on the cheek.

"Now wouldn't life be dull if you always knew what I was going to do?" she teases as she sits down with her cup of coffee.

"I want what you two have," Lizzie says, looking at her parents. "You two are the relationship goals everyone wants to reach."

They hug and both look at their daughter. "It's not always perfect," Gabby says.

"Or easy," Peter concurs, "but it's more than worth it." He walks over and takes a leash off a hook and clips it on to Daisy's collar. "Come on girl, let's get you out for a little walk."

"Be careful out there, honey, it looks pretty slippery," Gabby cautions.

Peter slips into his heavy-treaded boots, "Will do! Be right back," he says as he and a very happy Daisy head outside.

Gabby sits down with her coffee, and she and Lizzie look out at the snow that's still coming down, but now more just flurries. "I'm usually pretty grumpy about March snow, but for some reason, not today," she says, sitting back and putting her feet up on an empty chair near her. "A lot of things that used to make me grumpy don't anymore."

"And to what do you attribute this new-found sunny attitude?" Lizzie asks, smiling at her mom.

"I just feel so lucky, I have both of my children, their partners and my granddaughter here. I have friends, I love this community, mostly," she says laughing. "I'm just feeling very grateful."

"I am too," Lizzie says. "Though deadlines looming over me daily might keep me feeling quite as sunshiny, but I know what you mean. Yesterday I was looking at Jack, and sometimes it still hits me that we might never have gotten back together. I feel very lucky that we did, and that we've both found meaningful work here. Projects we're passionate about, and have good friends."

"How are you feeling about the meeting tonight?" Gabby ventures.

"Good. Mostly good?" Lizzie corrects herself. "I'm worried about the old guard, folks like Billy Taylor and Bud Mackelroy.

They love to stir up controversy and I've been hearing that they're coming prepared to raise some hell. But maybe that's just the Cranberry Harbor rumor mill. I hope so."

She gets up and takes her cup to the sink and rinses it before putting it in the dishwasher. "How are you feeling about the high school renovation? You think it will pass?"

Gabby gets up too. She's quiet for a moment, pondering the question. "I think so?" She leans against the counter and sighs. "I have a little speech in my back pocket I'm prepared to deliver if the need arises. I have no problem pulling on some heartstrings."

"Oh, if anyone can appeal to people's hearts it's you for sure," Lizzie says, joining her mom in leaning against the counter.

"Well you two look deep in thought," Peter says, coming in with the dog who shakes, scattering snowy droplets everywhere. "Everything okay?" He unclips the leash, hangs it up and slips off his snowy boots, oblivious to the wet floor. Gabby gets up and drags a dish towel around the floor with her foot wiping up the water.

"Sorry," Peter whispers, smacking his head as Gabby smiles and pats his shoulder, used to him being oblivious.

"Yeah," Lizzie says, "We're just talking about tonight, that's all."

"I have a good feeling," Peter says. "And as you know, I am not always the most optimistic of fellas given my experience in covering town politics for decades. But I think most people have seen the help wanted signs up year-round now, and they know this town needs housing, and we need to find a way to keep young people here. I also think all those pieces we ran by students at the high school made a real impact. The stories of brown water in the gym showers, and no windows in some classrooms really shocked folks. People know it's time. It's more than time."

"I hope you're right Dad, I really do," says Lizzie. "Okay, I'm going to go take a shower and head to the office. You?"

"Same. I'll see you there in a little bit. Well, if I don't see you right back here before that," he smiles at her.

As Lizzie starts to go upstairs Peter calls after her.

"Hey, so this is all working okay for you? You're not sick of me? Not yet anyway?" he asks.

Lizzie turns around and comes back, and hugs her dad. "Not

tired of you yet. Not by a long-shot. It's all good." She kisses him on the cheek and goes upstairs. She picks her phone up off the nightstand where it's been charging all night and sees she's missed four calls and three texts from Jack. "Call me ASAP," says the text. Her stomach drops as she calls and waits for him to pick up.

"Hey, are you okay?" she asks, trying to not panic.

"Depends on how you define okay," he says. "I'm not sick or anything, but apparently Bud Mackelroy and Billy Taylor have been organizing some people to come out and protest the project. He's determined to sink it."

Lizzie can hear the panic in his voice. "Okay, everyone knows that they are both malcontents that are never for anything. I can't imagine they'll find much of a following. I mean, I haven't done official polling, but in all the stories we've done, and all the people I talk to all the time, I have heard nothing but excitement over your project and the high school renovation."

"Well, he's apparently making up all kinds of things about how this is all a big ruse on my part and how I plan to bring in all these people from Silicon Valley and there won't really be any local jobs realized." He's silent for a minute. "And then he's dredging up all this stuff from the past, when my startup failed and I moved to California. He's making me out to be some kind of carpetbagger who's going to somehow take all this money from the town and leave people stranded."

"Oh my god, he's such a jerk! Nothing is further from the truth, and you've been nothing but completely open and transparent about what happened, and how this isn't the same thing at all."

Lizzie can tell that more than anything Jack is hurt, and he's revisiting a past business failing that he still feels so much guilt about. She struggles to find the right thing to say, while also wanting to go find those two men and throttle them for stirring up so much trouble.

"You know those two are idiots, right?" she says to no response. "Remember when years ago the town was all for building a community center and those two knuckleheads got up at town meeting and said it was going to attract 'criminals and hooligans.' I remember it because the entire room erupted in laughter. Yes, having a place where your grandmother could play tennis, and your kids could take swimming lessons was really going to destroy the town."

"Oh my god, I'd forgotten all about that," Jack says, chuckling.

Lizzie feels better, getting him to laugh was her goal, though even she's now feeling a little concerned, but she's certainly not going to share that with Jack.

"Both the Terra Marique and high school projects are things this community needs, Jack, and the people who really love Cranberry Harbor know that," she says. The high school is over 50 years old, and everyone knows we need housing, and we are not going to survive if we don't start doing some innovative things around housing and jobs. We're going to be Sunset Pines in a few years if we don't find a way to help younger people stay here and build businesses, buy homes and raise families."

"I sure hope you're right," he says, sounding a little less frantic. "I'm really glad you and your parents are going to be there. I'm going to need all the support I can get."

"We will all be there, and I don't care about optics, if those guys do something stupid I'm speaking up," Lizzie says. "I love you, but that's almost beside the point, the town needs this, and Billy and Bud can take a flying leap as far as I'm concerned."

"Ha! Well, one thing is for sure, it's not going to be a dull meeting," Jack says, and takes a deep breath. "I love you too. Maybe lunch later?"

"Sounds good. I've got to get myself in the shower and to the office. Text me when you're nearby later and we'll make a plan."

"Okay. And hey, thanks for talking me off the ledge. I was so upset. You're the best. I'm so lucky."

"I'm lucky too. It's going to be all good. I promise. I'll see you later. Love you."

Lizzie puts down her phone and stands by her bed for a second. "I sure hope I'm right," she says out loud to herself. "I just have to be.

CHAPTER 6

PER HER USUAL ROUTINE, Lizzie stopped in at Sea Coast for a warm beverage before going to the paper. Depending on what she'd had at home, one or two cups of coffee, she'd either have her second cup there, or a decaf green tea. She tried hard to manage her caffeine intake lest she get too wired which made it very hard to focus.

When she'd been working at the Sentinel in Boston she had gotten into some very unhealthy habits - too much caffeine, too much sugar, and way too much stress. When she was in the middle of it she didn't see how completely unbalanced her life was. Little time for exercise, friends, or just relaxing. Since she'd been home, Dr. Gabby Martin, aka, Mom, had been subtly and not always so subtly, working on Lizzie's choices, and quietly instilling some changes. Like the caffeine, and sugar was down to a rare treat, there was of course the thrice weekly yoga classes, and Gabby had even sneaked a mindfulness app onto her phone. All these small steps added up to big changes, and Lizzie felt better than she had in a long time. Of course, Hope's cookies at Sea Coast were a constant temptation, but she (mostly) resisted them.

When she walked into the only slightly crowded coffee shop, she was excited to see Alexis, childhood and present best friend seated at a table, laptop open, and a notebook covered in sticky notes.

"Hey friend, would I ruin your flow if I grabbed a tea and sat for a moment?" Lizzie asks, not wanting to intrude.

"Oh my gosh, no, you'd be saving me from the writer's block I am currently experiencing, please! Save me from my brain not cooperating with my deadline!" Alexis pleads.

Lizzie orders her tea and is back in a flash. She pulls out a chair, takes off her coat and sits down. "What are you working on?"

"Jack asked me to have something prepared for tonight, just in case I need to make the argument for the project from a community well-being point of view. And it's not like we don't all talk about all this stuff all the time, but the thought of having to get up in front of the whole town and talk is freaking me out, I don't want to freeze and screw this up for Jack, and everyone else involved," Alexis says, sitting back with the rest of her freshly baked spinach and cheddar scone.

"First of all, you won't because I've heard you at all these other meetings and you are always amazing. You are smart, focused, succinct and articulate. So stop with that dialogue." She sits back too. "Take a deep breath," she takes a breath along with Alexis. "Now let it out slowly..." They both exhale and relax their bodies. "Feel better?"

"Yeah, surprisingly I do!" Alexis moves her head around a little, relaxing her shoulders. "Thank you. It's always amazing how when we're stressed we forget to breathe, huh?"

"Totally! I've actually caught myself basically holding my breath sometimes! My shoulders scrunched up to my ears, heart racing. Now, when I feel that way I just close my eyes and breathe. I have my mom to thank for that. She used all sorts of tools like that with her patients, she even went to training to learn how to help her patients with heart issues and how to use mindfulness based stress reduction to change their lifestyles."

"Your mom is just the coolest," Alexis says.

"She definitely is, way cooler than me," Lizzie says. "So what is it that you think is the most important message to get across to voters tonight about why we need both the high school renovation and Terra Marique?" She takes a sip of her tea and looks at Alexis, hoping to instill some confidence in her.

"I think we are at a crossroads as a community. There is a future where Cranberry Harbor is all about the summer visitors, the second home owners, and older retirees. The other is, making the families, young adults, the farmers, artists and those who make a living from the sea a priority, because without them, we cease to exist as a viable, healthy year-round community and there's nothing for tourists to come here for. No stores, no restaurants, nothing. In order to thrive we need balance. Balance economically and balance in our population.With no families, no children, no young adults starting and maintaining businesses, we will become a mere shell of what we used to be. We have to find a way to stop catering to the wealthy, and embrace who we are at our core - a small town that cares about its members. Remember our history, our legacy."

"Bingo. You nailed it, my friend," Lizzie says, choking back some tears. "Wow," she says, wiping her eyes.

"Really?" Alexis isn't so sure. "I figured it probably wasn't good to say something about how there is no one to date here because everyone is old, married or I dated them in high school," Alexis jokes.

"Yeah, probably best to leave that out," Lizzie laughs too. "But oh my gosh, it's so true! If we don't get some younger people moving here we'll have to host a reality show or something. 'Bachelors and Bachelorettes By the Sea,' I can see it now, dates where you learn to surf, or go clamming-"

"Oh! Or cranberry picking!" Alexis jokes. "Seriously, I cannot remember the last time I went on a date. Like an actual, someone called me up and asked me out, picked me up and took me someplace date. And hey, I am totally willing to ask a guy out, but there's no one to ask!"

"Ugh, I hear you. I see it with all my single friends here," Lizzie looks down at her tea, "It makes me feel guilty that I have Jack, because I want everyone who wants to meet someone to have that chance."

"Do not feel guilty!" Alexis insists. "You two give me hope, so stop feeling bad!"

"Have you gone to any events in other towns? Like Wellfleet or Brewster? Do they have more going on?" Lizzie asks.

"Oh, I'm totally willing to travel for a social life, but they don't seem to have a whole lot more going on than we do here," Alexis laments. She shakes her head. "This is not what we need to be focused on today. Today we need to think about Town Meeting and getting these projects passed."

"Okay, but I know there's more we can be doing. Let's stick a pin in this and we will circle back once we can relax about these projects," Lizzie says.

"Well, speaking of coupledom, here comes your guy," Alexis says, looking toward the door. "Hey Jack! And yes, I am working on what I'm going to say tonight. Lizzie is actually helping me. I'm not goofing off talking about the lack of eligible men around here to date. Not at all." She goes back to looking at her computer screen, looks up at him and smiles.

Jack laughs. "Oh my god, am I that horrible a taskmaster that I make people feel guilty and nervous when I show up?" He smacks his forehead with his hand. "I'm so sorry!"

"I'm totally teasing you, not to worry, it's all good," Alexis says. "Though this better pass or I'm going to have to seriously consider moving to a place where the median age is not 65, and the closest I've come to holding a man's hand isn't helping 91-year-old Mr. Farnham across the street last week."

Both Lizzie and Jack laugh. "Well that's just tragic, helpful and kind, but tragic," Jack says. "We must know someone who would be worthy of Alexis, don't we?" he asks, looking at Lizzie.

"Um, we know all the same people I think. Unless you've been hiding a few people from me that I don't know about. Cranberry Harbor is in desperate need of new and young blood," Lizzie says.

"Once this passes we are going to be seeing a whole bunch of new people coming here, I can almost guarantee it," Jack says.

"Hey, I don't know if I'm going to get up at Town Meeting for 'almost,' Alexis says, laughing. "Look, I am having fun kidding about my social life, or rather lack of a social life, but I am well aware that we have a lot more at stake here than me getting a date. So let's stop talking about my dating situation and get pumped to crush these folks tonight who don't want to let this happen. Alright?!"

Lizzie and Jack both nod in agreement, and they all high five.

"Wow, so that was a little lame, let's not do that tonight. We need to look a little cool, right?" Jack says, laughing. "Not that I've ever been cool."

"Yeah, let's make a pact - tonight will be a high-five-free zone, okay?" Lizzie says.

"Yes!" They all concur.

"I'm typing that into my notes - 'no matter how excited do not high five.'" Alexis says.

"Okay, well with that decided, I am going to get going to the office and see what kind of trouble my dad has gotten himself into with the new program we're using," Lizzie says, standing up. She puts on her coat, picks up her tea and is ready to go. "I will see you two later. We've got this."

Jack stands up too. "Mind if I walk you to the office?" Not waiting for an answer he puts on his jacket and wraps a scarf around his neck. "Sorry? Am I being a pushy jerk? You okay with me walking with you?"

"Of course, I'd love it. But I do have to actually get to work, so no attempts to distract me, okay?" She smiles at him. "Because you are very distracting."

"Ugh, would you two leave? Seriously, I do not need to be reminded how much my love life stinks. Shoo! Get out of here with all your moony-eyes mushiness!" Alexis feigns disgust and waves them off.

"I do believe we made our friend feel ill with our display of affection," Lizzie teases. "Fine, we will not offend you anymore with our shenanigans."

"We seriously need to find her a date, and soon," Jack says, loud enough for Alexis to hear as they walk to the door. "She is seriously getting crabby!" He turns to her, waves and smiles, while Alexis pretends to be annoyed, shaking her head and then laughing.

It had gotten a little chillier since Lizzie had walked into Sea Coast, she wasn't prepared for the briskness. "So wait a minute," she says, looking at her parked car. "I drove here from home, I need to get my car to the office so it's there when I leave."

"I want to walk with you," Jack insists, "I tell you what, I'll walk back and get your car and drive it to the office and walk back to get mine."

"That seems like an awful lot of work just to walk me to the office," Lizzie says.

"I just want to walk with you, okay?" Jack is sounding a little testy. "Sorry, I didn't mean for that to come out that way. I'm a little stressed."

"I know you are, we all are, it's okay, I get it," she takes his hand and squeezes it. "So let's walk."

They walk along, side by side in complete silence in the slushy snow for a block. Lizzie is confused, he wanted to do *this?* To walk in silence? And she's very glad that she had decided to go with boots, not sneakers today. She pulls her coat tighter around her, it's cold , gray and damp, not exactly the walking weather she enjoys. She's not sure what's going on, but given Jack's mood she decides to leave well enough alone. As they get near the Gazette building Jack puts his hand on her arm to get her to stop walking.

"Yes?" she says.

He clears his throat. "I just wanted to say I know I've been really preoccupied and not the best boyfriend in the world these last few weeks, well months actually. I just wanted to say I'm sorry for being neglectful and if, no, *when* this passes I promise to do better."

"Jack, you don't owe me an apology, I work all the time too. I understand. We're not 17, we both have busy careers that are demanding a whole lot from us right now, it won't always be like this." She looks at him, and kisses him. "It won't, right?" she teases.

"No, it won't. And I promise you, I am thinking about the future, our future, not just the town's. I just want you to know that," he says, looking incredibly serious and earnest. "There is a future here. At least for me, anyway."

"Really? Because I thought this was just a summer fling, oh wait, it's March, it's a pre-spring fling," she laughs at how silly that sounds. "Jack, I understand what you're trying to do here, because in a very different way, in different fields we're both building something for the future with our work. I'm here, I'm not going anywhere."

"Okay, because I was even thinking of getting a placeholder ring or something," he says, looking at the ground.

"A placeholder ring? I've never heard of such a thing," she says, trying not to laugh because he looks so serious.

"You know, like I'm not proposing *right now,* but I will be in the not-too-distant future, but this isn't the best time, so hold on to this, and we will circle back. And when I do it will be so much better than whatever I'm doing here, right now," he looks incredibly uncomfortable and even squats down, and jumps up quickly, startling Lizzie. "Arrgghh!" he says.

"Wow, honey, this isn't a big deal. And really, that's a whole lot for a 'placeholder ring' to say," she says, still trying not to laugh and hurt his feelings, and thinking how not romantic 'circle back' sounds, but it was all still very endearing. This apparently was a pre-proposal proposal. Not that there was such a thing, but she was certainly touched. "Jack, we're good. I don't need a 'placeholder ring', there's nothing to worry about. When it's the right time, it will be the right time. Until then it's all good. Okay?"

She can see he looks visibly relieved. "Okay." He nods. "I've gotten myself so twisted up, it's hard to relax about anything. I'm sorry for being a nut."

She hugs him, and pats his back. "Oh, it's fine. You're my little nut and I'm grateful for you. Now I have to get in there and do some work and I'm sure you have a lot to do today too. Are you going to be okay?" She digs her keys out of her pocket and hands them to him. "I think a little more walking will do you good," she says.

Jack nods, kisses her, and shakes the keys. "I shall return," he says, heading back to Sea Coast.

"You better be, I'm going to need that car. I love you, you nut!"

"I love you too," he calls out as he walks away and she can see he's shaking his head.

As strange as that whole exchange was, it was still pretty sweet. He truly did love her, she knew that. And they were going to get married. She knew that too. Someday, when he circled back to it. She laughed to herself and headed inside.

CHAPTER 7

"Hey Dad," she says, hanging her damp coat on the coat rack and sliding into her chair.

"So what are you working on?" she asks. He's deep in concentration mode.

"Ah, this story about the fire department having a hard time finding new help to replace the three people who are retiring." He sits back in his chair, "I tell you, the housing crisis here is impacting absolutely everything."

"It sure is," Lizzie opens her computer. "Hey, it might not be a bad idea if you can get Captain Ellis to come tonight and say something. Appeal to the voters?"

"You think the captain of the fire department would come and put a pitch in for Jack's project?" Peter asks, looking unsure.

"Well, he wouldn't be talking about Terra Marique, per se, but just speak to the shortage of affordable housing, that houses are so expensive that even a young adult with a good full time job can't afford to live here," Lizzie offers.

"Hmmm, I can maybe ask, I certainly know Dave," he still looks unsure. "I just don't want to put the head of the fire department in the position of having to be political."

"Dad, everything is political, the town allocates money for the department, it's all politics. And if the town becoming completely unaffordable for his staff is a problem, then he should speak to the town about it!" Lizzie is feeling adamant. "Everyone knows there's a problem, but unless we actually talk about it it's not ever going to change. This didn't happen overnight, it happened over decades of decisions being made and too many officials turning a blind eye to what was happening to Cranberry Harbor. We've seen bubble after bubble, but the town elders just shrugged their shoulders and thought it would fix itself." She stops and takes a deep breath. "Sorry, I'm very wound up about this right now. I'm so scared about what's going to happen if this doesn't work out."

"I know, honey, I am too." They're both quiet. "Okay, I'll give him a call. Thanks for the pep talk."

"Any time," she says. "Okay, so I think I hit all my deadlines. Is there anything I can help you with to lessen some of your pressure?"

"Good question. I have been thinking ahead to Easter. We should probably see what's going on around town. The Chamber of Commerce might be a good place to start. See what they've got planned for the egg hunt, and any other activities that might be happening." He begins rummaging through some papers on his very messy half of their partner desk. "Wait, as a matter of fact I think Tall Tales has some things going on." He keeps going through papers. "Ah! Here it is! Anika and Jay Patel sent me this flyer," he hands it over to Lizzie.

"Hmm, this looks fun. They're doing some story telling, egg coloring, and oh!" she keeps reading, "The Easter bunny is going to be there too. We should definitely advance this event." She looks over at the calendar. "Gosh I got so caught up in this meeting tonight that I kind of lost track of dates and what's happening. Maybe I should run over there and talk to Jay and Anika so we can get going on helping promote this. What do you think?"

"I think that sounds good, and like a nice change of pace from writing about school renovations and housing problems," Peter says.

"Kind of exactly what I was thinking to be honest," she says. "Maybe I'll run over there now, you okay with that?"

"Yes, go! Get out of here! Get some fresh air and change the channel. This meeting is going to be what it is, we've done everything we can possibly do. Let's find something a little bit lighter to talk about. I'm betting readers could use a change too."

"Okay! I'm out of here!" Lizzie jumps up and gets ready to head out. "Oh wait..."

"What's wrong?"

"Jack was supposed to bring my car back," she looks at her dad. "It's kind of a long story."

Just then the door opens and Jack runs in and tosses Lizzie her car keys. "Sorry! When I was walking back to get your car I ran into Sean and we got talking."

"No problem, I wasn't worried." She puts her coat on and walks toward the door. "How's Sean?"

"He's good," he waves at Lizzie's dad. "Hey Peter!"

"Hi!" Peter says, gaze still on his screen.

"I'll be back Dad, you want anything?" Lizzie calls on her way out.

"Nope, I'm good."

Lizzie and Jack walk outside where it's now drizzling a cold and wet mess. She pulls up the hood on her coat and shivers.

"Get in, I'm driving you back to your car," Lizzie says. They both get in the car, she starts it up and begins to back up. "So you didn't say how Sean is," she asks again.

"Oh, he's good." He's looking out the window. "He kind of talked me off the ledge."

"You were on the ledge again?" she teases. "I hadn't noticed," she turns and smiles at him as she shifts her car into park when she's pulled into the small lot near Tall Tales and Sea Coast.

Jack shakes his head and laughs. "Just a little bit."

Lizzie unclips her seatbelt, shifts in her seat and turns to face Jack. "So what kind of wisdom did Sean impart on you? I could use some too!"

Jack undoes his seatbelt too. "He told me I was overthinking everything and to just focus on one thing at a time."

"Like in *City Slickers* when Jack Palance told Billy Crystal that life was about one thing?" Lizzie smiles at him, pointing her index finger upward.

"Ha, I had forgotten all about that. Yeah, I guess, it's sort of the same thing." He stops for a moment and looks out the windshield.

"I was feeling like this was all going to unravel like the last time, when my startup crashed and we broke up. Sean reminded me that this isn't three years ago, that it's a completely different project, that I have solid investors, and a lot of the town behind me."

"Well, he's right about all those things. I feel bad that I didn't think to tell you that, I guess I didn't know, until you started talking about placeholder rings that you were that stressed out about everything. I'm sorry."

"No, there's no need to apologize. I've been keeping a lot of my crazy worry to myself, you had no way of knowing what I was thinking." He leans over and kisses her. "And he reminded me that you and I are on very solid ground, and that I don't need to worry that things are going to fall apart."

"That Sean is one smart fella." She kisses him. "I'm so glad you bumped into him. Totally meant to be. And I'm really glad you're feeling a bit less stressed. It's going to be tense tonight, but no matter what happens, we're going to be okay. I am very secure in knowing that. We have each other, we each have lots of skills, if this doesn't go our way we will lick our wounds, take some time, and come up with a new project. But I really don't think that's going to happen. I'm feeling pretty good about this."

"From your lips, sweetie." Jack kisses her one more time. "And now I am going to get out of your hair and let you get back to work."

They both step out of the car. "I love you," Lizzie says as Jack walks back toward Sea Coast. "Do yourself a favor? Get a decaf!" she calls to him, to which he replies with a nod and a thumb's up.

Lizzie walks over to Tall Tales and opens the door, jangling the bell on it. She loves that sound. It's the same bell that's been there since, well, it had been there her whole life and makes the store feel like home. This was and always would be her absolute favorite bookstore. It was warm, cozy, and overflowing with books, and had the perfect cozy reading area in the corner. Being there always made her feel more calm and happy.

"Hi!" Jay Patel calls out from behind the counter. "This is a nice surprise. I thought you'd be caught up in town news stuff all day. Nice tweets by the way, a great reminder to get people to turn out."

"Yeah, my biggest fear is that the people who want these

projects to happen will think it's a slam dunk and stay home. I also wanted to make sure that young parents knew there was free childcare too. Fingers crossed it's all going to go well," Lizzie says. "So I came by because my dad showed me the Easter flyer and I thought I'd talk to you and Anika about what's going to be happening so we could begin to promote it. And count on us to post on our social media accounts too."

"Oh, thanks so much, that's great," he says. "Let me get Anika, she's in the back unpacking some new books, she's the one who really knows what's happening. The events are all her, the mundane is all me," he laughs. "I'll be right back."

While Jay goes out back Lizzie wanders around seeing what new books have arrived. She picks up one, *The 20 Questions to Ask,* Lizzie is about to flip it open when Anika comes over and gives her a big hug.

"Hey, this is a nice surprise!" Anika says. "Oh my gosh, that book is so fun," she says, pointing at the book Lizzie is still holding. "I think it's such a good ice breaker. And in times where we can feel like we have more things dividing us than bringing us together, it shows that at our core we are often much more alike than we think."

"You are so right, Anika." Lizzie flips open the book, "Hmmm, yeah, like this question, 'Your favorite ways to spend a rainy day,' that's not the same old boring chit chat." She keeps flipping through, "Oh, I like this, 'what's something that instantly makes your day better.' This is fun. You know, this isn't why I'm here, but it gives me an idea," she says, looking intently at Anika.

"I can tell looking at your face you're up to something," Anika laughs.

"We can talk more about this another time, but this makes me think about a conversation Alexis and I were having earlier about how hard it is to meet anyone to date here, and I was just thinking, wouldn't it be fun to have a night for singles here where people can ask a question - kind of like speed dating, but with more depth than, 'so what do you do?'"

"I love it! My only concern would be, getting women to come would be pretty easy, but how do we entice guys to come? Most of the ones I know aren't exactly chatty," Anika rightly assesses.

"Yeah, good point. We'll have to think about that," Lizzie agrees. "So, I should get back to the reason I came here in the first place - Easter! I saw the flyer and thought we could advance the event in the paper, and on our social media, and get the word out."

"Thank you! That would be so great. It's coming up faster than I thought and I'm worried no one is going to show," Ankia says, walking them toward the cozy reading area perfectly appointed with colorful comfy chairs and leather couch.

Lizzie takes out her reporter's notebook and pen. "First off, do you need volunteers? It's always good to put out the word early on that."

"Actually, I think we're good. Several parents from the school parent group have offered to help, so that's good. I'm so impressed at how willing the parents here are to help out. It's amazing, even with jobs, kids, school, often for themselves, people are always so good about pitching in," Anika says.

"That would be a good story to write sometime," Lizzie says. "We should make sure we're shouting out all the people in this town who show up to help others. And goodness knows, this town loves its special events!" Lizzie is writing everything down. "Are you good with supplies too?"

"Yup, Bradfords is giving us eggs to dye, and the art supply store special ordered us dyes that are safe and also won't ruin clothes, which I know parents will appreciate. And Leah offered to supply us with some snacks and drinks. All we really need is kids to come."

"Well let us worry about that, I will get right on this and get it in this week's edition. Between the paper and our social media we will definitely let everyone know." Lizzie says, standing up.

Anika walks her to the door. "So are you ready for tonight? Thank you by the way for making sure there is childcare, now both Jay and I can go. I heard that was all you."

Lizzie shrugs, "Actually it was me and Shannon, she knows a lot of teens through the library, and they offer that babysitting class so it was super easy. We have to make sure everyone who has kids can come. You're the future of Cranberry Harbor."

"Well, thank your wonderful sister-in-law, for us," Anika says.

Lizzie opens the door, "I will be sure to. Thank you again for

Easter information, and let's make a plan to get together and talk about a book lovers singles event, I'll get Alexis to come too."

"Oh! 'Book Lovers,' I love it! That's what we should call it!" Ankia says, excited. "And let's do it before too long, before the summer season. It would be nice to keep this for locals."

"Agreed, I'll be in touch!" Lizzie says as she leaves.

As she walks to her car, Lizzie feels excited about all the things she can envision for Cranberry Harbor. More young people, more young families, places for everyone to live, and fun, happy events. It's possible, she thinks. But it all depends on tonight.

CHAPTER 8

BY THE TIME Lizzie arrived home from work at around 5:30, Gabby had dinner waiting on the kitchen counter, and was geared up and ready to go.

"I cheated and got us some wraps from Bradford's," Gabby says, almost apologetically.

"Mom, I don't expect you to provide me with food, I'm an adult, stop being hard on yourself." She puts her things down, "That said, these do look delicious." Lizzie chooses one that appears to be hummus with lots of veggies, and she picks up a handful of carrot sticks as well and puts them on her plate. "Thank you so much for doing this, I probably would have just had some cereal or something." She sits down on one of the stools and starts to eat. "Are you going to join me?" she asks her mom.

"I had one already, but I will nibble on some cucumber and carrot sticks with you," she says, pulling out a chair and sitting down. "So how are you doing?" Gabby asks as she picks up a carrot stick and takes a bite.

Lizzie finishes chewing, swallows, and shakes her head. "Honestly? Between you and me? I'm really nervous. We've seen what these naysayers are like, they might not be in the majority, but they are loud and command attention. I'm just worried about anyone on the fence, or anyone easily swayed by lies -you know they're going to try to scare the bejeezus out of the much older folks, tell them life as they know it will end, their taxes are going to go through the roof and they won't be allowed to go to church anymore."

"Ugh, I know. The level of disinformation is staggering," Gabby says. She gets up, I'm going to make some tea to bring, you want me to make you a travel mug too?"

"Sure, thank you. Though depending on how this meeting goes I might prefer there to be some wine in that mug," Lizzie says, finishing up her sandwich. She takes her plate and puts it in the dishwasher.

Gabby's phone dings and she picks it up. "Huh, it's your dad, he says he's running over to the meeting, apparently there are people out front with signs protesting already."

"Oh dear lord, I'll bet my last dollar that it's being led by Billy and Bud," Lizzie says, shaking her head. "I should get over there too." She stops in her tracks, "Should I call Jack and tell him? He's so nervous already, I hate to stress him out more."

Gabby finishes her text to Peter, then looks up. "Honestly? I think it's better if he's prepared rather than blindsided when he pulls up."

"My thoughts exactly," Lizzie says, putting on her coat. She's shaking her head and looking at her mom. "What is wrong with these people? Why can't they see that this is all for the good of Cranberry Harbor, the high school renovation is not going to raise taxes more than ten dollars a year per resident, and Jack's project is all being funded by grants, angel donors and federal money earmarked for environmental projects. It's a total win/win!"

Gabby walks over and hugs her. "There are more of us than there are of them. Billy and Bud may be loud, but their following is limited, and I do believe we will prevail."

Lizzie picks up her keys, her phone and her purse. "From your lips, Mom," she turns to go. "Sorry to eat and run, thank you so much for the sandwich. Oh, should I bring one to Dad?"

"You get going, I'll wrap one up and bring it. I'm going to head out as soon as I take Daisy for a quick walk, you get going."

"Okay, thanks Mom, I don't know what I'd do without your calm presence," Lizzie says. As she gets in her car she takes a deep breath, holds it for a couple of seconds, and lets it out. She does it a second time, just like her mom taught her. She feels calmer. She puts in her earbuds and calls Jack. He picks up on the first ring.

"You're calling about the protesters, right?" he says, not even saying hello.

"So you heard," she says, pulling out onto the street. "I don't have details, are there many of them? I'm on my way over now."

"Yeah, me too," Jack says. "I don't know how many there are, but it's worrying me. I just have to remind myself to stay calm, because the last thing that will help is me losing my temper and yelling at these people." He's quiet for a moment and Lizzie knows him well enough to give him a minute. "Because there's nothing that upsets me more than misinformation. If you think the project isn't good for some logical reason, fine! Don't vote for it! But if it's because of some lie designed to just scare you that makes me furious."

"I agree completely," Lizzie says, pulling into the school parking lot. "And those two have been spreading all sorts of disinformation about taxes, about how Terra Marique will cause more pollution not less, and how my dad and I are being paid to write positive stories about the project."

"Really? They said that? Arrggghh, I just want to deck that guy," he says. This is precisely why Lizzie hasn't mentioned it before. "I'm pulling in to your left."

They hang up and each get out of their cars.

"I can take care of myself, don't get into it with the town bully, especially since that's exactly what he wants," Lizzie says, hugging him. "While I appreciate the instinct to protect me, I've got this, okay?"

They start walking toward the building. "I know, I know, he just infuriates me," he says.

"You and half the town, more than half," Lizzie agrees.

As they get closer they can hear a few muffled voices chanting, as they keep walking it becomes clear, *Save Our Town! Save Our School! Vote No and Save Your Tax Bill Too!*

"Uh, none of what they're saying makes sense," Jack says, as they walk around the ten or so protesters.

"I know, I know," says Lizzie, hoping they can sneak by unnoticed. As soon as she thinks that someone spots them.

"It's all their fault!" Bud Mackelroy shouts. "You washashores just go home!"

Lizzie starts laughing. "Bud, I was born here, and you know that, and so was he," she says pointing at Jack. "I know you like making stuff up, but everyone here knows you're the real washashore, you moved here in high school."

"What happened to not engaging them," Jack says under his breath, leading Lizzie away.

"Ugh, I know! They just make me so mad! At least be accurate!" she says to them, turning around and getting one last dig in.

"Save it for the meeting, we're probably going to need to push back a little bit, or a lot, depending on the veracity of their presence," he says, opening the door to the school. "We need to be on our game and not let them throw us off."

"Yes sir," she gives a little salute, "I am here to be a team player, I will save my passion for when we need it."

Jack finds a seat in the gym and puts his coat on the back. It's filling up quickly, which he hopes is a good sign. "This good for you?" he asks.

"Hmm, do you think it's a good idea for us to sit together? It might make our case for the Gazette being neutral a little suspect, don't you think?"

"Good point, we can wave to each other," he says, smiling nervously at her.

"Yeah, I think I should sit with my dad and Stan," she says. "I should go find my dad and check-in." She leans over and hugs Jack. "I'm with you in spirit, okay? Your parents will be here soon, right?"

"Yes, they will," he says. "Let's hope we are heading to Murphy's in a couple of hours to celebrate, okay?" Jack says.

"Yes! Here's to clinking glasses over our success, fingers crossed!" Lizzie says, turning to go find her dad. "We can text too, if you're getting stressed!" Jack gives her a thumb's up and sits down.

"There you are," she says to her dad who has saved her and the family seats. "You hear anything from anyone about how it's looking?"

Peter shrugs his shoulders, "I think it's looking good for both projects, but Billy and Bud are doing their level best to sidetrack people and make them think this is too good to be true, that somehow they're being lied to."

"About what? That their taxes aren't going to go up much at all? That this building isn't over 50 years old and in dire need of repairs? That we're losing people in droves because they can't afford to live here?" Lizzie feels her pulse quicken and takes another deep breath, letting it out slowly. "I've got to stay calm, getting upset isn't going to help anyone." She sits down, takes off her jacket and puts it on her lap.

Peter joins her, and then sees Gabby, Shannon and Matt crossing the gymnasium. He stands up and waves them over, "I've saved seats for all of you," he says, gesturing to the three seats with various items, pens, notebooks, and a hat marking them as saved.

"Here's a sandwich for you, and some herbal tea," she says to Peter, handing him an insulated bag and a travel mug. "You need to take a break and eat something," she gestures for him to sit down.

Matt, sitting on the other side of their parents, leans over to Lizzie. "Bud and Billy are certainly in rare form tonight. They yelled at me that I am 'in the pocket of big alternative energy,'" he says laughing. "I don't even know what that means!"

Lizzie laughs, "Oh, he called me a washashore, and Jack too. This is going to be an interesting night," she says, shaking her head.

Gabby takes another travel mug out of her NPR tote and gives it to Lizzie. "Here's a decaf green tea with one dollop of honey, just how you like it," she says as she hands her the mug.

"Thanks, Mom, you're the best." She's surveying the room and is heartened to see lots of younger adults, and even some teens. She recognizes many of the farmers, artists and fishermen and women from all the stories she's been writing about Terra Marique. We may just do this yet, she thinks.

There's a hush as the selectboard members and the planning board come in and take their seats at the front of the room behind a long table. The town moderator, Sharon Mackenzie, takes her place at a lecturn adjacent to the table and she swings her gavel.

"Welcome everyone to the Spring Town Meeting, we're very happy to see so many of you here tonight to vote on these two important projects for Cranberry Harbor."

"The two projects you are shoving down the throats of our citizens!" Someone yells.

Peter leans over to Lizzie, "I'd recognize Billy's bellow anywhere," he says, rolling his eyes.

Sharon pounds her gavel loudly, startling everyone. "Outbursts like that will not be permitted, Mr. Taylor, if that happens again you will be escorted out of the building."

Lizzie's phone vibrates with a text from Jack. "And...it's going to be that kind of night!" He included an eye rolling emoji.

She looks across the gym at him and nods.

"We have several people who want to speak, and we're going to try to keep this as brief, and as civil as we can. Is that clear?"

Sharon has clearly prepared herself for what the night could bring, and she's not accepting any challenges for power or anyone being out of order. She is just not having it.

"Alright, so the first item on the agenda is the renovation of the high school. Mr. Mackelroy has requested the floor, so he will open the public comments. Sir, you have three minutes."

"Three minutes?!" He practically bellows, then calms himself down as he sees a police officer move a little closer. "Fine, I can say what I need to say in one minute. This is a total waste of our tax dollars! These kids don't need computer labs, fancy new classrooms, locker rooms, and such. This school was good enough for me, and it's good enough for them. Our taxes are going to double!" There's a collective groan and some booing from the crowd. Sharon once again wields her gavel.

"That's enough," she says to the crowd. "Let him have his three minutes, and then you can have your turn."

"Mr. Mackelroy, you can continue," she says.

"And you have to know that the Gazette is in cahoots with the powers that be because they haven't run one of my letters that I wrote talking about how lots of us feel about this boondoggle."

Lizzie leans over to her dad, "'Cahoots' and 'boondoggle' in one sentence. That's got to be some kind of record."

"And maybe if all his letters weren't full of threats, expletives and lies we would have run them," Peter replies.

"So in closing, I just want to say I don't even recognize this town anymore," he's starting to sputter a bit, clearly, if he had notes he's not using them. "I want things to stay like they were when I was a kid. Change isn't good. So I say let's keep Cranberry Harbor like the Norman Rockwell place it's always been. And if you don't want your taxes to triple, vote no!"

Peter leans over to Lizzie, "Wow, not one swearing tirade, I'm surprised!

Lizzie laughs. "Yeah, that was a whole bunch of nothing, maybe this won't be as vitriolic as we feared."

She looks over at Jack who is nervously running his hands through his hair.

"Does anyone else have comments?" Sharon asks. She looks up and sees a line has formed behind the microphone in the aisle. "Oh, apparently there are many of you..." She clears her throat. "Okay, same rules, three minutes."

A very nervous young man moves toward the mic. "Uh, hi, my name is Mike Lowell, I graduated last year from this school, and I am here to say-"

"Are you registered to vote, Mr. Lowell? And where do you live?" Sharon asks.

"Yes. I mean, yes ma'am, I am registered to vote, and I live with my parents when I'm not at college? Becky and Tyler Lowell? We live at 36 Sea Street, Cranberry Harbor."

"Okay, please continue," she says.

"So, anyway, I just wanted to say, I went all through school here, and I wanted to voice my support for this renovation. In my opinion it's way overdue. I played sports all four years and all of us stopped taking showers here because the water was so gross. It was like, brown. I had three classes my senior year in classrooms with no windows, and the heat didn't work, and there was no AC. So we froze all winter and were so hot in the last weeks of school our teacher had us meet in the cafeteria. The kids in Cranberry Harbor deserve and need a place that is clean and safe. Thank you."

The crowd bursts into applause. "Thank you, Mr. Lowell," Sharon says, motioning to the next speaker. Person after person talks about how needed the renovations are, for every five people who are pro renovation, there's one negative one that is always met with stony silence, quite a contrast to the cheers and woots for the pro folks.

An hour into testimonies, Sharon levels her gavel and asks if everyone is ready for the vote. Everyone holds up their voter cards, save a few outliers who seem to want more debate.

"The ayes have it," she says. She then reads the formal proposal, the budget, and gives the directions. "Everyone keep your card up until the person counting your section signals you to put it down."

"It's pretty amazing isn't it that we still run our government that way they did two hundred years ago?" Lizzie says, getting ready to vote yes. "I think that's good?" she says to her father.

"Ha, I have to say I sometimes wonder if we'd be better off stepping into the twenty-first century, you know, electronic counters or something," Peter says.

Lizzie is stunned. "Really? The guy who calls Twitter, Tweeter, thinks we should be more plugged in at Town Meeting?"

"Well, maybe I'm getting a little more with it," he laughs.

"Well, we welcome you to this century, sir," Lizzie jokes.

Lizzie's phone dings, it's a text from Jack.

I think the naysayers are saving their strength to fight our project. #worried

Lizzie looks over to him, and does a hugging gesture, and tilts her head.

She texts him back. *Try to stay positive. There's a lot of young people here. I've never seen so many people under 60 at a meeting. Love you xo*

Jack is holding up his voter card with one hand and reading his phone with his other. He looks over at Lizzie, smiles, and nods.

Section by section puts their hands down as the counters signal them to do so. The people counting have these hand-held counting devices, and Lizzie prays everyone is accurate.

"It's going to take a few minutes to get the count tallied," Sharon says from her lectern. "Why don't we all take a few moments to stretch our legs, and regroup before the next item, the development called, 'Terra Marique,'" she reads from her notes.

"It's a socialist plot to take over the town!" Bud Mackelroy is at it again. Lizzie rolls her eyes, and looks over at Jack who is walking toward her.

"Hi Peter," he says to Lizzie's dad.

"You hanging in there okay?" he asks Jack.

He nods, "As well as I could have expected," he says. "Though I think things are about to get a lot more heated. I said to Lizzie that I think they gave up fighting the school project because they were so outnumbered. This may be a horse of a different color," he says, evoking the *Wizard of Oz,* to Lizzie's surprise. She smiles at him.

"Okay, can everyone return to their seats?" Sharon asks, having returned to her post.

It takes a few moments for everyone to walk back to their seats and get settled.

Once the room is quiet, Sharon opens up a folded piece of paper. She clears her throat and begins to read. "We have 1678 yays for the renovation project, and 49 nays. The town has spoken, the yays have it!" She slams her gavel and the gym erupts in applause, foot stomping and cheers.

Lizzie, Peter, Gabby, Shannon and Matt all burst into applause as well. Matt jumps up and high-fives Lizzie. Her phone buzzes.

Hey, thought we agreed, no high-fives! Jack texted. They look at each other across the room and laugh. Lizzie shrugs.

I did not instigate the high-five I was a mere recipient, she texts back. They smile, and get ready for the next item on the agenda. Their project. Something tells Lizzie the path isn't going to be quite so easy for them.

CHAPTER 9

"ALRIGHT, we now move on to item two. The proposal is regarding the parcel of land presently owned by the town to be turned over to a new nonprofit that would be overseen by a board of directors, all from the town, and the project to be managed by Jack Cahoon. The purpose of this nonprofit is to provide housing, farming, workspace and alternative energy sources which will include a discrete turbine, solar panels and state-of-the-art storage batteries, making the entire enterprise completely energy self-sufficient. The goal is to provide housing for 100 families and individuals. Mr. Cahoon states that the intention is to keep much of the aesthetic beauty to the property, make as little of an environmental impact as possible, while providing much needed housing and opportunities for as many year-round jobs as possible."

Sharon looks up from her papers. "Mr. Cahoon has asked for a few minutes to speak to better explain what he and his investors envision for this project."

Lizzie looks over at Jack as he makes his way to a mic stand in the aisle near him. Lizzie is posting the highlights of the meeting on the paper's social media - mostly Instagram and X, but also some posts on Facebook too for the older demographic still hooked on Facebook. Doing this was a nice distraction from worrying and obsessing.

"He's going to turn this place into Silicon Valley! Vote no!" Someone, most likely, Bud yells.

"Thank you, Madam Moderator. And to answer that comment, no, this will not turn our beloved community into Silicon Valley, but if we keep going the way we are we are going to turn into Sunset Pines, South Hampton, or some other community that is not right for us. And I will dispel the inaccurate notion that this will raise your taxes. It will not. This endeavor is being funded by a handful of investors and grants. Anything else you've heard is a lie. " He pauses and looks around the room, and takes a breath. "We are at a crossroads here in Cranberry Harbor, my friends. The median price for a house is well beyond the means of an average person. We are in danger of losing our future, of losing all the young people who will be graduating from this wonderful new high school and leaving because they can't afford it, and there's no future for them here. We have teachers, police and firefighters who live with their parents. We have frontline people who work in our supermarkets and restaurants, who have to travel almost an hour because there is no place for them to live here. We have always been a community that yes, while we had some wealthy second home owners, and retirees, we also had folks like my parents who worked hard their whole lives, my mom as an accountant and my dad as an electrician. But they could buy a house here, they could raise a family here. Now, with the median cost of a home closing in on a million dollars, that dream is no longer possible." He pauses again. "Add to this the threat of climate change," there's a loud boo from a very small faction, "and life as we know it on Cape Cod, and here in Cranberry Harbor could be coming to an end. Now I know this little nonprofit isn't going to save Cape Cod, and it's certainly not going to save the planet, but it's a start. It's a step in the right direction. What we envision is a place where science and living off the land, and the creative genius of this special place can come together and create a self-sufficient community that will benefit us all." There is wild applause and cheering. "I ask you to please vote yes for this project, and take a step toward envisioning a new, greener, and more equitable future for Cranberry Harbor."

Lizzie's eyes well up and she leaps to her feet. "Yes!" she yells.

She then catches herself not exactly being an impartial journalist and sits down, and puts her hands on her lap and sits quietly.

"Thank you, Mr. Cahoon, I can see there are some others who wish to speak, Mr. Taylor, you may have the floor for three minutes," Sharon says.

"I just wanna say that project will be the worst thing to happen to Cranberry Harbor ever." Lizzie can feel her face getting hot. "He," he says, pointing at Jack, "is nothing but a carpetbagger who is going to take that land, build a bunch of places for his fancy California tech buddies and leave us hanging. I know his type, he doesn't care about this town, not one little bit. Nothing needs to change here, we're doing just fine. We don't need any outsiders coming in and changing everything!" he inexplicably yells.

Jack jumps to his feet and heads to the nearest mic. "Excuse me? Can I have a quick rebuttal?" Sharon nods.

"I'll be quick. First, I'm a native Cape Codder, I was actually born in an ambulance on our front lawn, a true native Cranberry Harbor resident, Mr.Taylor, and you know that. Second, this is housing for people who live here. There may be a few tech people I bring in to help run the project, but priority for all the housing, farming, and commercial art and kitchen space is for residents, those who have small businesses, and those who work fulltime in town. Mr. Taylor and his group have been spreading misinformation from the get-go. They have been invited time and again to sit in on meetings but have always declined. Instead they prefer to craft the fictional narrative they are feeding to all of you." He stops and looks around the room. "Look, I love this town. Ever since I moved away three years ago I have spent every day planning how I could get back here, and how I could do something good for the town. Terra Marique is that dream come to fruition. I am committed to this project, but more than that I am committed to this community. I plan to raise my own family here, and I would do nothing to harm it.Thank you." Jack turns and heads back to his seat.

There is much applause, but there is still a little booing. Jack sits down and looks over at Lizzie. She's having a hard time hearing Jack being attacked. She is literally sitting on her hands to avoid wildly gesturing to the crowd. She also felt a flutter in her chest at his mention of raising a family there. It's what she wants too.

"Are you doing okay?" her dad leans over and asks.

"Yeah, I just get so mad," she says. "I'm hoping some positive folks will get up."

As soon as she says that, Leah steps up to the mic. She's been running Sea Coast Coffee for her grandmother for the last couple of years, and is also a big proponent of Cranberry Harbor becoming greener.

"Hello, I am Leah Alden. I live at 14 Main Street. Other than my four years away at college, I have lived my entire life on this little peninsula. I love this town. As most of you know, I am now running the business my grandmother started decades ago, Sea Coast Coffee. If I didn't have family to live with, and if I hadn't had an established business to join, I wouldn't be able to be here." She stops, looks down and takes a breath. "A lot of you are new residents, and I am not saying that because I think we locals are better, or should have more rights, but I only say it because you probably don't have the history we do. And with that history is the commitment to stay and make it work, not just for yourself, but for the people coming up behind you. As someone who runs a small business here, I know how hard it is for us to find help because no one can afford to live here." She pauses again. "Many of you probably also don't know that we didn't used to get the kinds of heat and storms we do now. Maybe some of you are aware of how much shoreline we are losing every year, but I'm betting a lot of you don't think about how we can change that. Your first experience of that reality may have been when the Snack Shack at Sea Meadow Beach got washed into the ocean three years ago during a winter nor'easter. But this is something I think about every day, and it's something Jack Cahoon and his team have also put a tremendous amount of thought into. I went to college to study environmental science, I didn't plan on taking over the coffee shop. I know what trouble we're in if we don't make some big changes, nationally, and locally. Like Jack said, this one project won't change the course of the planet, but it's a start. It also won't solve all our housing needs, but it's a start. We need to start somewhere, right? Please vote yes."

There's much applause as Leah walks back to her seat and sits down. Lizzie looks over at her and can see her letting out a big breath and letting go of the stress of speaking up.

Next up is an older woman Lizzie can't place. She slowly makes her way to the mic using a cane.

At first her voice is barely audible as she's too far from the microphone.

"Miss Millie, you need to stand closer," says a young man sitting nearby. He gets up and helps her.

"Thank you, dear," she says.

Now Lizzie knows who she is, she's Millicent Maguire, always called Miss Millie, she was the town librarian all through Lizzie's school years in Cranberry Harbor. She was always kind and encouraging when Lizzie was writing for the Gazette in high school and college, sometimes finding information for her stored on microfiche in long-forgotten places in the library.

"I won't take but a minute," she says, "But I just had to speak up." Lizzie finds herself sitting on the edge of her seat wondering what she will say, if she will be pro or con.

"I just wanted to say that I am 97-years-old, and this is the only place I have ever lived. I was here before cars, why, there were lots of houses that didn't even have electricity when I was a girl. I've seen people, businesses and ideas come and go. I'm betting most of you don't even know we once had a bustling train station." She pauses for a moment, and Lizzie is worried she's feeling unsteady, but actually she's far from it. "The one constant has always been a solid year-round community. We were always there for each other in hard times, like the Depression, wars, storms and personal losses. If we lose our young people, if we don't have them starting businesses, raising families, buying and building homes, what will we be? Last month I fell down and the rescue squad was there in minutes. The young paramedic who helped me told me she lives almost an hour away because there are no places to rent year-round here. She wants to live here more than anything. All of you people booing and saying bad things about little Jack Cahoon?" Lizzie smiles and looks over at Jack who is clearly blushing, "you have no idea how lucky we are to have someone like him who wants to help us. If it was up to you fellas, Billy and Bud, we'd be stuck in the era I grew up in, which I wouldn't wish on anyone! Well, except for maybe the weather which was not nearly as dramatic," She laughs. Oh my gosh, Lizzie thinks, she's still sassy and so present. She knows she probably shouldn't but she applauds and the room joins her in thunderous support. "If you love this town, and I'm sure you do, you will vote yes on this project and let these smart young folks begin the work to save our economy, our shoreline and our community. Thank you. And now I have to get back to my seat and sit down, because this is a lot for a little old lady," she smiles. Three different people get up to help her, including Alexis who takes her arm and leads her back to her seat.

Lizzie quickly types a text to Jack.

Well if that doesn't put this over the top I don't know what will.

Jack looks at his phone, and then at Lizzie and makes a little prayer gesture.

"Is there anyone else who wishes to speak?" Sharon Mackenzie asks from the front of the room.

A few people had been lined up, but Lizzie senses they've read the room and have all sat back down.

"Well then, let's take a vote to decide if public debate is over and if we will stop debate and take a vote," she says.

Just then there is a lone, deep voice from the crowd.

"I got something to say," says the deep baritone, Lizzie is straining but can't see who it is.

"Okay, sir, make your way to one of the microphones and you have three minutes," Sharon says.

A man makes his way down the center aisle. He's wearing a red plaid, flannel shirt, black knit cap, well-worn jeans and equally well-worn work boots. He has a hand-carved cane and is walking with a bit of a limp. Lizzie looks over at her dad wondering who this is. He doesn't look at all familiar to her.

Peter looks shocked, and mouths to Lizzie, "Oh my god." Lizzie turns back to see the man remove the cap, allowing a cascade of white hair to tumble out. She looks back at her dad.

"I thought he was long dead," he whispers to her. "That's Shadrach Nickerson, I haven't seen him in years."

"Who is he?" Lizzie whispers.

"A cranberry farmer, a fisherman, bricklayer, you name it, he did it," Peter says.

"I've never seen him," she says.

"Well, neither have I, in decades, I can't imagine what he's got to say."

Lizzie has been so distracted whispering with her dad that she hadn't noticed the other whispers circling around the room. Apparently they are not the only curious people there.

Sharon gently strikes her gavel, signaling to everyone to be quiet.

"Ma'am, I have not spoken up about anything in this town in, well, I've never spoken up. I just keep to myself. But I had to come out for this. I am Shadrach Nickerson. I live down at the end of Nickerson Road. Lived there all my 87 years." He looks around the room. "My family has been a part of this town for four hundred years, my ancestors built many of the buildings you all use every day. Nickerson is one of the oldest names in Cranberry Harbor. I don't like change. I don't like new fangled things like the internet, but I'm smart enough to know what I don't know. What these young folks have in mind though isn't all new. Using the sun and the wind for energy is about as old as it gets. Somewhere along the line humanity went off the rails thinking they could outsmart science and nature and use up and pollute the planet and not have to pay the piper down the road. Well folks, the bill has come due, and we have to do something. And we have to do it now if we are going to save this town. We are drowning in plastic, we are heating up this planet so much that it's trying to throw us off like so many fleas on a dog." Lizzie looks down and smiles, shaking her head at how wonderful he is. "And if we don't do something now about making it so young people can afford to make a home here? Well, soon it's going to be me, Millie, and a few rich folks who I doubt are going to want to be stocking the shelves at Bradford's or driving a fire truck. So all you naysayers, I'm looking at you Bud and Billy, you two have never done a lick of anything to help this town, all you like to do is stir up trouble and try to make yourselves look like you big fish when you're nothing but chum. You need to sit down if you're not going to pitch in. You are going to be responsible for the death of this town all because you just need to shoot off your mouths. Well I'm telling you, for the sake of all of us here, just shut the heck up and let people who know a whole lot more than you do to help save us."

He pauses and the crowd begins to loudly clap and cheer him on.

Once again the sound of the gavel breaks through the noise. "Quiet, please, Mr. Nickerson, you need to wind this up," Moderator Mackenzie says.

"Yes, ma'am. I've said all I need to." He pauses and looks down. "There's been a lot of mistakes in the history of this town, beginning with how the Native Amercians were treated when families like mine arrived. We cannot undo the damage done by our ancestors, nor can we undo the damage done with poor planning for the influx of folks with so much money that they priced out the people who do all the living, working, and growing of this town. But we have the power to make changes now. We can start now to be the people who do the right thing. The right thing for the people, and the planet. Thank you."

With that the crowd jumps to its feet and not even the sound of the gavel can contain it.

"Quiet! Please, quiet! We need to take our seats," Sharon says. "By a show of hands, are we ready to take a vote?"

Practically every single hand goes up. "The majority has it, we will now take a vote to approve the town giving the land at the southern end of town, 45 acres, to the Terra Marique nonprofit corporation to build housing for no more than 300, and to include wind turbines, solar panels, acres for local farming, a commercial cooking facility for local vendors, and other outbuildings for community use. All of you know the protocol. I will ask who is voting for this project first, hold your cards up until the counter for your area signals you to put it down. We will then ask for the no votes, same procedure. We will now start the vote, all those in favor, please raise your card."

Lizzie looks around and it is a sea of blue cards raised over the heads of everyone. She and Jack look at each other from across the gym and are both shaking their leads in disbelief.

In under five minutes the cards are all down. "All those voting no, please raise your cards," she requests. There are a smattering of cards scattered across the vast room. The counters are done in about one minute.

It's clear the yes vote has it, but they of course have to wait for the final tally.

Keely from Town Hall brings a paper to Sharon who opens it. "Alright, so we have 1934 votes for the project, and 123 against. The proposal passes."

Lizzie doesn't care if she looks biased, she jumps up and runs over to Jack. "You did it! You really did it!" she says, hugging him tightly.

He squeezes her and lifts her off her feet. "Yes! We did it, not just me." He sets her down. "I'm so grateful to you and your dad for all the stories, all the op-ed pieces, and well, just being there for me. Thank you." He leans down and kisses her.

"This is a huge move forward for the town," Lizzie says. "Even if I didn't love you I'd be for this project. But since I do love you, it's even sweeter."

Alexis, Leah, Sean and Ben all come over and there are high-fives and hugs all around.

"Clearly they didn't get the high five memo," Lizzie jokes to Jack.

"I am all in for the high-fives now that we won," he says, kissing her again.

Their revelry however is cut short when Billy and Bud strut on over, pushing their way into their happy circle.

"Yeah, you go ahead and celebrate now, Cahoon," Billy says. "You may have won this battle, but the war is just beginning."

"Billy, I don't want to be at war with you, or anyone," Jack says, extending his hand. "Why don't we all just move forward and let bygones be bygones. Clearly the town wants this."

"They don't know what they want," says Bud.

"You just watch your back," Billy says, walking away.

"Yeah, what he said," Bud chimes in.

The group of friends all look at each other in stoney silence.

"Um, he just threatened you and we all heard it," Alexis says.

"Yeah, that was definitely a threat," Lizzie agrees. "Maybe we should talk to the police?"

"No, I'm going to chalk this up to the heat of the moment and being sore losers," Jack says. "I don't want to start this project with police and charges of threats. Let's hope as time goes on they'll see that the town really wants this and we can all move forward. Peacefully."

"Okay, but we've all got your back, Jack," Ben says, "And I did not intend to make that a rhyme," everyone laughs, easing the tension of the moment.

The group breaks up after deciding to go to Murphy's to celebrate.

As Jack and Lizzie head to their cars, after saying goodnight to their families, Lizzie takes Jack's arm. "I'm a little scared about those guys. You really think that they're going to calm down and not do anything?"

Jack stops and looks at her. "Yeah, I really think they'll move on to something else in due time." Lizzie knows Jack well enough to know when he's trying to reassure her about something, so she decides not to press the subject.

"Well, if you're not worried I won't be either," she lies, hugging him before she gets in her car. She starts her car, fastens her seatbelt and thinks, he may be certain, but she's not, and she's going to keep her eye on those two. They're up to something, she doesn't know what, but between her and her dad they have decades of investigative journalism, and she's going to find out.

CHAPTER 10

SEAN AND BEN were so thrilled to be out, having gotten a sitter for baby Ollie, that they were the first ones to arrive at Murphy's and had secured a table for all of them before they got there. They'd missed this cozy neighborhood place, right down to the red checkered tablecloths.

Once they all have their drinks of choice, Ben raises his glass. He clears his throat, "Huh, I'm feeling very emotional about this," he says, choking up a little. "I'll be honest, when you first started talking about this, it felt impossible-"

"It hasn't been built yet, my friend," Jack jokes.

Ben laughs. "True, but the fact that you got it this far, past all the people who never want anything to change, the Billys and Buds, and the last-ones-over-the-bridge who want to live in the image that has been their fantasy of Cranberry Harbor forever, it's really unbelievable. But as excited as I am to have Terra Marique become a reality, I am by far more excited about having my old friends back in town for what I hope is a long, long time. So, to Jack, Lizzie, Alexis, Leah, here's to many more gatherings, time spent together, and growing Cranberry Harbor in a positive way."

They all clink glasses, "Thank goodness you wrapped that up, I was getting ready to grab the hook!" Sean teases, as only a spouse can. Ben looks sad. "I'm kidding, honey, I felt like we were all going to dissolve into tears and I had to lighten things up."

"Well I thought it was lovely," Lizzie says. "And I feel very emotional too. I'm so grateful both those projects passed, and I'm excited for the future of Cranberry Harbor, for you Jack, for the paper, and for all of us. But I'm also really happy and feel so lucky to have come back here. It's the last thing I ever envisioned for my life, but here we are! And I couldn't be happier."

"To Cranberry Harbor, old friends and new, and to the future!" Alexis toasts. They all clink glasses again.

"Wow, we really have become our parents, haven't we?" Jack laughs. "We're all squishy, and emotional…"

"Hey, there are worse things, all our families are pretty darn great," Lizzie mock protests.

"Yes, they are," Jack agrees.

Their food all arrives, a smattering of many items on the menu - everything from cheeseburgers to chowder to fish tacos, and some of Murphy's famous fries and onion rings as well, and while they eat things fall silent for a little bit.

"I haven't eaten an entire meal for at least two weeks," Jack says, finishing up his fish tacos. "I don't think I completely realized just how stressed out I've been." He sits back in his chair and sighs. "That tasted so good."

"Yeah, I've been living on coffee and scones from Sea Coast," Leah says. "Occupational hazard," she jokes. "I know I'm not as invested as you three," she says, speaking to Jack, Lizzie, and Alexis, "but I wanted this to happen so much. I want to stay here, I want to run the shop, I also want to maybe someday get married, have a family, and have my kids grow up here. The way things have been going, it's been looking more and more like a total pipe dream. Now though, maybe not so much. I can't thank you enough, Jack, for giving me something I haven't had a lot of since I moved back here, hope."

"Wow, Leah, thank you," Jack says, now he's choked up. "All you've been doing, all on your own, making your business more sustainable, pushing the town to think in new ways environmentally, that all paved the way for what we're going to be doing. Honestly, if you hadn't done all you have, this never would have passed. So thank you for all your hard work."

They all toast again, and Jack leans over and kisses Lizzie. "I love you so much," he says quietly. "You have no idea how much," he kisses her again.

Everyone is so emotional, it's been a long year of planning, researching, writing, meeting, praying and some begging too, to get them to this very moment.

"Does anyone else feel like they could sleep for a week?" Alexis asks, looking around the table. "Well, you two probably always feel that way," she says, pointing to Ben and Sean, "I don't have a baby but I kind of feel like this project has been kind of a collective baby for all of us, and I am ready to take a couple of days off and rest!"

Just then Jack's phone rings, it's an unfamiliar number so he lets it go to voicemail. A minute later his phone alerts him to a message. He presses the phone to his ear to listen above the din of Murphy's.

Hi Mr. Cahoon, this is Sam Blackburn from the Boston Sentinel. Rumor has it you are breaking down some barriers there building a new green community on the outskirts of Cranberry Harbor, We'd love to do a story about it. Please call me, my number is 323-555-2313. I look forward to hearing from you.

"Well that's weird, a reporter from the Sentinel just called me, they want to do a story, but he gave me an L.A. area code," Jack says, putting his phone down on the table.

"They could have moved from California to work at the Sentinel," Leah says. "Lots of my friends here don't have a local number."

"Yeah, it could be," Lizzie says, 'but I know they have no local reporters at the Boston office. Chances are pretty good this person-"

"Sam Blackburn," Jack says.

"...that Sam is living in California, freelancing and writing stories about Massachusetts," Lizzie says, shrugging her shoulders.

"Wow, how can they do that and get any kind of feel for the community?" Sean asks.

"They can't. They may be brilliant writers, but they don't get what the community is all about, who the people are who are involved, the impacts, and what it means. It's incredibly generic newspaper writing that has lost all sense of local journalism. It's really sad," Lizzie says. "And even sadder is how rare it is that people are doing what my dad and I are. If we didn't have the angel investors we do, we wouldn't still be here. It's sad, but it's going to take people with money and a commitment to journalism to make an investment in communities like ours".

She looks at Jack. "So what are you going to do?"

"I don't want to talk to a guy in L.A., but I suppose I should call and see what's up. I also don't like that paper at all since they laid you off, so I'm already biased."

"This guy probably isn't going to be the last reporter calling you," Ben says, "so you'd better get used to being in demand. This is a big deal, and as the country begins to pivot more and more green, this project is going to be an example of what communities can do."

"Yikes, like I didn't already feel a lot of pressure! Now I'm going to be the face of this project?" Jack says, looking a little worried. "I'm a tech guy, I'm not someone who ever aspired to be on morning television or the front page of a national newspaper."

Lizzie puts her arm around his shoulders. "No one is expecting you to do that, as the project gets going you can have other people do the press for you, take care of social media, and just manage all of that for you. You won't have time to be posting on Instagram or fielding calls. We'll all help you, so don't think you're doing this all by yourself. You're not. You've got a team, and we're the first line of defense. Okay?"

For the first time in several minutes Jack smiles. He lets out a deep breath. "Okay, you're right. I just kind of panicked a little bit."

The evening winds down pretty early. Everyone is exhausted from the stress of the evening, not to mention the build up to it.

"We have definitely lost our ability to stay out late," says Sean, glancing at the clock on the wall which says 10:02." He sighs, "Ah, the reality of parenthood."

"And we wouldn't trade it for anything," Ben says, putting his arm around Sean. "It's exhausting, but it is the best thing we've ever done."

They all gather their coats, Jack has paid the tab, despite many protests that it's his night and he shouldn't pay, so they make up for it by all putting down cash and leaving an enormous tip for their server.

The group spills out of Murphy's and heads to their cars, after saying their goodnights and sharing hugs. Jack walks Lizzie to her car.

"Well that was quite an evening. If I kept a diary I'd go home and write about it," Jack says, leaning against her car.

"Well, I think today most people call them 'journals?'" she laughs, "and I do have a journal, not a diary, and will make sure to make note of the date and time when all this came to fruition, lest we get so busy we forget."

"I'm so grateful to have you," Jack says, pulling her close to him. "I know there's a lot to do in the next weeks, months,-"

"Years," Lizzie interrupts, "Sorry, you were saying..."

He laughs, "Yeah, you're probably right. But now the funding will begin to kick in and I'll be able to get more help, and spread some of the tasks around. First order of business is going to be hiring an assistant. Someone I can delegate things to. That will help."

"Maybe then we'll finally be able to get away for a weekend!" Lizzie posits, hopeful.

"Yes! We need a couple of nights away for sure," he agrees.

"Though, it's hard to think of being too far away because, well, stuff keeps happening and we're both in charge of so much, and I'd worry-"

"I know, me too." he says. They stand there in the chilly March air, both leaning on her car. "I know, what if we went to the Cape's End Inn, in Provincetown? This time of year it's not too crowded, and it's close enough that if either of us was really needed we could be back here in 40 minutes."

"But it also feels like a different world...I think that's perfect! This weekend?" Lizzie asks, hopeful. She could really use a break.

"Yeah! I think before things get really crazy we should just go for it," he says.

"I'll call tomorrow and see if they have any rooms available," Lizzie says. She's getting cold and as much as she loves Jack, she wants to get home and in her pajamas, so she reaches for the door handle.

"I can call, you don't have to," Jack says.

"That's okay, I kind of know the guy at the front desk, he's super nice, and maybe he can make sure we get in," she says, smiling.

"Ah, always the one with the connections," he says, kissing her on the cheek.

"It's all about relationships," she opens the car door and before she gets in, kisses Jack. "Good night, my love, I will talk to you in the morning."

"Good night. I love you, Lizzie Martin. You are the best."

"Well, I'm not so sure about that, but I'm glad you think so."

With that she closes the door, starts the car, fastens her seatbelt and drives off giving Jack a wave.

"This is going to be the best weekend getaway ever, Miss Martin, just you wait," he says, smiling to himself, as he watches her drive off. "I am going to make this something for that journal, that's for sure."

CHAPTER 11

Lizzie slept better than she had in weeks. She knew she'd been stressed, but had no idea just how much it was affecting her whole self. From not sleeping well, to feeling less patient and snippy, to not eating as well as she should, all the worry had taken its toll.

When she woke up, extremely late for her at 7:45, she stretched and smiled and felt more relaxed than she'd felt in, well, forever. As she stirred in bed, yawning, stretching and sighing a little her mom was walking by, and just happened to have a cup of coffee in hand.

"Ah, you're awake!" Gabby says, placing the coffee on the nightstand. "I'm so glad you slept! I've been hearing you up at night, and then waking early in the morning and I was beginning to worry about you."

Lizzie sits up, fluffs her pillows behind her and leans back. She picks up the coffee mug and takes a sip. "Hmmm, this is so good, thank you Mom. And I hope I haven't been keeping you up with all my insomnia, I'm so sorry about that."

"No, I was awake too! I hated that you were as well." She sits down on the floor, cross legged and hugs Daisy who's jumped onto her lap. "I'm just so glad this is over and that we can all move forward and start obsessing about something else," she laughs.

"I know, right? I have a feeling it's always going to be something," Lizzie says, continuing to drink her coffee. "So Jack and I decided to get away for a couple of nights. We're going to Provincetown."

"Oh! That's wonderful! Cape's End Inn I assume?" Gabby says. It's a family favorite for a close, but very special getaway.

"Of course! I know Rusty gets to work at about 8:30, so I'm going to call and see if he can help us. I'd really like to go sooner than later, so I hope they've got something." She finishes the coffee and puts the mug back on the night table.

"I'm betting your chances are pretty good," Gabby says, standing up. "There's no holidays this week, and the weather predictions aren't the best, so I doubt too many people will be clamoring to come to the Cape this week, or weekend."

"I hope you're right, because we definitely need a couple of days to unplug and relax," She tosses the covers aside and gets up, stretches and hugs her mom. "Thank you so much for the coffee, and for being such a great support these last few weeks. And, well, forever. You are a rock, for sure."

Gabby squeezes her right back. "It's very nice to be appreciated, but I love having you here, and I love being able to help you in any little ways I can. It makes me happy, honey."

"You are very much appreciated, that is for sure," Lizzie says. "I'm going to take a quick shower, then call Rusty, and head to the paper." She hadn't checked their social media yet. That was bound to be a place where folks like Billy and Bud would take their ire, and she had to be more fully awake before she started dealing with them. Her standard approach was to stand back and let people have their say, but step in if it got too personal or ugly. That fortunately had only happened a few times, and usually around silly things like a new rotary, or the recent ban on yard pesticides which came when the town had qualified as a "Blue Community," meaning they were making water quality and safety a priority.

Lizzie was out of the shower in no time, and while still in her robe, towel on her head, she called the inn.

Rusty answered on the second ring.

"Cape's End Inn," he says, very chipper for so early in the morning.

"Hi Rusty, it's Lizzie Martin, how are you?"

"Hey, sweetie, I'm excellent! You?"

"I'm good, a little burned out and tired, but good. To that end, Jack and I were looking to get away for a night or two, how are things looking down there? Are you fully booked?" she asks, quietly praying he says they have a room for them.

"Well, someone just beat you to the last room, the tower room no less," he says.

"Oh no! Darn!"

"But thankfully, it was your guy, Jack, so…" he laughs a little. "Sorry, that was probably kind of mean."

"It was downright cruel, sir! You do not tease a woman in desperate need of a couple of days away," she laughs. "I can't believe he did that! I told him I'd take care of it. He's too sweet."

"He said you were going to call but he wanted to do this for you, so the phone was actually ringing when I walked in at 8:15."

"I'm so excited! I think I've only stayed in the Tower Room one time, after I finished my Master's Degree, and Mom and Dad got it for me and I think Shannon and Alexis. It's a pretty amazing room, I can't wait!"

"Well it will be all ready for you by late this afternoon, my dear. I can't wait to see you, it's been way too long!" Rusty says.

"I know, I feel terrible that I haven't gotten down there to see you. Are you still playing music out? I haven't seen you perform in forever!" Lizzie says.

"I am! I'm playing with another guy, Luke, and we've got a good sound. As a matter of fact we're playing tomorrow night at the Beachfront, if you two feel like coming out, I'd love to see you there!" he says.

"Oh! That would be so fun! I'm not sure if Jack has anything in mind, but I will definitely see if he's up for it. He's been so tired. These last few months have been crazy, and I know I'm tired, but he's super tired."

"Yeah, I've been following everything on the Gazette's social media and in the paper of course. I'm always a loyal subscriber" he jokes.

"You are the best, Rusty, thank you. I guess I should call Jack and see when we're headed your way. I can't wait to see you!"

"We will have the room all spiffed up and ready for you! We'll see you later, hon." he says.

"Thank you again for everything," Lizzie says. "See you soon, bye!"

Lizzie smiles and feels so excited. The Tower room! This is going to be such a great getaway. She calls Jack.

"Hey, I was just going to call you," he says. "Good morning, by the way," he sounds cheerier than he has in weeks, months actually.

"Good morning to you too! So Rusty informs me that we are booked for the Tower room, I can't believe you did that! Thank you so much! I'm so excited! This is going to be awesome!"

"You do so much of the day to day planning and executing for us, I wanted to do something for you that would be a little bit of a surprise," he says.

"That was a wonderful surprise for sure! What's your day like? Are you free to go this afternoon? I could make it work if you can," she says, hopeful he will say yes.

"Yeah, I cleared my calendar for the next couple of days, so we're good to go."

"Yay! I'm so excited, Jack! We're finally getting some time away!" Lizzie is positively giddy. "I'm going to run to the paper in a few minutes, clear my desk, and I can be ready to leave by noon. You?"

"Yeah, that sounds perfect. I'll pick you up at noon and off we'll go," he says.

"I will be ready!"

Lizzie puts her phone down, and gets up and pulls her suitcase out from under her bed. It's positively dusty from lack of use. She puts it on her bed, opens it, and goes to her closet.

"Hmmm, probably two dinners out, but it's off-season, so we're not talking very dressy," she says out loud to herself.

Her mom knocks on the door, "Ohhh, you're packing! So this is really happening!" Gabby says.

"It is indeed. Jack booked the Tower Room, so I am super excited! Now I'm just trying to figure out what to bring."

"It's off-season, and pretty chilly, so probably err on the side of function more than fashion, but I'm also not 33, so I may be more practical than you!" she laughs.

"Oh, I'm being plenty practical. Nothing can ruin having fun more than the wrong choice in clothes or footwear. I've learned that lesson the hard way. It's why I hardly ever wear heels anymore,

I got tired of being in pain and not being able to walk more than a few yards!"

Gabby laughs, "I see you have the practical gene, and besides, you look beautiful and stylish in anything you wear, so be comfortable and warm!"

"I appreciate that lie, Mom. I do not look particularly stylish or beautiful in my joggers, but I appreciate you thinking I do." She pulls out a pretty, but simple black jersey dress that is a classic, plus it's thick enough to be warm, and looks great with boots. She holds it up for her mom to see. "What about this for going out to dinner tonight?"

"Oh, I love that! And I have several pashminas in different colors. If you want one to wrap around your neck, sometimes restaurants can be drafty. I'll go grab a few to see if there's one you like." She leaves and goes down the hall to her room and is back in a flash.

"Okay, so there's this one, a nice cream color, but that might be too dull, and then there's this soft rose color, and this pretty blue." She lays them all on the bed.

"Gosh, they're all so pretty," she holds each one up to her. "Which one do you think looks best on me?" She says, doing her best impersonation of a model, turning and smiling.

"I like the blue best," Gabby says, "it brings out your eyes beautifully."

"Then blue it is. Thanks Mom!" Lizzie moves on to practical items like some leggings, jeans, and a couple of sweaters. "Oh! I have to remember some slippers too because I love hanging out by the fireplace in the communal living room there, in pajamas and slippers of course. It's always so cozy and you meet such interesting people." She puts her cozy pajamas and slippers in the suitcase. "There's something equalizing about meeting people in your jammies, I think," she says, taking out a toiletry bag. "Everyone is relaxed and themselves. I love it."

"It is a wonderful spot for sure. And the views!" Gabby is almost as excited as Lizzie is.

"I know! It's been years, but I remember the incredible view. I can't wait to see the sunset from there," Lizzie says.

Gabby sits down on the bed and refolds some of the things

Lizzie has just tossed in. "I am so happy for you and Jack to be getting out of town for a little bit. You two have definitely earned a couple of days away."

"We have for sure." Lizzie sits down next to her. "Honestly? I'm a little nervous about what the next phase of this is going to look like. There's going to be so much work, and a lot of scrutiny, but one step at a time, right?" She stands up. "Okay, I think I have most everything. After I put my makeup on in the bathroom I'll grab that, my toothbrush and toothpaste, and my hairbrush." She stands there looking around.

"Yes?" her mom asks, looking at her.

"I'm just thinking, for a minute, that's all," Lizzie says, looking pensive.

"About?"

She shrugs. "I don't know, Jack was being a little mysterious about this getaway. It got me thinking..." she shakes her head, "Ugh, nevermind."

"What? What are you thinking, honey? Are you okay?" Gabby asks.

She shakes her head again, "Oh yeah! I'm great, really, Mom, don't worry."

Lizzie finishes packing, zips her bag shut and stands it up on the floor near the door. "Okay, so I am going to go to the office and check in with Dad, and be back here before noon. She looks at the clock, it's now 9:45. "I'd better get going. Thanks for your help, Mom, I'll be back soon."

When Lizzie arrived at the paper Peter was already hard at work, looking very serious sitting at his overflowing desk, jacket still on.

"Hey," she says, taking off her coat and putting down her bag. "Everything okay, you look very intense?"

"The phone's been ringing off the hook, and I'm trying to make deadline, it's just-"

Lizzie sits down. "I'm sorry, Dad, I didn't know it would be so busy today, which seems clueless on my part. I'll field the calls for a while." She opens her computer and logs on. "So who's calling?"

"Papers from all over the country, some cable news outlets,

some Boston TV stations, and a couple of national magazines too. Everyone seems to have heard about Terra Marique and wants to report on it."

"Wow, color me naive, but I had no idea our project in a small town on Cape Cod would garner so much national attention," Lizzie says.

"Actually international attention," Peter says, leaning back in his chair. "I forgot, I heard from a paper from Oslo and a reporter from Auckland. It's crazy!"

"I can't believe it! That's a little scary!" Lizzie says. "I mean, it's just a lot of eyes on our little town." She's quiet for a minute. "It's just, I hope this doesn't become a 'be careful what you wish for' moment in history for Cranberry Harbor. I want this to be for the people who live here, not another tourist attraction. This is all going to be good, right?" Lizzie feels like she's ten years old, looking for reassurance from her dad.

"Yes, it's a hot story now, but you know how long the attention span of the public is, it's miniscule, they will move on to the next big story they see on social media or cable news and move on in no time."

"I sure hope so," Lizzie says. "So given what's going on I'm wondering if Jack and I should be going away right now. I hate to leave you in the lurch–"

"No way are you not going. You are not leaving me in the lurch, and you two need to get away. You have both been working non-stop since you moved back here. You need to have some fun," Peter protests.

"Hey, we have fun," Lizzie fake-pouts.

"Yeah? When was the last time you went to a movie? You went to trivia night last month at Murphy's only because you were writing about it for the paper. You need to get out of town for a couple of days. I won't hear of you not going."

"Yes, sir," she says, trying to look serious, but then laughing. "Boy, our lives do sound very bleak when you put it like that. Fine, we will go away and have tons of fun, Okay? Does that make you happy?"

"It makes me very happy, honey." He pauses. "You know, if

there's one bit of advice I could give you, it's don't get so busy that you miss it."

"Miss what?" Lizzie asks.

"Your life. Your life with Jack, a family, if you choose to have one, but just, just don't miss it, okay?"

"Okay." She's looking at her dad who looks so pensive. "Do you feel like you missed it? Because I don't feel like you weren't there for us."

"No, yes, sort of?" He says. "All the above! It just all goes by so fast, I want you to be happy, that's all.

"I am, Dad, I really am. And I always knew you were there for me, Dad, I really did."

"Good, I'm glad to hear it," and with that the phone rings.

Lizzie puts up her hand, before Peter can reach for it. "Good morning, Cranberry Harbor Gazette?" She's nodding and looking at Peter and then mouths, "Iceland!" to him.

By the time Lizzie is ready to leave at 11:30, she's fielded calls from Los Angeles, New York, London and China. In between calls Lizzie quickly assembled a press kit they could easily send out to those making inquiries that would give them all the information, including contact numbers and emails for sources for quotes if they so desired. Jack was only going to be available if a very big paper or news station was looking for an interview. Luckily, there were now others on board who could answer the basic questions and give good quotes, leaving Jack free to be the lead on executing the project, plan, and get two days away.

"Okay, I am out of here, Dad," Lizzie says, walking around to his side of their partner desk. "And if anything comes up, you know you can–"

"Nope, I am not calling you, no way, no how," he says, standing up and hugging her. "You and Jack go and have fun and forget about all this for a couple of days. It will all be here when you get back, I promise." He smiles, hugs her again and gives her a kiss. "Now scoot!"

"Aye, aye sir," she says, turning on her heel, grabbing her coat, slipping it on, and as she picks up her purse she leans over to pick up her laptop,

"Nope, you leave that right here, no laptops allowed!" Peter scolds.

Lizzie sighs, "but what if–"

"No, back away from the computer and leave the building…" he says smiling at her.

She puts her hands up, "Fine! You win." She backs up to the door, waves to her dad and leaves. Feeling a little anxious, but proud of herself for leaving the laptop behind. She is truly taking the weekend off. At least that's the plan.

CHAPTER 12

JACK WAS ALREADY THERE when she pulled in. She rushed into the house, and found him happily sitting at the kitchen counter having a coffee with her mom. They looked so cozy, leaning on the butcher block, drinking coffee from locally made mugs, of course.

"I'm all packed! It will only take me a second to run up and get my suitcase," she says, rushing by him. He grabs her hand. "Hey, this mini-break starts right now. Stop, take a deep breath,". Lizzie obliges. "Okay, we're done rushing for two days, yeah?"

She smiles and nods. "Yes!" She closes her eyes, takes another deep breath and does a quick mountain pose from yoga class. "Alright, I will now slowly, very slowly, go upstairs and get my bag." She gives him a kiss. "Oh, hi Mom," she says, laughing as she heads upstairs.

"I know, I know, I'm invisible," Gabby laughs.

"You could never be invisible, Mom," Lizzie calls from the stairs.

She's back in a flash with her luggage. "Okay! I am ready to go and start this vacation so we can come back and get back to work as soon as possible!" She teases.

Jack looks at Gabby, "What are we going to do with her?" he says, shaking his head. "I thought I was a workaholic until I worked alongside this one," he says, pointing to Lizzie.

"Scoot! You two go and have a wonderful time!"

Lizzie gives her mom a hug, "We're out of here!" she says.

Jack carries Lizzie's suitcase out to his car and puts it in the back. They both get in, and Lizzie leans in to kiss Jack. "I am so excited!" They each fasten their seatbelts.

"Me too!" Says Jack. He backs out of the driveway, and they head off.

Lizzie looks out the window as they drive through a very quiet downtown Cranberry Harbor, and head to Route 6 and the Outer Cape, the towns at the tip of the Cape. She feels her body start to relax. She closes her eyes for a second, then turns to look at Jack.

"So how are you?" she asks Jack. "I haven't even asked you! You sleep okay last night?"

"I fell asleep great," he says, merging onto the highway from the rotary. "But then I woke up around 4 and started thinking, you know, all the 'holy moly, what have I started?', kinds of thoughts. You know, the kinds that haunt you at 4 in the morning."

"Ugh, I hate those thoughts. There's nothing lonelier than the middle of the night. I'm sorry that happened. I was shocked that I slept great, though when I did wake up I was mostly just excited about getting out of Cranberry Harbor for a couple of days."

Provincetown was only about 40 minutes from Cranberry Harbor, and before Lizzie knew it they were at the town line welcoming them to Provincetown. It was all water and dunes on the right, and little cottages that dotted the other side of the highway on their left. Before she knew it they were turning off the highway and driving down Commercial Street.

"This is my absolute favorite time of year to come to Provincetown," Lizzie says, looking at the light dusting of snow on the sidewalks and the empty streets. All the beautiful older homes, cozily next to each other, lining either side of the street, it was a world away, and not far, all at the same time.

"Me too, it's been way too long since I've gotten down here," Jack says, slowing down in front of Provincetown Marketplace, a little market that also has great to-go food, and several cozy little tables. "Hey, it looks like they're open," he looks at the clock, "We can't check in for another hour, you up for a little bit of lunch?

"Yeah! That would be great! I totally forgot to eat today, I'm so hungry!"

Jack pulls into a parking spot and they get out, and head to the door. Before they go in Jack turns Lizzie toward him. "Hey, I'm so glad we're doing this, and I am so glad I have you to...well, to do anything with." He kisses her.

"Aw, that's so sweet," she kisses him back. "I'm happy to be with you too," she says.

They walk in and the place is pretty quiet, looks like a few regulars, there aren't many tourists this time of year, and there are several empty tables.

Lizzie puts her coat over the back of a chair at one to claim it, not that there will be a rush, and joins Jack who's walked over to the take-out counter at the back of the shop.

"Hmmm, everything looks so good," he says. "Are you in the mood for anything special?"

"I have to say, I remember from the past that their mac and cheese is pretty exceptional, on a chilly day that and some tea sound pretty good," Lizzie says.

"I may join you in that," he says.

"Can I help you?" says the man behind the counter.

"Yes, could we please have two servings of the mac and cheese, warmed up to eat here, and one tea and one..." he's looking at the menu. "Um, a café au lait?"

"Coming right up," the man says, "I'll buzz you when it's ready," he says, handing them a saucer-shaped beeper.

"Great, thanks so much," Lizzie says as they walk over to their table.

They pick up some napkins and two forks from the island by the tables, and sit down. "Just don't tell my mom we didn't have any vegetables with our lunch, I will never hear the end of it," Lizzie jokes.

"My lips are sealed," Jack says. "I don't know about you, but I hardly know what to do with myself without a huge to-do list. Are you feeling a little weird too? Like you forgot something really important at home?"

Lizzie lets out a big sigh. "Yes! I thought it was just me!" I kept looking over at you as we were driving here, and you looked like a normal person on a day off and I kept thinking, 'what's wrong with me? Look at him, he's so chill!'"

Jack laughs. "So not chill!" He sits back and sighs too. "We are the worst at relaxing!" he laughs.

"Well, we haven't exactly given the whole relaxing thing a fair shake yet I don't think," Lizzie says. "We've been out of Cranberry Harbor for all of about an hour," they both laugh at this realization. "I've read a lot about this whole topic, and most people say it takes them a few days to unwind. I think we're putting a lot of pressure on ourselves to automatically relax, which seems pretty counter-intuitive."

Jack laughs. "Very good point, it's like trying to meditate and getting mad at yourself for not doing it right instead of just feeling good that you're trying." The buzzer buzzes on the table, and Jack gets up. "I'll go get everything."

Lizzie finds herself reaching for her phone to check it, but instead takes a deep breath and looks out the window at the lovely view of Commercial Street. There's always dogs being walked, no matter the weather, Lizzie smiles as she sees a few, each dressed for the cold weather in cute sweaters, leading their humans down the street. This detoxing from work is not for the faint of heart, but it feels good.

Jack is back in a flash and takes their food and drinks off the tray and sits down. They clink forks. "Here's to a relaxing 48 hours," he says.

"Yes! To relaxing!" And with that she toasts him with a forkful of the warm and creamy mac and cheese. "Okay, this does not disappoint, this is the best mac and cheese ever. I wonder how they make it so creamy?"

"They stir in some cream cheese," says the woman reading the paper at the neighboring table who smiles at them.

"That would do it," says Jack, digging into his own dish. "Yup, this is amazing for sure," he says, taking another bite. "We will have to try to replicate this sometime. When your mom isn't home to look at us scornfully for using cream cheese, and telling how it's going to clog our arteries, of course," he smiles at Lizzie. "I love your mom, but hey, we all need some fat and sugar sometimes."

They are both done in no time at all. "Speaking of fat and sugar, I was thinking about getting one of their giant crinkled chocolate chip cookies," Lizzie says, standing up. "Want to split one? I think it's much healthier for you if you split it with someone,the calories disappear because you're being so kind," she jokes.

"It would be irresponsible of me to not share it with you, you know, for our health and mental well-being and all," Jack says.

Lizzie gets up and goes to the counter to buy the cookie.

"I think I saw your picture on the news this morning," the woman next to them says. "You're that guy building that new neighborhood in Cranberry Harbor, right?"

Jack is surprised at being recognized. "Uh, yes, I'm Jack Cahoon,' he reaches out his hand.

"It's lovely to meet you. I'm Delia MacFayden."

Jack pauses for a moment. "Wait, you're not *the* Delia MacFayden the film director are you?"

She looks down, a little embarrassed and nods. She looks up again, "Yes, I am, though I have not made a film in several years. I retired here, to Provincetown."

Lizzie comes back with the cookie, and smiles at the woman. "Hi," she says, "I'm Lizzie Martin," she says.

"Lizzie, this is Delia MacFayden," Jack says, still in shock.

"What?!" Lizzie exclaims, and is then embarrassed. "I'm sorry, it's just, well, we both love your work so, so much. You live in Provincetown now?"

Delia nods. "Yes I do, and I don't miss the pressure of working for studios, living in L.A. or worrying about box office numbers in the least!"

"I cannot imagine the pressure, and you wrote almost all your movies too," says Jack, "so there was always that too."

Lizzie is hesitant, but can't resist asking. "I will understand completely if you say no, but I'm the co-editor and owner of the Cranberry Harbor Gazette, and I'd love to interview you sometime, but please, no pressure!" She nervously shakes her head. "I know it's not exactly the New York or Los Angeles Times, but we're pretty proud of what we do. Anyway, I shouldn't have even asked, don't worry about it."

Lizzie is feeling very flustered, and is embarrassed that she bothered this poor woman who is just sitting, enjoying her newspaper, tea and blueberry muffin.

Delia nods, taking a sip of her tea. "Perhaps, though I don't have much to talk about. This," she says, gesturing to the contents of her table, "is about as exciting as it gets for me these days," she laughs.

"Are you kidding? You are one of the most fascinating women I have ever known of!" Lizzie gushes. "You have no idea how your movies, your writing, your entire career has inspired me. And I think I speak for lots and lots of women-"

"Not just women," Jack says. "Your movie, *When We Met,* slayed me. Just thinking about it chokes me up. Your movies are smart, funny, emotional and so beautifully shot. I bet I've seen it ten times. At least."

Lizzie smiles and takes Jack's hand. "We don't always agree about movies to watch, he's more action, I'm more drama, but we can always agree on one of your movies." Lizzie pauses. "Sorry, we're gushing, we don't mean to put you on the spot. Enjoy your tea and muffin."

"I can't thank you both enough," Delia says. "You completely made my day. It's very easy, even after a somewhat illustrious career-"

"Two Oscars, and several Golden Globes is hardly 'somewhat illustrious,'"Jack interjects. "Sorry to interrupt, you were saying…"

Delia laughs. "Okay, point taken. Thank you both. It's easy to almost forget what one has done, especially out here, in February," she smiles and looks out the window as it's starting to snow a bit. "Well, I am going to head home before the snow gets any worse." She stands up and gathers her things. "I may have lived here for a few years, but I am still very unsure of myself driving in the snow."

Lizzie looks out and sees that it's not sticking to the ground yet. "Good idea, I don't think it's supposed to get bad, but better to be safe. And I hope we didn't ruin your quiet time here with all our chatter. We're just such big fans."

Delia shakes her head. "Oh, not at all, it was a complete delight. I'd love to stay in touch with you about your project," she says. "I'm fascinated."

Jack pulls a card out of his wallet. "All my information is on there, please, reach out anytime, we'd love to give you a tour."

She tucks the card in her purse. "I would love that. I will be in touch." And then she's gone.

"Whoa, can you believe that?" Jack says.

"Not really," Lizzie says, shaking her head.

"Do you feel, and I know this is going to sound weird, and not really like me, but that we were sort of supposed to run into her?"

"That doesn't sound weird at all. You know, I read something recently that her son is becoming quite well known as a documentary filmmaker...Ian MacFayden is his name, I'm pretty sure."

They look at each other.

"Maybe that's why she wanted the card?" Lizzie says, her mind going a million miles an hour.

"Okay," he stands up. "This is supposed to be our big getaway, let's stick a pin in this and revisit it when we go home."

"Hmm, I'm predicting that will not be possible, but, yeah, let's aim for that." She stands up, puts on her coat and picks up her purse. "I'm betting our room should be ready by now," she says, walking toward the door, "let's say we go check in."

She holds the door open for Jack as they step out into a snow squall.

"I sure hope Delia doesn't live too far from here," Jack says as they walk to his car.

Lizzie pretends to look at her non-existent watch and makes a buzzer sound, "Well, that, my dear, lasted all of not even thirty seconds."

"Yup, not talking about meeting Delia MacFayden is going to be hard," Jack says getting in the car.

"Well, let's keep it to only one mention an hour, how about that?" Lizzie offers.

"I'd say doable." He starts the car and they begin the short drive to the Cape's End Inn. "Can you imagine if we could get him to want to shoot this? Terra Marique could become a template for communities like it all across the country!"

"Okay, that's twice in five minutes, I'm going to need a ruling from the Swiss judge on this," Lizzie teases.

"Argh, I am the worst. I promise that's it, for at least an hour." he replies. To which Lizzie nods and smiles.

They're silent for the rest of the short ride, the snow is coming down harder now and they're both focused on that.

"This wasn't in the forecast," Jack says. "I checked right before we left."

"Maybe it's just some ocean effect snow and will clear out soon?" Lizzie says. A part of her really doesn't mind. There are worse places to be snowed in than one of the most beautiful inns in Provincetown, heck, in New England. "No matter what, it will be perfect."

They head up the steep hill to the inn, fish-tailing a little bit, but arrive safely.

"Ahhhh. We are finally here. No more work, No more thinking about work-" Jack says, leaning back, then Lizzie interrupts his sliding into nirvana.

"But I was thinking about what you said," Lizzie says.

"Nope, we're on vacation. We will think about that tomorrow, Miss Scarlett," Jack says and kisses her.

She nods, smiles, and kisses him right back. It's going to be a great night, snowstorm or no snow storm. Anything else can wait.

CHAPTER 13

JACK GETS their bags out of the back of the car, and Lizzie retrieves her purse and Jack's backpack from the back seat.

They carefully make their way up the porch stairs which haven't been shoveled yet. There's only an inch or so, but it is really starting to come down. When they get to the top a guy comes out, shovel and bucket of salt in his hands.

"Oh my gosh, sorry, I was just going to do this, hope it wasn't too slippery," he says apologetically.

"Nah, not bad at all," Jack says. "We're all good, thank you."

Jack holds the stained glass door for Lizzie and they enter. Almost immediately Lizzie feels herself relax. She can smell the fireplace in the other room, it's cozy, warm, and welcoming.

As soon as Rusty, who's working behind the desk spies them he jumps up and comes around to hug them both. They've been friends for years, and through those years he has helped them both many times –Lizzie with stories, and working briefly for Jack at his start-up.

"Oh my god, it's so good to see you both!" Rusty hugs them again. "It's been way, way too long."

"It sure has," Lizzie says, putting down her things to be able to hug him back. "I hope you're good."

"Very good! I'm now the manager here, which brought a lot more security, benefits, and heck, more money which is always good. And we all know how crazy house prices are out here, so it was a fantastic bonus that it also came with the cottage-"

"Oh my gosh, that amazing cottage on the other side of the property here? The fairy tale cottage?!" Lizzie exclaims.

Rusty smiles and nods. "Yup! Stewart and I moved in two months ago, and he's able to write from home, and I work here. The job is so demanding it's nice to be able to take small breaks and go home for a little breather." He goes back behind the desk. "So, you two are all set in the Tower Room. It's all ready, so you can go right up."

"Have you heard anything about the snow?" Jack asks, a little concerned. "We were going to go out to dinner later, so I wondered if it's supposed to get worse."

"Yeah, a few people called and canceled, they were all coming from off-Cape. This seems to be a Cape-only storm, and last I heard they were talking six to eight inches and high winds. I'm not so sure you're going to want to go out tonight. I'm so sorry."

"Damn, I made reservations, I wonder if I should cancel? What do you want to do, honey?" he asks Lizzie.

"I'm good staying in, though we could get a little hungry later," she says.

"Oh, don't worry, if you're good with a tapas-type of situation we could make it work, you won't go hungry, I promise," Rusty says.

Lizzie pauses and looks around. This inn is always on all the top 10 lists not just for the Cape, but the East Coast. It's filled with so many unique antiques, Tiffany-style lamps, and beautiful furniture. No matter how many times she's been there, she always finds something new to admire.

While Rusty is giving Jack the keys to their room she wanders into the communal living room area and is immediately entranced by the crackling fire in the big, fieldstone fireplace. All she wants to do is curl up in front of it in some comfy clothes and relax.

Jack wanders in, bags and keys in hand. "Wow, this is not too shabby, huh?" he says, beaming at her.

"Yeah, I think staying here, eating cheese and crackers, drinking some wine... this could be the perfect evening, don't you think?" she says.

"Yeah, and it's looking like we may be the only people here, two more couples canceled while I was talking to Rusty, and he said the other two couples who were here left already because they have early flights out of Boston in the morning. I'm pretty psyched about that," he says.

"Wow!" She turns and looks at him, smiling slyly. "Are you sure you didn't just buy the place out for us," she says.

"Ha! Yeah, I wish! Maybe someday, but not on this entrepreneur's salary!" He picks up the bags. "Shall we?"

"Yes! I cannot wait to see that room again!" Lizzie says, following Jack to the stairs.

They quickly ascend the stairs, Jack takes out the key, and Lizzie finds herself holding her breath as he unlocks and opens the door.

It's even more beautiful than she remembers. The windows give a 360-degree panoramic view of the east end of Commercial Street, all the way out to the ocean. The sun is still up, though it's gray and snowy, causing the room to be a bit dark. Jack goes to turn some lights on, but Lizzie stops him. "Wait, I just want to look out for another couple of minutes. We won't be able to see as well once the lights are on."

She walks around the room, looking out from all the angles. It's just as spectacular as she imagined from the photos she's seen, which hardly do the space justice.

"Okay, you can turn on some lights now," she says, smiling. "I just wanted to take it all in." She walks over and gives Jack a hug. "Thank you for arranging all this. I cannot imagine anything more lovely and wonderful." They kiss, and Jack yawns. "Oh, am I boring you?" she laughs.

"I'm so sorry! I just hardly got any sleep last night, it's not you," he says, embarrassed.

"Stop, I'm tired too. I vote for a nap on this dreamy big bed, what do you say?"

Jack puts the suitcases out of the way, takes his shoes off, and jumps onto the giant king-sized bed. "Oh, thank you for suggesting that, I was going to try to power through with some more coffee, but this is much better."

Lizzie crawls onto the bed too, and they pull the thick down comforter folded at the bottom of the bed over them. Jack yawns again and closes his eyes. He's asleep in just a couple of minutes, but Lizzie is too excited to fall asleep.

She props herself up on her elbows, looking around at the gorgeous antique dressers, the stained glass lamps, and amazing art on the walls. Every room at the Cape's End is completely unique unto itself, and like little jewel-filled boxes is full of beautiful treasures. One of the paintings, on the far end of the room, is of some storefronts on Commercial Street on a day just like this. You can practically hear the silence looking at the empty, snow-covered street.

Laying back and looking up, she hadn't even noticed the actual tower that is right over the bed. She lies back and gazes up at the inside of the tower. It's only about six, maybe eight feet tall, but it's incredible to look at. As she lies there she begins to feel sleepy too. Thoughts about work, her parents, and their project run through her head, but before long she drifts off.

When Lizzie wakes up Jack is propped up on his elbow looking at her, smiling. She feels groggy, naps always do that to her, and she's not quite ready to interact with anyone else.

"Hey there, you really conked out," he says.

"What, what time is it?" she groggily asks.

"It's 6:15," he says, looking at his phone.

"What?" She sits up with a start. "I slept for almost three hours? I never nap, that's crazy!"

She starts to get up, "We need to unpack, figure out dinner, We need to…"

"Shhhh," he says. "We don't need to do anything. It's still snowing, we're not going anywhere. It's all good."

"What about our reservations?"

"I snuck downstairs and called to cancel," Jack says. "And Rusty showed me where everything is in the kitchen. He was so nice, he made up an amazing platter for us of all sorts of things. Cheeses, a fresh baguette, some fruit, and an antipasto plate he was going to serve tonight during the wine and appetizer hour, but since we're now the only ones here, we get to have it!"

"Wow," Lizzie says, still trying to rouse herself. Apparently, she was much more tired than she had realized. "That sounds wonderful."

"I was thinking since there's no one to dress up for, how about you take a nice hot bath, soak for a bit, and then we just put on our most comfortable clothes and go have that feast by the fire? Rusty even showed me how to connect to the Bluetooth so we can have music too."

"That sounds perfect," she says, kissing Jack. "You know how I love a nice bath."

"I noticed there's even a really cool clawfoot tub in the bathroom, you need to take advantage of that while you can," he says.

Lizzie gets up and walks over to her suitcase which she puts on the end of the bed and zips it open. "I did bring some cozy yoga pants and a sweatshirt, you're sure you're all in for comfort, not glamor? Because I also have a nice dress?"

"I'm sure. Why dress up? Let's be ourselves and be comfortable." He gets up and gets his suitcase as well. "I brought some sweats I'm going to put on and get comfortable too." He opens his suitcases and takes out his sweatpants and zip-up hoodie. "Want me to draw your bath, madam?" He says, grandly.

Lizzie laughs. "Uh, I think I'm good, but thanks for the offer." She heads into the bathroom and before closing the door she calls to him, "I won't be too long, promise."

"Take your time. While you soak I am going to get things set up downstairs," he says.

There's an assortment of bath bombs and lotions in a basket next to the tub on a little wicker stool. Lizzie leans over, starts the water running, and when it feels just right, closes the drain. She chooses a chamomile and lavender bath bomb and drops it in. The scent fills the air immediately. Lizzie undresses and carefully gets into the tub, wincing for a moment at the heat.

Within minutes she is completely comfortable and relaxed. She's so relaxed that it isn't until the water starts to get cold, about a half hour later, that she rouses herself out of the tub.

She dries herself with the fluffiest towel she's ever used, applies some of the rich, creamy lotion in the basket of toiletries, and slips on a plush terry robe that's hanging on the door.

"I don't know about you, but I'm getting hungry…" she says as she enters the room, but Jack is gone. She picks up a note he left on top of the comfortable clothes she'd left out to wear.

I'm downstairs by the fire, get dressed and come meet me.

Lizzie smiles, she quickly puts on her yoga pants and tank top, then runs a brush through her hair and applies a swipe of lip balm. She puts on the slippers she brought and slips on a slouchy sweater. She gives herself a cursory glance in the mirror, and smiles, "This is so much more fun than going out," she says out loud, and then happily heads down to meet Jack.

CHAPTER 14

WHEN SHE COMES DOWNSTAIRS and turns the corner into the living room, she audibly gasps. There must be at least fifty, no, maybe one hundred candles all around the room. The fire is crackling, and Jack has laid out a beautiful picnic on a cozy blanket on the floor in front of the fireplace.

"How, what...um…" She's positively speechless.

Jack walks over and takes her hand. "I had some help," he says, beaming at her. "Rusty is the best." He leads her to some pillows on the blanket, and gestures for her to sit down. She follows his lead and sits.

Lizzie can see he's nervous, and suddenly this is all starting to make sense. Immediately, she's self-conscious about what she's wearing, but then, looking at Jack, who's equally casual, it all seems okay.

Jack sits down next to her and clears his throat.

"You okay?" she asks, feeling nervous.

"Yeah, I'm good." He reaches behind him to the coffee table that has a bottle and two poured glasses of red wine. "Here, it's a 2010 Merlot that Rusty opened for us." They each take a sip.

"Wow, this is so good," Lizzie says, and takes another sip. She's starting to feel as uncomfortable as Jack looks.

"Uh, so, I wanted to…" Jack takes another sip of wine, then he takes both their glasses and puts them back on the table. "This isn't exactly how I expected tonight to go," he says. The words are no sooner out of his mouth than the power goes out, leaving them illuminated only by the fireplace and candles. They both laugh. "Could this night get any more cliche?" he jokes.

"Cliche?" Lizzie asks.

"You know, two people, stuck in a snowstorm, drinking wine in front of a fireplace, the lights go out…"

"Let's hope this is a romantic cliche and not a scary movie cliche!" Lizzie says.

"Totally the former and not the latter," Jack says. "So anyway, as I was trying to say." He pauses. "I love you Lizzie. I've loved you since high school. I know I blew it when I left to go to California-"

She shakes her head and takes his hand. "Water under the bridge, it's all in the past."

"I know, but I will always feel bad about it." He takes a deep breath. "My plan had been to do this at the restaurant tonight. To have the waiter bring this," he takes a box out of his pocket,"on your dessert plate. But here we are."

"This is totally better," she says, smiling.

"I think so too." He moves onto his knee. "Lizzie, you are the most amazing person I know. And you would make me the happiest man in the world if you would say yes again to me. I know I am nowhere deserving of having you say yes twice to me, but I am nothing if not adventurous and am asking you, if you, Elizabeth Martin, will please do me the extreme honor of marrying me? If you say yes, I will go out tomorrow and buy a lottery ticket because it will mean I am the luckiest man in the world and should spread that luck around."

Lizzie's eyes immediately well up and she moves, kneeling, facing him, and hugs him hard. "No," she says, and Jack's face falls. "Oh! No, I didn't mean no to the proposal! Oh god, no! Now I can't stop saying no! What I meant was, you're not the luckiest person, I am!"

"Oh my god," Jack says, grabbing his chest, and sitting back on his heels. "I thought, 'Dude, you have been reading this relationship completely wrong!'" He sits down on the blanket and sighs. "So that's a yes? Amidst all those nos there was a yes, right?"

"Oh my god, I am so terrible at this!" Lizzie laughs. "Yes! Absolutely yes!" She says, kissing him.

"Phew, now maybe my heart will start beating again." He opens the box and reveals a beautiful art deco-style ring. "So I got this at Jess's Vintage Bridal Shop, she's started carrying some vintage jewelry as well." He slips it on her finger. "It's from the 1920s, and I thought it was beautiful, but if you don't like it Jess said I could-"

"Oh my gosh, not like it? I love it! And it fits perfectly! How did you do that?" Lizzie is moving her hand around admiring the ring.

"Your parents," he says.

"My parents?"

"Yes. I went to see them a few weeks ago to do the traditional thing, you know, get their blessing, and to apologize again for how things turned out last time, which they graciously told me wasn't necessary, but it was for me. Anyway, when I mentioned I was looking for a ring, and your mom gave me one from your collection that she knew fit you well, and loaned it to me."

"And this ring was the perfect size?" Lizzie says, unable to stop admiring it.

"Not exactly, I had it resized, and it seems they did a good job because you could get it on, and it's also not falling off," he laughs.

"So you've been planning this for quite a while," she says. "And at the same time trying to get this enormous project passed. How was I so oblivious to all of this?" she says.

"That makes me feel great, that you were oblivious, I kept thinking I was going to say or do something to tip my hand, but apparently, unless you're just being kind, I did not. I really wanted this to be a surprise for you."

"Well, you succeeded! You could definitely knock me over with a feather!" Lizzie feels so exquisitely happy. She has never been a woman who felt incomplete not being married, or desperate in any way to land a guy, but everything with Jack has felt so good, so solid and happy over the last year, that this just feels...right. Definitely meant to be.

"So I know I've had a lot of time to think about all this, and you haven't, but I have been thinking about when would be the perfect time to get married on the Cape," Jack says, looking unsure about already talking dates for a wedding. "But there's no pressure, none at all, I'll do whatever you think is best."

"Actually, there is a time that I happen to think would be perfect," she says. Then, they both at the same time say, "Soon!" Lizzie nods, "We both screwed it up last time, so maybe we should just do it-'

"No, that was all me, I'm the one who left," Jack protests. "I screwed it up."

"But I didn't see what you were going through, and I'm sorry for that,' Lizzie takes his hands. "I promise to be a better partner."

"Me too," Jack says, kissing her. "We're a lot smarter than we were three years ago," he says, laughing.

"So...why wait?" Lizzie says. "We might as well do it as soon as possible?"

"I totally agree! Though the, 'we might as well do it' doesn't exactly scream romance," Jack jokes. "How long does it take to throw a wedding together anyway?"

Lizzie laughs. "Uh, generally one does not 'throw a wedding together,' babe. Honestly, it can take like a year.' She pauses. "I'm just worried about all you're going to have going on with breaking ground and getting Terra Marique going, do you think you're really going to have the bandwidth to be part of planning this? I bet most wedding planners would say trying to do this before summer is crazy," Lizzie says.

"Really? I have no idea about any of this, but I'm willing to learn and don't want to be one of those guys who is no help in making decisions and just shows up on the day. I don't expect you to do it all," he says.

"How very twenty-first century of you, sweetie," Lizzie says, teasing him.

"Hey, I'm a guy who can choose flowers and music with the best of them!" Jack replies. "How hard could this be?"

Lizzie is a little concerned that Jack's being so casual about planning their wedding. She's never had the desire to have anything huge and fancy, but does want it to be a notch above a neighborhood clambake.

"Well, it's a *little* hard, which is why there's a $62 billion-dollar a year industry devoted completely to wedding planning," she gently offers. She shrugs. "I wrote a story about Cape weddings last fall."

Jack laughs. "Yes! I know, but I really think there has to be a way to keep it simple with no-drama, don't you?"

She takes a deep breath, and pauses before replying. 'Okay, simple and no drama will be our theme. And not too big," Lizzie adds.

"The only one I need there is you," says Jack.

"My parents might find that a little hard to accept..." she says.

"Oh, mine too, but I love the idea of sharing this just with the people that mean the most to us," Jack says.

"I totally agree," Lizzie says.

"Wow, so we're actually doing this," he says, embracing Lizzie and laughing.

"Yes, apparently we are," she says, hugging him right back.

"I cannot wait to be married to you," Jack says, reaching again for their wine glasses. "We are going to have the best time. I know not all the time of course, I'm not stupid, but I think we're good together. Like really good. Right?"

"Yes, definitely right. I look forward to spending my life with you, Mr. Cahoon. I think it will be a fun adventure." She takes her glass and clinks it to his. "To us, and to happiness, challenges, and the whole catastrophe."

"Hoping for more happiness than catastrophe," Jack says, smiling at her. "But yes to all of it. I love you, Lizzie."

"And I love you too," she says, kissing him. She then looks down at her ring. She's so happy, but feels a little twinge of worry. Let's hope this turns out differently from last time, she thinks, and then quickly dismisses the thought. It's going to be fine. I hope it is, she thinks.

CHAPTER 15

Lizzie woke up before Jack, and not wanting to disturb him, grabs a sweater, puts on her slippers, and quietly exits the room.

As she makes her way downstairs she can see it's a gorgeous, sunny day. The snow has stopped, the sky is blue, and it looks like a postcard.

They'd sat in front of the fire for a couple of hours last night, eating the feast of the snacks Jack and Rusty had laid out, making plans for the future as they snuggled by the fire. But, being the responsible types they were, they'd then spent a good 45 minutes tidying, and had cleaned everything up, leaving the living room in pristine shape.

"Well, you're up early," Rusty says, coming into the room carrying a tray laden with breakfast items he put on the buffet. Lizzie joins him to help set things up. "Are congratulations in order?" he asks, smiling a knowing smile at her. "I sure hope so after all the work we did!" he jokes.

She lifts her left hand up, and sassily twirls her hand back and forth. "Yes, I said yes!" she beams, doing her best '*Single Ladies* put a ring on it' posing. "Thank you for helping make it such a special night. It was truly magical and the most romantic thing that's ever happened to me, that's for sure. I really appreciate you helping make it so special."

Rusty puts his hands up. "Hey, it was all Jack, I just provided some crackers, cheese, and charcuterie," he laughs. "Oh, and the 2010 merlot." He hugs her. "I'm so happy for you two, you make a fantastic couple, and an amazing team. There's not going to be any stopping the two of you. I very much look forward to seeing all you create together."

Rusty hurries back to the kitchen to get another tray, this one with some mugs and a small carton of half and half. Lizzie starts helping him get the coffee station ready. She pours the cream into a pitcher he has put out, and then suddenly thinks, wait, they're the only ones at the inn.

"Rusty, is all this just for us?"

"Yeah, and the staff. When no one is here we sometimes have a group breakfast. We won't get in your way, though, we'll eat in the kitchen."

Lizzie bursts out laughing and shakes her head, "Who do you think we are? The Crawleys at *Downton Abbey*?" She can't stop laughing. "We would love to have breakfast with you, and whoever else is here. You will not, I repeat not relegate yourselves to the kitchen! Though I cannot guarantee when Jack will wake up, he's been working so hard, I tiptoed out so he could sleep." No sooner does she say that, when he appears.

"You know I can't sleep past 8," he says, giving her a kiss. "Morning, Rusty. I see you have met my fiance," he teases. "I have been dying to say that word ever since we got engaged," he looks at his watch, "Ten or so hours ago." He goes to the sideboard where the coffee is, "You want some?" he asks Lizzie as he pours a cup.

"Yes!" she walks over and takes the mug from him.

"Did you tell your parents yet?" Jack asks, pouring himself a cup. "Rusty, you want some?" Rusty nods, walks over and Jack hands him a coffee. When they've all got their coffee they sit down on two sofas facing each other.

"I did not," Lizzie says. "Did you call yours?"

Jack shakes his head, takes a sip of coffee and sits back on the couch. "This is really good, Rusty, thanks. Nah, I think I'll wait until we get back. I'm kind of enjoying our little bubble here. Once we get back to Cranberry Harbor you know it will be all over town in two minutes, and we won't have any privacy about anything. I'm kind of enjoying this just being us. And Rusty of course," he says laughing and raising his mug to Rusty.

"I am honored to be the only other person in the know," he says. "Though I did post it on all the inn's social media accounts," he teases. "It's good PR for us, 'come get engaged at the Cape's End Inn,' posted with a photo of the two of you I took in secret. You're cool with that, right?" he says as he laughs.

"Oh totally cool," Lizzie says. "If it's not on the 'Gram it didn't happen, right?"

Jack laughs, "'The 'Gram?' I think you should never utter that word again."

"Yeah, as soon as I said it I thought it sounded very stupid coming out of my mouth. Maybe if I was 14, but yeah, even in jest it sounds dumb." She gets up to pop a bagel in the toaster. "You want anything you two?"

"I feel like I'm really imposing being here," says Rusty, starting to get up.

"No!" Jack and Lizzie both say, not meaning to yell, but they kind of do.

"Whoa!" Rusty says, sitting back down. "Alright, I guess I'm staying!" he laughs.

"I didn't mean to yell," Lizzie says, apologetically, "It's just we love seeing you and having you here." After she puts some cream cheese on her bagel she sits down. "We had our lovely evening last night, and we're enjoying hanging out with you."

"Agreed" says Jack, getting up, and surveying the breakfast offerings on the table. He chooses a small Greek yogurt, a banana and some granola that he pours into a bowl. He brings them all back and assembles his breakfast on the coffee table in front of them.

"Your selection looks much healthier than mine," she says as she takes the last bite of her bagel. "All carbs and fat." She gets up and puts a hard boiled egg in a bowl and comes back to the couch. "Protein," she says, as she takes a bite.

While they sit by the fire, which Rusty adds some wood to, a few more employees come in. They hesitate to join in, but the three of them encourage them all, and soon it's a lovely party.

"I'm suddenly aware that we're the only ones in pajamas," Jack says. "Usually at least half the folks sitting here are equally attired, this feels a little weird."

"Eh, we don't care, in all honesty I didn't even notice," says Katrina, the woman they just met who's in charge of housekeeping. "You wouldn't believe some of the outfits we've seen," she says, looking at her fellow employees with a knowing glance.

"Oh my god, that couple who came down in their underwear who needed to tell us they sleep naked and therefore had no pajamas-" Rusty says.

"And you went and got them two robes out of the dryer," says Katrina.

"Okay, so my flannel pajama pants and t-shirt aren't looking so bad now," Jack says, mock-wiping his brow.

"Oh no, you two look positively dressed to the nines compared to many!" says Rusty. He stands up and cautiously looks at Lizzie and Jack, "I'm not leaving because I feel I'm interloping, I have to actually get to work. Okay?" he teases.

"Yes, you have spent an adequate amount of time with us, you have permission to leave," Lizzie says, smiling at him. "Thank you, Rusty, for this, and well, for everything." She gets up and gives him a hug. "You helped make this a very memorable time." She kisses him on the cheek.

"Aw, shucks, tisn't nothing, ma'am," he hugs her back. "So happy to have gotten to be part of something so special."

And with his exit, everyone else gets up as well.

"I have to say I feel kind of lazy," Lizzie says, watching them all head off.

"Uh, when was the last time you took a day off? Not an hour to get a haircut, or do an errand, but an actual whole day off?" Jack asks her.

"Um," she sits on the couch and thinks. "I honestly can't remember."

"Well there you go, you have nothing to feel guilty about." He leans back on the couch and puts his arm around her, and she sighs a sigh of relaxation. "That's it, you can do this, I know you can!" he jokes.

She snuggles in closer to him and hugs him. "I could get used to this," she says. "Is this what married life will be like?" she says, laughing.

"Exactly. Every single day!" Jack replies.

"Good, then I'm all in," she says.

"You weren't before?" Jack says, mocking concern.

"I was mostly all in, but this clinches it."

"Well good, it does for me too," he says, squeezing her tightly. "Anything you want to do today?"

"I think I'm already doing it," she says. "But maybe in a little while we can go for a walk?"

"Good idea." Jack says. "But not yet," he says, hugging her again.

CHAPTER 16

BY NOON they had both showered, gotten dressed and were ready to go explore wintertime Provincetown.

After leaving the inn they drive down to Herring Cove to check out the beach. Lizzie loved beaches in wintertime, not only were they almost always completely empty, there was something just so magical about a snow-covered beach. They'd both worn their boots so they parked and took the short trek from the parking lot to the beach. The waves, enhanced by the storm the day before, were big, and intense.

Lizzie takes out her phone and grabs a couple of photos. "I know, I shouldn't have brought my phone as we unplug, but I want to have some photos to-"

"Oh, I want photos too!" Jack says, taking his phone out too, then putting his arm around Lizzie, takes a quick selfie. "These will be photos we will show our families, 'this is when we decided to get married!'"

"Aw, that's very sweet of you, honey," she says, taking a selfie as well. "Who knew a tech guy could be so sentimental?"

"Hey, that's a stereotype I have witnessed in real life that doesn't always fit. I've seen many a techie cry at a puppy video," he says, smiling at her.

"Well, who hasn't cried at a puppy video? I mean, unless you're completely dead inside." replies Lizzie. They walk for a while, but as the wind picks up, causing the cold to start stinging their faces, they turn around and head back to the car.

"Whoa! That was a sudden change!" says Lizzie, shivering as she fastens her seatbelt.

Jack is shivering too, "you know what they say about New England weather, just wait five minutes…"

"That's probably true everywhere," Lizzie says, "but the ocean does make it particularly unpredictable. Where to now?"

"Want to go grab some lunch?" Jack says, driving them back toward the town center. "Maybe some pizza at Tony's?"

"You do not need to ask me again, I can think of no better way to warm up than a hot slice of pizza," Lizzie says.

There's no line at Tony's, the gift of coming in the off-season, and in no time they are sitting in a booth enjoying their pizza - mozzarella with basil for her, and feta with black olives for him.

"So I have to ask you," Jack says between bites, "Have you really been able to not look at your email or check messages?"

Lizzie narrows her eyes. "Are you cheating on our deal? Already? We haven't even been engaged for 24 hours, and I am finding out you're not trustworthy?" she says, teasing him.

"I have not cheated. I've been very tempted to check my emails, but I have not, and I didn't pick up when my phone rang and it was a New York number. Even though I thought it could be the New York Times wanting to talk to me," Jack says, starting in on his second slice.

Now her curiosity is piqued. "Did they leave a voicemail? Ugh! No! I am getting sucked back in!" she laughs. "It's so seductive and such a slippery slope!"

"I know! It is truly almost impossible." He pauses, looks back and forth, like they're in a spy novel. "What if...nah, nevermind."

"No! You can't do that! You can't tempt me with something and then not finish the thought!" she says.

"Okay, what if, as, you know, responsible adults with demanding jobs, we allowed ourselves one half-hour to check in with our jobs? I'll be honest, the not-knowing is driving me crazy and keeping me from really relaxing."

"I know, I find I keep thinking about all the inquiries that are probably coming into the Gazette and how it's probably overwhelming for my dad," Lizzie says. "So okay, how about, we walk around Commercial Street for the next half-hour or hour, head back to the inn and make some calls? Check some emails? Sound good?"

"Yes, perfect, but let's put a limit on it, no more than an hour?" Jack says.

"Deal!" Lizzie says.

It didn't take too long to exhaust the open businesses on Commercial Street. Most were closed for the winter, and other than the Provincetown Bookstore, and Sea Side Records, there weren't too many spots that interested the both of them. Lizzie picked up a copy of a Mary Oliver book of poetry at the bookshop, and Jack snagged a vintage copy of *Meet the Beatles* on vinyl.

It began to snow a little bit again, so to add to the coziness of the afternoon they grabbed two hot cocoas at Cafe Nirvana on the way back to the inn.

Once they got back to their room, they took off their boots, Lizzie pulled out her laptop that she'd smuggled in underneath her clothes in her suitcase, and made herself comfortable on the bed sitting cross legged and snuggled up against the pillows she propped up behind her.

"I'm going to head downstairs, are you okay with that?"Jack asks Lizzie, pulling out his laptop, power cord and notebook.

"Yeah, that's fine," she says dismissively as she watches a day and a half's worth of emails appear in her inbox. She sighs. "Oy, okay, an hour, right? Good luck to us!"

As soon as Jack leaves Lizzie grabs her cell and calls her dad. He picks up on the first ring.

"Okay, so what are you doing calling me," he says instead of hello. "You're supposed to be relaxing."

Lizzie laughs. "I know, I know, we've given each other permission to check in and see what's up for an hour, so don't waste my time, Peter Martin.," she jokes. "What's going on? What's the 411?"

He doesn't say anything right away which concerns her.

"Dad?"

"Yeah, I'm here. I didn't want to ruin your time away with the drama here," he says.

"Drama? What drama? Is Mom okay?" She's getting concerned.

"Yes, she's fine...But, well, it seems Billy and Bud are not taking their defeat very well, and they…" There he goes hesitating again.

"Dad! You're freaking me out, just tell me what's going on," she asks, worried.

"They've encamped themselves down at the property, and last I knew Billy had chained himself to a tree saying he's doing this to, 'save Cranberry Harbor from ruin.'"

"You're kidding me," Lizzie says, incredulous. "They lost the vote by a landslide," she says. "Almost every single person voted for it. I just can't believe this."

"Well, they're saying the vote was wrong, they want a recount-"

Lizzie bursts out laughing. "A recount? We all saw how everyone voted, there's no recounting an overwhelming win on an in-person vote. He's totally lost his mind," Lizzie says.

"That he has, it has drawn some press however, mostly from the not the most reliable sort of press, the fringe kind out outlets from the dark recesses of the internet," Peter says. "I'm sorry honey. I promised your mom I wouldn't call you and tell you. But you called me, so…"

"No, I needed to know this," and right then Jack comes bursting into the room.

"Billy and Bud are at the property and Billy is chained to a tree!" he blurts out.

She points to her phone, "Yeah, Dad just told me."

"We need to head back," they both say at the same time.

"No, you two need to stay and celebrate, I mean relax," Peter says.

"Dad. I know you know," finally something for Lizzie to smile about. "Jack told me he asked you and Mom for my hand," she teases. "Were there any goats or exchanges of money involved?" she laughs.

"No, and I'm disappointed. I've been waiting and waiting for you to get married so I can finally get some goats. Thanks a lot," he shoots back, laughing. "Seriously, I'm assuming you said yes?"

"Indeed I did. Is this where you say you're not 'losing a daughter, but gaining a son?'", she asks, kidding him.

"Nah, we don't care much for him, you're on your own with this one, missy." They both laugh. "You know honey, we are absolutely thrilled. We love Jack like he's one of our own, but mostly we love that he makes you so happy. We think the two of you are so good together, we're thrilled that you found your way back to each other. Congratulations, sweetheart."

"Well, good, that's a relief, I wasn't looking forward to eloping and you know, never speaking to you and Mom. That would have made the partner's desk situation at the office very awkward," Lizzie says, smiling as she's talking to him. She looks over at Jack who is frantically typing on his laptop. Their little dreamy bubble seems to have been burst, and by the two biggest pains in everyone's neck in Cranberry Harbor.

"I should go, Dad, we need to figure out what to do. I think we're going to head back soon,". As he hears her say this, Jack nods, gets up, takes his suitcase out of the closet, places it on the bed, opens it and starts putting his clothes in.

"Okay, I'll probably come straight there when we get back,". She's quiet while listening to him as she watches Jack pack up. "I know Dad, but we really think we need to be there, especially Jack, this is his baby and he needs to be there to deal with Billy and Bud." She glances at Jack and rolls her eyes a little. "Uh huh, well okay, I should go Dad, I've got to pack. Love you, see you soon." She puts her phone down. "He doesn't want us cutting this getaway short, he thinks we should stay," she says, pulling her suitcase out from under the bed.

"I'm sorry, do you want to stay? Am I pushing you?" Jack says, stopping mid-fold, concerned.

"No! That's him, I definitely think we need to be back there. I want to control the narrative coming out on our social media. Dad won't be posting anything, and I want to stave off any panic in the town about what's happening." she says, as she goes into the bathroom to gather her things.

"Good, because I want to get together with some of my board members, maybe even the police and some selectboard members to see how to handle this. We don't want him turned into some sort of sympathetic character and have others join him," Jack says, putting the last of his clothes, phone charger and toiletries in his suitcase and zipping it closed. He then sighs and sinks onto the bed. "I'm so sorry, sweetie, I am beyond bummed that our break ended this way. I really wanted another evening here with you, to actually go out to dinner since we didn't get to last night. And in all honesty, to have a day and evening where I wasn't a nervous wreck thinking about proposing."

She stops her packing, walks over to him and gives him a hug. "Jack, it's fine, I want to head back as much as you do. We've managed to have an amazing 24 hours, and I am very grateful for that." She gives him a kiss, and he pulls her onto his lap. They fall back on the bed and begin to laugh. "How many people can say they had their engagement weekend ruined by Billy Taylor?"

Jack laughs, "I don't know, I have a sneaky suspicion we are not the first."

Lizzie gets up to finish packing. "I think you are probably right."

Once they're packed, before they leave the room, Jack puts down his bag, and takes Lizzie's out of her hand. "I just want to say, again, I love you so much, and cannot wait to marry you."

Lizzie throws her arms around him. "Me either, and let's do ourselves a favor and not invite Billy…"

"Or Bud," he says, kissing her.

"Oh, he's totally off the list," she says laughing as they close the door to the room. "Though I do wonder what kind of gift he would have gotten us."

CHAPTER 17

RUSTY INSISTED on giving them a refund for the second night, and with the knowledge that someone had just called asking if the tower room was available, and knowing the inn wasn't losing any money on the deal, and having left a very generous tip on the dresser in their room, they somewhat reluctantly accepted his offer.

As soon as they were on their way Lizzie called her dad alerting him to their plans. Lizzie puts him on speaker.

"Crikey, I feel so bad you two are cutting your time away short, but I admit I'm a little relieved, things are kind of heating up here," he says. Lizzie knows her dad and can tell when he's holding back. He's overwhelmed and that's not like him.

"Dad, what aren't you telling us?" Lizzie asks.

"Well, oh gosh, there's TV news crews, there's newspaper reporters from all over, it's a little crazy," he says. "I can't say I'm not very relieved you're coming back," Peter says.

"We'll be there in 40 minutes, Dad. I'll have Jack drop me at the office, and he's going to–" she looks at him because they hadn't really formulated a plan.

"I'll drop you and then I'll go out to the property and see if I can talk some sense into Billy, who I am betting is loving all this attention," Jack says. Just then his phone rings, he quickly glances at it, sees an unknown number, but answers it.

"Hello?" he says, wondering if it's a reporter or someone from the town.

"Hey, Jack, this is Ian, Ian MacFayden? My mom met you yesterday?"

Jack looks over at Lizzie, and widens his eyes and mouths 'It's Ian MacFayden!

"Dad, I have to go, I'll see you soon," Lizzie hangs up with her dad and is staring at Jack.

"Hey, nice to sort-of meet you. What's up?" Jack shakes his head at himself, thinking he doesn't exactly sound articulate, but he's got a lot going on. He switches the phone to speaker so Lizzie can hear too. She takes Jack's phone and holds it while he drives. "Just so you know, I've got you on speaker, my fiance, Lizzie Martin and I are presently driving back to Cranberry Harbor."

"Nice to speak with you too, Lizzie. Well, to get to it, I've been following your whole journey in the Gazette, and now I'm reading updates on the New York Times website–"

"What? The Times is posting about it?" Jack says, looking nervously over at Lizzie.

"So, yeah, with this guy now chained to a tree it's become a bit of a scene. I am actually there," he says, having buried the lede. "I've got my camera and I wanted to ask your permission to do some filming? Your business associate, Alexis, said I should ask you first, she didn't want to give the go-ahead without your okay."

Lizzie and Jack look at each other. Lizzie whispers, "Alexis is there?!" to which Jack shrugs his shoulders.

"Look, we're about a half hour out from Cranberry Harbor, I'm going to drop Lizzie at her office, and then I'll be right there. Can you hang tight for that half hour?"

"For sure," he says. "Alexis is giving me some background on the project, and I'm just getting a feel for the property. She's going to show me around a bit. I'm good."

"Alright, thanks for reaching out, I'll see you soon," Jack says. Lizzie puts his phone on the dashboard, and Jack shakes his head. "This day keeps getting more and more surreal, can you believe this?"

"No, who would have thought us getting engaged wouldn't be the biggest Cranberry Harbor news of the day?" Lizzie jokes.

"Wow. You think he's going to want to make a movie about all this? That would be pretty crazy."

"Yeah, a part of me gets nervous thinking about too much attention being thrown at the town, I don't want it to become another tourist attraction and end up making things worse for everyone," he says.

"Well, let's jump off that bridge when we get to it. Until then, let's just take it one step at a time. Okay?"

Jack takes a deep breath and nods. "Bird by bird."

"Yup, bird by bird," Lizzie concurs. She's quiet for a moment, and picks up her phone from the console. "I'm thinking I'm going to call my dad and tell him I should go to the property with you, scope out what's happening, and plan our social media posts and the next issue accordingly."

"Whatever you think is best," Jack says. "I would actually really like that. The closer we get to Cranberry Harbor the more nervous I get." He doesn't say anything more, and neither does Lizzie. She wants to give him space to gather his thoughts. "What if by trying to help the town I instead ruined it?"

He's said it. He's said the big thing he's been thinking, but has been too worried to verbalize. Lizzie knows this about him. She puts her hand on his leg, "You're getting way ahead of yourself, honey, nothing has happened that is going to ruin Cranberry Harbor. Two guys who can't stand to lose are having a tantrum. As soon as fishing season opens they'll get distracted and forget all about this. And as soon as they see that they're completely in the minority in how they feel and start to experience the freeze out of the community, I'm sure they'll give up. Remember when they protested the traffic light on Bog Hill Road? That was over as soon as they weren't invited to enter their ribs into the July 4th barbeque contest."

Jack smiles for the first time in a while. "Okay, so we pray for the power of the freeze out, huh?" he asks.

"Oh, there's nothing like being frozen out by our small, year-round community," Lizzie says. "Remember when Carl was weighing selling his store to that chain from Rhode Island, and Cranberry Harbor Hardware was going to become a dollar store? He couldn't go anywhere without getting the cold shoulder. The pain is real, my friend, the power of freezing someone out is huge."

"I'd forgotten all about that, and he ended up passing the store on to his daughter, Maggie."

"Yup, so once Billy and Bud find no one will listen to their fantasies about how the vote was stolen, or how it's going to raise taxes, cause more pollution, and ruin the aesthetic of the town–"

"Wait, there's no way either one of those guys said anything about the 'aesthetic' of the town," Jack laughs. They're just crossing the town line into Cranberry Harbor.

"Fine, I was embellishing for effect," Lizzie says, "But you know what I mean, once people dismiss them at the post office, at Sea Coast, or heck, on Main Street, they'll get the hint."

"I sure hope you're right," Jack says. They're on Main Street now, headed out to the land.

"Oh! I forgot to call my dad!" Lizzie says. She picks up her phone, "Call Dad," she says and waits a moment. "Hey, Dad, I decided to head out to the land with Jack before I come into the office. I think I should check it out, maybe take some pictures, and then we can talk about what we want to put on our social media and how to respond to all the inquiries coming from other places."

"Sounds good, honey, he says. "You watch out for yourself, I don't trust those two as far as I can throw them."

Lizzie grows a little concerned. "Have they said they're going to do anything?"

"No, but they're loose cannons individually, put those knuckleheads together, and well, you don't know what they might do."

"Got it. We'll be careful, Dad, promise," she says.

"When we finally all get home I want to celebrate - we haven't even had a chance to talk about your news," he says, she can hear his smile through the phone.

"Yes, we will have lots to discuss. Let me just say, your input and help is much appreciated, and I can't wait to hug you and Mom."

"Okay, I'll see you in a little bit," Peter says. "Remember to be careful."

"Will do, bye."

As she hangs up they enter the property. There aren't as many cars there as they'd feared, and there, in the distance, they see Billy and his chain.

Jack parks and they both get out. Alexis makes a beeline for them with a guy Lizzie assumes is Ian MacFayden.

"Hey, guys," Alexis says. "This is Ian, Ian this is Jack and Lizzie."

"Hi, it's nice to meet you both," Ian says, shaking their hands. "This is an amazing parcel of land you have here. I had no idea it had the views it does, it's just incredible."

"Thanks, we're pretty excited about it," Jack says, looking over at Lizzie and feeling unsure about what to say next. "So you want to shoot a little video here? Do you mind me asking, to what end?"

"Of course! I'd expect you to ask," Ian says. He's a tall, handsome guy, Lizzie notes. With the Brad Pitt scruff and blonde hair he's got happening, it's hard to not notice. "I've been working on a film about climate change for a couple of years. I've been all over the world seeing how different countries are handling it, some much better than others, and I have been finding small projects that have the potential to make big differences, and could help influence policy. Because that's where the real change will come in."

Lizzie is nervous about butting in since it's really Jack's project, but as a journalist she has questions. "Our concern," she says, looking over at Jack, "is that this would bring lots more people to Cranberry Harbor who want to see where that movie was filmed, or something?"

"I understand the concern completely. I'm not making this for commercial release," Ian says. "I was actually hired by a philanthropist who wants to have a record of all these ideas and projects and present the film to the U.N. So not to worry, this isn't going to be streaming into everyone's living room, or at the multiplex down the street. It's in my contract that it will not be widely released because all too often the message gets muddied with companies looking to make a profit. This isn't something for profit, it's just for education and to hopefully inspire change within global leadership. The family funding it are long-time environmentalists. They're good people."

Lizzie and Jack nod. Alexis looks at them, she looks comfortable with the situation as well.

"If you decide to let me do some filming over the next few months, I will put all of that in writing for you," Ian says.

"Okay, well, first off, why don't I show you around, and check in on our protesters," Jack says.

The two of them start walking ahead, and Alexis pulls Lizzie's sleeve. "So, I didn't want to say anything in front of Ian, but I couldn't help but notice a new piece of jewelry on your hand! Is that what I think it is?" Alexis says, beaming.

Lizzie lifts her hand and shows her the ring. "Yes, ma'am, I am indeed betrothed!"

"Oh my god!" Alexis yells, loud enough that Ian and Jack turn around. "Oops, sorry!" she says to them. "I know we can't talk now, but soon, and I mean very soon, I want all the details, where, what he said, what you were wearing...I want it all!"

Lizzie laughs, "I will gladly fill you in very soon, but this is not the moment."

"Oh, not at all, we will have to make a Sea Coast date soon," Alexis says, hooking her arm with Lizzie's. "I am so happy for the both of you, you totally give me hope that there is a chance to find great love out there. Even in tiny Cranberry Harbor, where the median age is–"

"Nope, don't say it," Lizzie laughs. "It only takes one guy, and all these older folks? They have sons, grandsons, nephews..." Lizzie gets closer to Alexis and whispers. "Ian MacFayden sure is handsome!"

Alexis shakes her head and acts embarrassed, enough so that Lizzie knows she agrees. She brushes off the thought.

"What? An Oscar-winning documentary filmmaker, not good enough for you?" she teases. "One who looks an awful lot like a movie star?"

"Stop it! I do not need some rich guy who grew up in Hollywood, I'm looking for a regular guy. He seems nice and all, but–" Alexis isn't finished but Ian speaks up and interrupts her.

He turns around, but keeps walking. "I'm pretty regular," he says. "Grew up in a small town in the Berkshires, my mom didn't want us growing up in Hollywood," he looks at Alexis and smiles.

"Oh my god, how did he hear us?!" Alexis is mortified. "I feel like I'm in ninth grade!" She starts to pull away from Lizzie like she's going to leave.

"No, you are here with me, you're not going anywhere," Lizzie says, pulling her back. "And how did he hear that? He's got superhuman hearing!"

"I just want to crawl under a rock, or maybe chain myself to a tree," Alexis says.

"Please don't do that," Ian says, turning around again. "Then you couldn't have coffee with me later. You know, if you'd like to?"

"She'd like to," Lizzie says, laughing.

Through her embarrassment it's clear Alexis is not unhappy at the prospect of having coffee with Ian. Lizzie looks at her and smiles, and she knows her friend well enough to know when she's a little smitten, but decides to drop the subject and move on to the issues at hand.

"So any idea what Billy wants?" Lizzie asks her as they get close to the spot where he's encamped himself.

"Attention? Relevance?" Alexis says. "Honestly, I don't think he really thought this through. He doesn't have any supplies, he's already freezing, and Bud left quite a while ago saying he couldn't allow himself to get arrested - something about a job at the post office that he's applied for? So he's kind of on his own."

"Interesting," Lizzie says. I wonder if there's a way to bring Billy on board? Hold on," she runs ahead to catch up to Jack and Ian. "Hey, I was thinking that Billy may be able to be convinced to give up this protest."

"How?" Jack asks, clearly not convinced.

"Alexis was just telling me that even Bud has left him in the dust, and well, I'm not seeing anyone else here supporting him. And, it's going to be getting dark and cold before long-'

"So he might be open to a change of heart?" Jack says.

"I'm just thinking, maybe approaching him in a more friendly way might help him let his guard down and we could all come out as winners, you know, let him have a little dignity, even though I'd like to throttle him for causing all this drama," Lizzie says.

"Okay, I'll be nice," Jack says, smiling at her. "I promise," he says, anticipating her next comment.

"Hey, it's worth a shot, right? More flies with honey and all?" she says. "I'm going to hang back and let you talk to him, he doesn't tend to like the press and I might agitate him a little more."

"Good idea," Jack takes a deep breath. "Wish me luck," he walks over to the small tree Billy is chained to. On closer inspection Lizzie sees the scene is nothing like she's envisioned. The chain actually looks like something for a small dog. Billy is sitting on a beach chair, and he looks less angry and more tired.

"Hey, Billy, can we talk for a minute?" Jack says as he walks over to him and sits down on a log Bud must have left there. Billy nods his head.

"I'd love to be a fly on the tree," Alexis says, the two men are talking quietly, and Billy doesn't look the least bit upset. Lizzie, Alexis and Ian are all trying to not stare, but doing a terrible job of it.

Within just a couple of minutes Jack is standing up and the two are shaking hands. Billy unlocks his chain and folds up his chair, He stretches, stiff from sitting on his dilapidated beach chair for hours.

"What the heck did you say to him?" Lizzie asks Jack when he walks back over, amazed at how easily and quickly the situation resolved itself.

"I just asked him if there was any more information I could give him. That I wanted to be completely transparent and if I could explain anything better I was here to listen. He was quiet for a minute and then said that sitting here for all that time he started to think about his family, people who'd been here generations ago, and how they would probably not be able to live here anymore either. And shocker, that he actually liked our ideas. But a lot of it was thinking about all the people he grew up with, and their kids not being able to stay here, and he realized how lucky he is to have a house and property largely because of the luck of the draw."

"Yeah, he lives in a house his family's had forever, he could never afford to buy it today," Alexis says.

"Wow, that was a lot of drama for such a quiet ending," Ian says.

Jack laughs, "Yeah, crisis averted. At least this one, I'm sure there will be many more to come."

"Hey, I'd love to discuss the possibility of doing some filming as this moves forward, would you all be available to go have a coffee to talk about it and maybe warm up? I spent too much of the last few years in California I'm afraid, I'm a weather wimp," Ian says.

Jack and Lizzie look at each other.

"Um, in all honesty, this day has not at all gone as planned," Lizzie says. "We're supposed to still be on our mini-vacation celebrating getting engaged last night," she looks at Jack and takes his arm. "So since we can't do that I'd at least like to go celebrate with family. I have a ring I have to show them," she blushes a bit, still getting acclimated to being engaged.

"Oh my gosh, congratulations!" Ian says. "I had no idea, please, go, we can do it another time. I feel terrible to have imposed on you!"

"No, Ian, it's fine, you didn't know!" Jack says. "I would love to sit and talk with you another time. Any other time, you just let me know what works for you."

Ian reaches out to shake Jack's hand. "I will definitely be in touch."

"Um, I can go and fill you in on some things?" Alexis says. "I don't know as much as Jack certainly, but I'm pretty much up to speed and could give you some idea of where the project is headed and the initial steps we'll be taking."

"That would be great," Ian says. "Where to?"

"Well, there's only one coffee place in town, Sea Coast, you can follow me," Alexis says. "I will see you two later," she says, giving Lizzie a hug. "We have lots of planning to do."

"Oh, you know it," Lizzie says. "Have fun!"

Jack turns to her. "Well, that turned out to be a whole lot of stress for nothing. I am so sorry it ruined everything."

Lizzie shakes her head, "Are you kidding?" She takes his hands. "I am so happy, I have everything I could ever want. Our escape may have only been 24 hours, but it was perfect." She leans in and kisses him.

"I can't believe how lucky I am to be marrying you, Lizzie Martin."

"You stole my line, sir," she says, kissing him again. "Well, except for the 'Lizzie Martin' part."

"What do you say, want to get out of here?"

"Yes! I have a ring to show my mom!" Lizzie says as they head to their car. She looks at it for the thousandth time. "She's going to love it!"

CHAPTER 18

AS SOON AS Jack starts driving Lizzie gets a text from her dad.

I got word that the crisis has been averted. Don't go to the office. Come home, I'm working from here. "Huh, okay, so my dad is working from home this afternoon apparently," she says. "So I guess that's where we're headed."

"Sounds good to me," Jack says, taking the turn that heads to the Martin's house.

As they turn the corner they see the driveway is full of cars, including Matt's work van.

"What the heck?" Lizzie says, unbuckling her seatbelt.

"I think maybe our families are up to something," Jack says, grabbing her luggage from the back of his car.

"Here, let me help," Lizzie says. She extends the handle on her suitcase and tries dragging the suitcase across the crushed shell driveway, she finally gives up the third time it tips over and picks it up.

As they arrive at the door, unsure of what awaits them inside, they each take a deep breath.

"You jump, I jump, Jack," Lizzie says. "Sorry, I have to stop saying that," she says laughing. Before either one of them has a chance to open the door it swings open. They look down and Lizzie's four-year-old niece, Sophie is standing there.

"Surprise, Aunt Wiz! Happy Birthday!" she exclaims.

Matt comes over and scoops her up, he's laughing. "Yeah, she couldn't quite get the concept down about congratulations, or best wishes, for her every celebration is either a birthday or Christmas." He leans in and gives his sister a one-armed hug. "Congratulations, Wiz."

"Okay, I'm cool with Sophie calling me Wiz? I'm not sure how I feel about this becoming a family thing," she says, mock-scolding him.

"Hey, man,welcome to the family," Matt says, giving Jack a big hug.

"I am very happy to be joining you," Jack says, smiling. "Thanks for having me!"

"Hey, we're just thrilled anyone is willing to take her on," Matt says, looking over at his sister and laughing.

Just then the rest of the family comes rushing over, now aware of their arrival.

"Oh my goodness!" Lizzie exclaims as her parents, and Jack's, and Matt's wife Shannon all emerge from the living room and rush them in a huge, group embrace. "I can't believe this!" Lizzie and Jack look at each other, stunned by the exuberant reaction.

Gabby and Peter, at the front of the pack, both envelop their daughter in a huge hug.

Gabby is teary, "I am so happy for you, honey! You and Jack are so good together, I couldn't be happier." She can't stop hugging her.

Peter hugs her, "I don't know what magic you two used to end that standoff, but thank goodness that's over!"

"I can't believe he gave up on his grudge so easily, but Jack is quite the charmer," she says, looking over at him and smiling.

Jack's parents, Jane and David have grabbed their son, and Lizzie smiles when sees his very quiet, and slightly reserved dad positively glowing and ruffling Jack's hair. It's sweet. And she's very relieved to have averted a crisis and be here now with their families.

As they all spill from the entry into the kitchen Lizzie and Jack are shocked to see the place completely decorated, and the island covered with amazing food.

"How did you ever pull this off?" Lizzie says, taking off her coat, which her dad immediately takes from her. "We didn't even know we were coming back today until a few hours ago!"

"I swear, the next time I need an event at the library organized I am calling all your parents," Shannon says. "They put this all together in about two hours. I can't believe it."

Gabby and Jane are standing with their arms around each other, and point to each other. "She did most of it," they both say, and then laugh.

"Peter and I are just good at following directions," David says. "It was a complete and total labor of love."

"We cannot thank you enough," Jack says. "We certainly aren't going to need a wedding planner with you four around."

"Okay, I don't know about *that*!" Gabby says, widening her eyes. "I think this is about my level of party planning. A few streamers, a pinata, and some takeout from Bradfords. I'm assuming you want a bit more than that." She pauses, "Is it too early to ask if you've set a date?"

Lizzie and Jack look at each other.

"Well, nothing definite, but we're thinking pretty soon?" Lizzie says. "We're thinking we've been engaged before, so why wait?" she says laughing.

"Definitely. We just want to get married already," Jack says.

"Spoken like a true romantic," his mother, Jane says, laughing.

"If we all work together we could totally pull that off. I mean, if you're not thinking big venue and all that," Shannon says.

"No," they both say at the same time.

"We definitely don't want a big, expensive, stiff event. We want fun, pretty small and relaxed, right?" Lizzie says.

"Yup, I couldn't stand to have a huge production. I want people to have fun and just be themselves. You know what would be cool? I once went to a wedding in Vermont where they had a grilled cheese bar, wouldn't that be fun?" Jack says, looking hopefully at Lizzie.

"Oh I love that!," Lizzie says, beaming. "This is going to be a lot of fun to plan. I want silly, and fun!"

"Oh! Games! We need games!" Matt says. "Like bocce, and croquet and-"

"No lawn darts," Peter jokes.

"Definitely no lawn darts," Matt says. "Maybe we could even have it at the property, depending on where you're at in building."

"Well, the crew is showing up tomorrow ready to break ground, we've amassed quite a large group, thanks to all our investors, and we had hoped by fall to have it mostly done, but we might be able to do something there, or there's always the Marshview," Jack says.

"Well now all you need is a date," says Jane.

Everyone pulls out their phones.

"What month are we looking at?" Matt asks.

"Hmmm, May?" Lizzie says, hesitantly, looking at Jack who nods in agreement.

"Wow, that's soon!" Gabby says. "Okay, so the 14th and the 21st or both Saturdays, and it's before Memorial Day weekend which is always packed in Cranberry Harbor," Gabby says.

"Do you have any preference? Does any day sound better to you?" Jack asks Lizzie.

"I'm kind of thinking the 21st sounds good, and gives us another week." She turns to Jack. "Are you sure just building Terra Marique isn't enough pressure without adding planning a wedding to the mix? We could just elope," she jokes, looking at their parents.

"No!" Peter, Gabby, Jane and David all exclaim.

Jack laughs. "Okay, no eloping. And it will be a great motivator, to get things as far along as we can," he jokes. "With the on-site manager and the crew we have, the project should go along well. We're also using some eco-friendly prefab parts, so that's going to move along the building process. I want to get people living there as soon as possible. And let the gardeners and farmers get to work before it gets too cold to get some fall plantings in. I think May 21 at Terra Marique or the Marshview sounds perfect. How do all of you feel?" He asks their assembled families.

Gabby has been handing out flutes of champagne to everyone as the discussion has been going on, so they are all ready to toast the happy couple.

"Yes!" They all raise their glasses, even Sophie, with her little cup of apple juice.

"Yes!" Sophie calls out a few seconds too late, but with more enthusiasm than everyone. "What are we yessing?" she then asks.

Lizzie crouches down, "Our wedding, honey," she says, toasting her with her glass. "I have a question, will you be my flower girl?"

"Yes!" She says, then turns to Shannon. "Mommy, what's a flower girl?"

"A flower girl is one of the most important people in a wedding," Lizzie says. "You wear a pretty dress, carry a basket of flower petals and drop them as you walk down a path. And then Uncle Jack and I will be married, like your mommy and daddy, and Grabby and Pop."

"Huh, okay, I'll do it." She's quiet for a second. "And no one will be mad that I made a mess with the flowers?"

Lizzie hugs her. "No, it will be a beautiful path outside and everyone will be happy. I promise!"

"Okay! I'm in!" Sophie says, hugging her back. Everyone oohs and ahhs and gets emotional.

"I have no idea where she got that!" Shannon laughs.

"We have an awful lot of food that is just sitting there," Gabby says. "How about we all wipe our eyes and celebrate!"

"Here, here," Peter says. "I'm famished! All this crying really works up an appetite!" He starts handing out plates to everyone as they que up.

Lizzie takes a plate from her dad and gives him a kiss on the cheek.

"Thanks, Dad," she says.

"For the plate?" he says, smiling at her.

She laughs. "Well, sure, but for everything else too. This is not where I could have ever imagined my life a year ago, and yet, here I am, back in Cranberry Harbor, working with you, engaged, again to Jack, it hardly seems real. I may have to pinch myself. I'm so grateful to have you and Mom in my corner."

"Always and forever, honey," he says, hugging her. "And yes, it is very real, honey, and I cannot begin to tell you how incredibly grateful I am for how it's all turned out. To see you this happy," he begins to choke up, "is everything to your Mom and me. All we ever wanted was that. Getting to work with you every day is just icing on the cake."

"Back at you," she says, as she places some vegetarian lasagna on her plate.

Peter goes back to being the host, and Lizzie takes a moment to look around at everyone. She and Jack catch each other's eyes and smile at one another from across the room. Cranberry Harbor does it again. In that moment she knows this is where she wants to be, with these people, with this man. And with that amazing looking cake her mother just put out on the table.

CHAPTER 19

STILL FLOATING on air Monday morning, Lizzie stopped by Sea Coast on her way to the paper hoping to catch Alexis who's been showing up there every morning, using it as her de facto office for the time being. Maybe it's because she's viewing the town through her newly engaged rose-colored glasses, but she smiles as she sees crocuses popping through the ground in the beds by the shop, and notices some daffodils inching their way up as well. Spring is finally coming.

As soon as she walks in she's happy to see Alexis already encamped at a round table for two, laptop open, papers spread about and deep in thought.

"Good morning!" Lizzie says, not meaning to startle her friend.

"Oh! Hey!"

"I don't want to interrupt your flow if you're in a groove," Lizzie says, hoping she will ask her to join her.

"No, please, I'm just answering some emails, please, sit!" Alexis says, closing her laptop and gathering her papers.

"I promise not to stay long, but I haven't had a chance to catch up with you since–"

"Since the big proposal? No you have not!" Alexis leans forward, excited to hear all the details.

"Cool, let me get my coffee and I'll be right back!" Lizzie takes her wallet out of her purse, and puts it on the chair. "Do you need a refill?"

Alexis, taking a sip, shakes her head no. "This is already cup number two, so I'm going to cut myself off for a while, thanks."

Lizzie is back quickly and sits down with her tea. "Are you still getting lots of press inquiries?"

"Not as many, I think most people were into the drama, now that Billy is no longer chained to a tree they've backed off," she says.

Lizzie shakes her head. "I really hate that that was what they were excited about, not the project itself. It says a lot about the state of the media in this country. It's all about clicks and getting people angry or outraged."

"Yup, it sure seems that way," Alexis agrees. "So enough about that, I want to hear about this," she says, taking Lizzie's hand and looking at her ring. "This is so beautiful! Where did he get it?"

"He actually got it at Jess's Bridal Shop, apparently she's starting to carry some vintage jewelry." She admires it herself, still getting used to seeing it on her hand. "This is from the 1920s. He had it sized for me and everything."

"So he's obviously been planning this for a while," Alexis says. "Was it all romantic and dreamy?"

"It was! The snowstorm kept us at the Cape's End Inn, but he and Rusty, an amazing guy who works there, made us this beautiful picnic in front of the fire. It was perfect, Alexis. Like out of a movie."

Alexis puts her hand on her heart. "Aw, I'm so happy for you, for the both of you. Like I've said, you give me hope that on this little sandbar, with hardly anyone our age around, you can find love."

"You most certainly can," she says. "So...speaking of cute guys-"

"No one said anything about cute guys," Alexis says, laughing.

"Fine, *I'm* bringing up cute guys, how was coffee with Ian after we left?" Lizzie takes a sip of her coffee and looks intently at Alexis.

By the way Alexis casts her eyes down, touches her brow and smiles, Lizzie immediately knows she enjoyed herself.

"He's a really interesting guy," she says.

"You're going to have to give me a lot more than 'interesting', my friend."

Alexis laughs. "Okay, he's smart, funny, creative and doing good things in the world. How's that?"

"Much better, though you did not say handsome. He looks like he could be Brad Pitt's stand in! He's gorgeous!" Lizzie says, pausing to take a sip of her coffee. "And yeah, he seemed really nice, like a good guy."

"He does. Of course I don't know him well at this point, but he certainly is someone I'd, um…"

Lizzie leans forward. "Someone you'd...want to get to know better?"

She's very squirmy which Lizzie finds adorable. "Um, yeah, sure."

"'Um, yeah, sure'? Lizzie laughs. "The guy is an award winning filmmaker who is handsome, and is also an environmentalist, and you yourself said, is nice, and funny. Could it be we've set the bar a little too high if you're not completely convinced he would be at the very least someone worth getting to know a little bit better?"

Alexis laughs too. "It could be I've just gotten so used to saying no to everyone that asks me out that the idea of a possible yes is a little scary. You know?"

"Oh I totally know," Lizzie says. "In those three years Jack and I were apart I dated a few people, most notably Ed, in Boston before I moved back here, but no one really struck my fancy. And I was terrified of getting hurt again, so I hear you about the fear of saying yes."

"Yup, and he didn't ask if I wanted to get together sometime, so there's also that," Alexis says, sounding a little disappointed.

"He may not have been sure of your relationship status, or was worried about overstepping since you may be working together a bit if he decides to film some of the project. It gets complicated for people to know what's the right thing to do and what's not, you know? But it was clear to me he liked you." Lizzie counters.

"Yeah? But he may have a girlfriend or fiance'…"

"I didn't get that feeling, he really seemed to want to spend time with you," Lizzie says.

"It is the twenty-first century, I could have asked him out too. Ugh, maybe I completely blew it!" Alexis shakes her head.

"Stop, you did not blow it. What are we? Seventh graders? He's a grown adult man, I doubt he's thinking anything other than perhaps, damn I blew it, I should have asked her out to dinner, or lunch, or a movie."

"True, he didn't seem like a delicate flower," they both laugh.

"Hardly, the guy is the son of one of the most successful women directors in the world. She's won Oscars, heck, he's won an Oscar. And they both survived the world of Hollywood, which, from what I've gathered in all my magazine reading, isn't exactly an easy place to make a go of it. So I'd say meeting you, my dear, dear friend would not terrify him." She's quiet for a second. "Unless of course he has already fallen madly in love with you, knows you are his true soul mate and can't live without you...that could be intimidating," she says, laughing.

"Alright, well now you're terrifying *me*! If any guy felt that way after meeting me once and having a cup of coffee, I would run, sprint, bolt to the highest peak possible," Alexis says, looking more relaxed.

"See? Playing out the most ridiculous, fantastical possibility kind of puts things in perspective, doesn't it? My diabolical plan worked!"

"You are evil! Pure evil," Alexis jokes. "And thank you for that. You're right, it's all good. I just need to calm down, and focus on the job at hand. Getting Terra Marique off the ground and that is not going to be any small feat."

"It is not. But if anyone can do it, Jack can, and with you, and all the other people he has lined up, it's all going to happen," Lizzie says in her best pep talk-speak. "You've got this."

Alexis looks at her a bit skeptically. "If you say, 'you go girl,' I am out of here," she laughs.

"Okay, you've stopped me just in time," Lizzie smiles at her.

"Phew, our friendship was hanging in the balance."

Lizzie finishes her coffee, "Okay, I am out of here," she says standing up.

"Wait, so you really think we've got this? I'm not going to fall flat on my face on my first job in my field?" Alexis asks, looking scared as she opens up her computer.

Lizzie stands tall and confidently, and looks her right in the eye.

"It's going to be amazing. You're going to be amazing. You've definitely got this. I know it. "

Alexis relaxes a little.

"You okay if I leave? I'm only a text away." Lizzie says.

Alexis nods and even smiles a little.

"Good," Lizzie turns to go, "Alright, and hey, never forget, you go girl!" She laughs and heads to the door. "Oh! Save May 21, it's our wedding date!"

"Wow! Soon! Of course I'm there!"

"Yup, why wait when you know it's meant to be?" Lizzie smiles and after holding the door for a mom and toddler coming in, leaves.

CHAPTER 20

PETER AND STAN are both at the paper when Lizzie arrives and she feels guilty that she spent so much time at Sea Coast on her way in.

"Sorry guys, I was getting the low down on things from Alexis." She hangs her coat on the antique rack and takes a seat. "Have I missed anything?"

"Nope, things are actually pretty quiet, which I have to say is a bit of a relief," Peter says, leaning back and putting his hands behind his head.

"Oh no, Stan, I think he's cursed us now! Take that back, Dad," Lizzie says, mostly joking but a little seriously too. She didn't like to admit to her superstitious side, but it was there. Without even thinking about it, she knocks the wooden desk. Just in case.

"Oh, Lizzie!" Stan says, standing up and rushing over to her and giving her a hug. "I'm sorry! I meant to say congratulations as soon as you came in! I'm so excited for you and Jack."

Lizzie hugs him back. "No apology needed, Stan, I didn't even think about it! I certainly hope you and Maggie will be at the wedding!"

"If we're invited we most certainly will be," he says, beaming.

"Of course you're invited, Stan, you're family!" Lizzie says.

Lizzie opens up her computer and begins checking her email. There's one from Anika Patel from Tall Tales Books.

Hey Lizzie,

Per our conversation the other day, I think I want to start planning the "Book Lovers Singles Night." Maybe you could help me a little bit with publicity and getting the word out? Between our social media, email list, the 'Cranberry Harbor Cast' podcast, and the Gazette, I think we could make it happen. I'm thinking in about three weeks? Thanks! Anika

Looking up from her computer Lizzie asks her dad and Stan, "Did I miss a beat here, who is hosting a Cranberry Harbor podcast?"

"Huh, this is the first I'm hearing about it," Peter says, while Stan just shrugs his shoulders. She should have known better than to think the two of them would be more in the loop than she.

"I need to find out about this podcast," she types, quickly writing Anika back.

"It's a really good idea, I'm kind of jealous I didn't think of it."

Lizzie takes out her phone and goes to her podcast app. She scrolls through the pop culture, crime, and news podcasts she follows and types in *Cranberry Harbor Cast.* "Hmm, it's Justine who works at Toy Works, and Leah, from Sea Coast Coffee." She can't imagine why they didn't tell her, they were just doing yoga a couple of days ago.

"I'm going to go and see what I can find out about this, and also stop at Tall Tales and see if I can get some ideas for helping Anika plan and promote a singles night at the bookstore," she says, getting up. "Unless there's something pressing here you need me to do?"

"Nope," her dad says. "A single night at the bookstore? That could be really good, maybe? Do you think people in town would come out for that?"

"I'm going to translate what you just said, Dad. What you're really asking is, do I think any guys will come out for that, right?" She smiles at him as she buttons her coat.

"Busted," he looks embarrassed. "Maybe I'm showing my age, I'm just not sure I know any guys who would go to a singles thing at a bookstore. Cape League Baseball game event? Heck yes. And I know I am probably completely wrong so don't go by me. I have not been on a date in a hundred years."

"At least one hundred," Stan jokes.

"I hear what you're saying, Dad. And it crossed our minds too when we thought of it. But you never know. Maybe there will be a few brave and bookish folks in Cranberry Harbor who will show. We won't know if we don't try, and the whole idea is to be inclusionary for sure."

"That sounds really good, honey. You go forth and find out what's up, and I will be very curious about that podcast," Peter says.

"There's only one episode up, so it's definitely a new thing. I'll see what I can find out. See you soon!" She calls to them both and heads out the door.

As she's walking down a still-sunny Main Street her phone rings, it's Jack. "Hey, I've been wondering what you're up to." she says, smiling ear to ear without even realizing it.

"Ah, I was doing the same thing, where are you?" Jack asks.

"I am walking from the paper to Tall Tales and then Sea Coast. Hey, did you know that there's a Cranberry Harbor podcast? It's called *Cranberry Harbor Cast*?"

"Huh, I did not. I have to say I'm surprised that someone started that before you had a chance to," he says. "Is it any good?"

"I haven't listened yet, it's Justine and Leah, I wonder why they didn't tell me?" Having reached the store she stops and takes a seat on the bench outside. It's chilly, but she doesn't want to end the call yet. And, it's kind of pretty out. After all the endless gray and rainy days they'd had, it was nice to take in the sunshine and look at the trees budding along Main Street.

"Maybe they just wanted to see how it went? How many episodes are up?" he says.

"Just one, so it's pretty new. I want to hear what they're doing, but I also want to talk to them about their plans," Lizzie is getting chilly. "Hey, so I'm outside the Tall Tales and getting cold, talk later? Oh wait, I didn't even ask you what you're up to!"

"Oh, just the usual, except I'm looking out from a trailer onto the land as bulldozers are starting some excavation," he says nonchalantly.

"What?! They're starting?! You have a trailer? Oh my gosh, this is real! I'm not sure when I can get out there, can you grab a few photos on your phone for me to use for the paper and our socials?"

"Of course, I've already taken a bunch. This is crazy, Lizzie, it's really happening!" Jack says with a sound of disbelief in his voice.

"It is all happening, honey, it really is!!" Lizzie feels choked up. "You made this all happen, Jack, I'm so excited for you, for us, for Cranberry Harbor!" She's so excited she hops up and down, then looks around feeling a bit self-conscious.

"It's pretty crazy for sure," he sighs. "Look, you get inside and get warm, I'll talk to you later on. In the meantime I'll send over some photos for you to post. I love you."

"I love you too, and congratulations on the start! I thought it would all be more ceremonial, like we'd have a ribbon cutting or something," she says.

"I thought of it, but they showed up three days early and I wasn't about to send them away, you know?"

"Heck no," Lizzie agrees. "Strike while the iron or excavator is hot, for sure. I'll call you when I'm done here and see where you're at."

"Sounds good," he says.

Lizzie slides her phone into her coat pocket and walks into the book store.

"Hey!" Anika says from behind the counter. "I didn't expect you to come running in," she says, walking over and giving Lizzie a hug. "I hear through the grapevine congratulations are in order!"

"Yes, thank you!" She reaches out her left hand to show Anika her ring. "It's official! And mark your calendar for May 21!"

"Oh, I will block out that day for sure!"

Lizzie takes off her coat and slings it over the back of the couch in the reading area and sits down. "So, how far have you gotten in planning the Book Lovers night?"

"Ah, well, I emailed you, and I messaged Justine and Leah, that's about it. Oh! And I've been playing around with a fun graphics app and making a poster." She gets up to grab her tablet from the counter. "Here, this is what I've got so far." She sits down on the couch next to Lizzie and shows her a poster featuring a few people in silhouette–standing with books, sitting with books, talking...with books, it looks a bit stiff.

Before Lizzie can say anything Anika blurts out, "This does not look like anything fun, does it? It's positively Edwardian."

Lizzie feels bad, but she's thinking the same thing. "Yeah...it's a little, well, um, old fashioned? If we wanted Mr. Darcy and Elizabth Bennet to come, it would be perfect!" They both laugh.

"Okay, back to the drawing board." Anika says.

"Hey, how about if we get Justine and Leah to come and have it be a podcast about being single in Cranberry Harbor? Or the Cape in general for that matter. From Sandwich to Provincetown. the off-season is spectacularly bleak dating-wise," Lizzie says. "It could be interactive, maybe some games, make it a real party!"

"Oh, that sounds fun!" Anika starts playing around with some graphics. "Hmm, before I get too into this, perhaps we should ask them if they'd be interested?"

"Good idea, though asking for forgiveness is often easier than asking permission, something my dad always said when it came to getting things done in town. Probably not applicable here though," Lizzie says. She gets up and puts her coat on. "I'm going to run over to Toy Works and see if Justine is there, and we can see what they think?"

"Okay, I will be here optimistically designing a poster for, hmmm, how about, 'Live From Tall Tales:Singles Night; Share Stories, Share Favorite Books...You Never Know Who You Might Meet...' Too hokey? I'll keep working on it," Anika says, now looking for fun graphics.

"I like it! Let me see what Justine and Leah say, then we can work out the details." and with that Lizzie runs over to Toy Works.

"Good morning, my friend!" Justine says cheerfully from behind the counter. "What brings you in? Something for Sophie? Oh my gosh! I forgot!" She gets off her stool and rushes around the counter to hug Lizzie. "Congratulations! I'm so excited for you and Jack! He is one lucky fella!"

Lizzie hugs her right back. "Oh, thanks so much. I think we're both pretty lucky!"

"Seriously, finding love in Cranberry Harbor, especially in the off-season? Next to impossible!" Leah says, straightening up a display of Legos. "So what brings you in?"

"Well, I heard through the grapevine that you and Leah are the masterminds and hosts behind the *Cranberry Harbor Cast*."

Justine blushes, and shakes her head. "Ah, yeah, we are. We so don't know what we're doing, we do not have the best equipment, but we're trying to learn all we can. Leah has a friend from college who's a podcast producer in New York, and she's giving us tips. But man, it's a little rough around the edges. That's why we haven't said anything. We wanted to get a few episodes up and then promote it more. We are totally in learning mode!"

"I haven't gotten to listen to it yet, but I'm betting it's better than you think it is."

"I would reserve your thinking on that," Justine says, laughing. "In the first episode Leah's dog went crazy seeing a squirrel outside and we didn't know how to edit anything out, so it's about three minutes of her chasing Munchkin and him barking, and me laughing. Not super professional!"

"No one expects *This American Life* out of the gate," Lizzie says. "I'm betting *This American Life* has had its rough moments too!" She clears her throat. "Okay, so Anika had this idea of a singles meet-up at Tall Tales, but we're worried no one will come, and we were trying to think of a way to make it fun, open to everyone, well, as long as you're single, and wondered if you and Leah would ever think of making it part of your podcast? 'Live from Tall Tales!' or something? We're trying to find a way to create something that doesn't feel like it's from another century and is fun. It's just a thought, no pressure at all!"

Justine is quiet, Lizzie can tell she's thinking, but doesn't know what she's thinking. She's hard to read.

"I think that's a fabulous idea!" she blurts out, startling Lizzie.

"Really?"

"Yeah! Let me run it by Leah, but I think it could be really fun! We could have some games - maybe book trivia, some storytelling, and then maybe a little speed dating segment?"

"Oh yeah, we thought of games and stories, but some speed dating could be great! I'm so glad you're on board!" Lizzie says, relieved that hopefully they will take over planning this and take the pressure off of her. Covering the beginning of Terra Marique being built, all the rest of the town news *and* planning a wedding was making her plate feel pretty darn full.

"I'll text Leah, and get back to you and Anika ASAP," Justine says.

"You are a godsend!" Lizzie says. There's nothing like the energy of some twentysomethings to get things moving. "Let me know if there's anything on my end I can do. I can certainly post things on the Gazette's social media, and we can do a story about it too. We're a little light on events this time of year, so we could give it some good coverage."

"Awesome! I will get back to you today, but I'd say I can pretty much guarantee it's a go on our end,"

"Thank you so, so much!" Lizzie says as she heads to the door. "I'll talk to you later!"

Lizzie heads back to Tall Tales and thinks if only every idea she had was this easy to pull off.

CHAPTER 21

AFTER TALKING to Anika and being relieved by her new and improved poster, Lizzie can't help herself, and even if she really doesn't have the time today, after she walks back to the paper, she decides she has to take a quick trip out to Terra Marique and see what's happening. And of course give her fiance' a big congratulatory hug.

She's there in just a couple of minutes and can't believe her eyes. These investors aren't fooling around. There are trucks and all sorts of heavy equipment everywhere. It's so busy there's even a police officer there to make sure people coming and going are safe.

After being directed to a spot to park near the construction team's trailer, Lizzie gets out of her car and is totally agog at all the action. Per the plans they are being very careful about tree removal, only taking out ones that absolutely have to go for construction, so there is no clear cutting going on like in so many developments where they fell every tree in sight. Over the last several weeks, being hopeful the project was going to pass at town meeting, a team has been optimistically putting bright yellow ties around the trees to be cut, bright pink for those to remain.

Lizzie has only been there a moment when Jack spots her through the window and comes bounding down the stairs from the trailer.

"Well, what do you think, huh?" He says, grinning from ear to ear.

"This is amazing! I thought they couldn't get all the machinery here until next week, what happened?" Lizzie asks, still staring in disbelief.

Jack shrugs, "Someone on the team made some calls. They certainly have a lot more pull than I do. I think I got hung up on three times, but then all of a sudden, bam, they were here." He puts his arm around her and hugs her close. "I know we talked about doing this whole groundbreaking ceremony with the paper here and everything, but after how hard it was to get them here I wasn't about to ask them to wait. I did get some good pictures though I think, which I emailed to you. So, it's not a complete loss."

Lizzie looks at all the work going on and is a little disappointed that they weren't able to have the guests she'd hoped for there to see this, to have some sense of ceremony around this momentous event. The governor had not said no, so she had been hoping she was coming… "I understand, I really do," which she meant, but still... "Maybe we can create another photo op a little bit down the road. It's okay." She puts her arm around his waist. "This is very exciting! I can't believe this is happening! I'm so proud and so happy for you, sweetie," she gives him a kiss, just as someone with a hardhat and some plans comes over.

"Excuse me, sorry to interrupt," he says, clearing his throat nervously. "We had some questions about a couple of the trees? Looking at the plans there are a couple of pink ones that look like they should be green, or they're going to be in the middle of someone's living room."

"You go, you have lots to do," Lizzie says. "I'll see you tonight, we'll celebrate."

He starts to walk away. He turns to her, "I have a feeling the next few months are going to be a little crazy. I'll call you when I'm done."

"Ah, so in like, six months?" She calls after him, smiling.

He keeps walking and gives her a thumbs up and nods.

She takes a couple of photos, but is aware that it's actually pretty dicey walking around. Trees are being cut down, the sound of chain saws is deafening, there's debris all over, and she's not exactly dressed with proper footwear or a hard hat for traipsing around a construction site. She jumps when not too far from her she hears a tree fall to the ground.

"Okay, so it's back to town for me," she says quietly to herself.

When Lizzie gets back to the office both her father and Stan are gone. The photographer she hired, Lisa, is there, but she's got headphones on and is busy editing some photos, so she doesn't bother her. That said, she can't seem to settle down. She's distracted and preoccupied.

Despite her lack of focus, she gets everything done she needs to. The photos Jack sent her are up on all their social media platforms. She's filed a story that she'd been close to done with, and had formatted page one. She sits back and sighs.

"Hey, I'm going to head out," she says to Lisa as she puts her coat on. Lisa, in the midst of editing photos from the latest high school hockey game, nods and waves.

Once in her car, Lizzie has no idea where she wants to go. So far her engagement hasn't exactly gone how one might think it should go. "You've been watching too many romcoms," she says to herself as she starts her car. And then, just like that, she knows exactly where she wants to go, and what she wants to do. She takes her cell phone out of her pocket and texts Alexis and her mom.

If you aren't too busy right now, would you both like to meet me for a very important errand?

She hits send and waits a moment.

Is this the errand I'm thinking it might be? Her mom writes right back.

Lizzie smiles and types back, *Yes! Can you both meet me at Jess's?*

I'm in!" Alexis tests back. *See you in five!*

Lizzie is now beaming as she heads to the bridal store.

She and Alexis arrive at the same time, and Alexis comes bounding down the sidewalk, "Yes! This is going to be so much fun!" she exclaims, hugging Lizzie.

Gabby then arrives, so excited she has to turn around when she gets out of her car because she forgot to close her door. "Oh my gosh! This is so fun!" she says, hugging both Lizzie and Alexis. "Shall we?"

Once they walk in, Lizzie's heart begins to race. She'd been so excited, but now, all of a sudden, she's feeling a little wobbly. Her mom immediately notices. So does Jess, the shop owner who busies herself behind the counter, not wanting to intrude.

"You okay, honey?" Gabby puts her arm around her and leads her to a couch. "What's going on?"

"I don't know... I, um, I was so excited to do this, then all of a sudden I feel really anxious, I don't know why, but, ugh," she shakes her hands. Alexis comes over and crouches down.

"What's up? You okay? You want to leave? We can get out of here right now if this isn't feeling good to you," she says, rubbing Lizzie's arm.

Lizzie takes a deep breath. "All of a sudden I was brought back to having put a dress on hold four years ago, and then having to call and say that I wouldn't be needing it." She leans into her mom who has her arm around as they sit. "That probably sounds insane, it's not like it was a huge trauma or anything, but yet, it kind of was. I didn't realize until right now how scared I am of that happening again. That he's going to leave again. Does that make me crazy?"

"No, it does not. It makes you perfectly human," says Gabby, kissing her on the head and stroking her hair. "That was a terrible time and you have done an amazing job moving past it, but of course, old feelings would come up as this next chapter becomes more real."

Alexis scoots onto the couch and joins them, Jess, who has probably seen it all being the owner of a bridal shop, is giving them their space. "Lizzie, I think you are incredibly brave, and strong and if today is not the day, it's just not the day. It's all good."

Lizzie sits up and dries her eyes with her sleeve before her mom can pull a tissue out of her pocket. "Thank you, both, no, I want to do this. Things are not the same as they were four years ago, Jack isn't the same, and neither am I. I'm not planning the wedding from four years ago, I'm planning the wedding for now." She sniffs, wipes her nose with the tissue her mom put on her lap and stands up. "Okay, so I have one question...what style?" She starts going through the racks. "Mermaid? Nah, not me, vintage?" She pulls a gorgeous dress from the 1950s section out and they all ooh and ahh over it.

"I can start a dressing room for you if you like?" says Jess, who sees the storm has passed and has come in to join them. "We also do couture alterations right here, so we can make any changes you need, even if it's just the hem, right here."

"Oh, that's so good to know, thank you!" says Gabby. "This wedding is coming up pretty quickly, in May, so it's important we can get things done right here in Cranberry Harbor."

"Jess," Lizzie says, standing up and walking over to her, and putting out her hand, "Thank you so much for helping Jack with this beautiful ring, I love it so much."

Jess takes her hand and smiles. "Oh my gosh, it looks fantastic! I'm so glad you love it." She lets go of Lizzie's hand and leans in. "Truth be told, this was my favorite out of all the rings I brought in." She turns to return to her task at hand. "Let me know if you need anything, I'll let you and your crew look around a bit."

Alexis pulls out a dress from the 1970s, a gorgeous crocheted, empire-waisted dress with bell sleeves. "Oh, look at this, it's so Cher circa 1972!" she says, holding it up and dancing with it. "What do you think?"

"Sure! Put it in the dressing room." Then, Lizzie sees it. It's a new dress, not vintage, but it has a certain something. It's not too frou-frou, it's a bit beachy, but not too bohemian.

"What are you looking at, honey," Gabby says, following her gaze. "Ohhh…that's beautiful!" Gabby takes it off the rack, "This is the first one you're trying on," she says leading the way.

Lizzie goes into the dressing room and peels off the many spring, but still winter layers she's wearing, and realizes the stretchy sports bra she has on is hardly the right undergarment for a wedding dress. But she slips on the dress and smiles when she sees herself in the mirror. She opens the curtain and steps out, her mother immediately starts to cry before she's even zipped up.

"Mom, now you're going to make me cry!" Lizzie steps up on the carpeted platform and turns to look at herself in the mirror, and promptly starts to cry too. "Now, look at what you've started," she says looking at her mother and laughing as she wipes her eyes.

Jess hands her a tissue, and zips her up. "This looks wonderful," she says as she fluffs the train out to give Lizzie the full effect.

"This can't be it, can it? The first dress? But I have to say, I sort of love it." Lizzie says, turning and looking critically at the dress and herself. "I surely need to try on like, ten, right?"

The dress is a beautiful ivory color, Lizzie has never been a fan of bright white, and while it's new, it has the lines and elegance of a vintage dress. It's not too poofy, but not too tight so it's easy to move in.

"I love the lace detail on the bodice, and the illusion fabric on the chest and shoulders, it looks like it's from the 1940s, but it also looks contemporary," Alexis says, she's choked up too. "Maybe this will sound funny, but, I don't know, it just looks like you," she shrugs her shoulders and grabs a tissue from the box Jess has kindly placed nearby.

"It's this wonderful line from New York," Jess says as she circles Lizzie, seeing how every aspect of the dress fits. "They do an incredible job of marrying old and new," she laughs. "Pardon the bridal pun."

"Mom? What do you think?" Lizzie asks.

Gabby blows her nose and nods, throwing up her hands and laughing,"Look at me, what do you think?" Then they all start to laugh.

"Should I try on a couple more? Just to be safe?" Lizzie asks the room.

"Hey, why not," Alexis says. "We're all here, you've got the ring and all," she smiles. She gets up and takes a dress off the rack. "I thought this one was really nice." She puts it over her arm and walks it over to Lizzie. "It's strapless, and you have such pretty shoulders from all your yoga," she says, smiling, and hands it to her.

"Sure," Lizzie says, "I'm game!" Jess takes the dress from her and puts it in the dressing room. She steps down from the platform, "Mom? Do you mind unzipping this for me?" She asks, pulling her hair to the side.

Gabby gets up, but before unzipping the gown gives Lizzie a

hug. "I'm not a mom who thinks the only way you're going to be complete is by getting married, you know," she says.

"Of course I know that, you've never pressured me at all," Lizzie says, feeling emotional.

"It's just, ugh, I don't know why I'm so teary," Gabby says, wiping her eyes again. "But you and Jack are so good together, and you two are such forces on your own, but you're even more together, and I just feel so grateful for us, for you, for Cranberry Harbor to have the two of you starting your life together right here. Okay, I'll shut up now." And with that she unzips the dress. "There you go! I promise to stop crying now," she jokes.

Lizzie slips into the dressing room and closes the curtain, and keeps talking. "You know, if I choose that dress I may be one of the only brides to choose the first dress they put on, is that right, Jess?"

"Well, you'd be in the minority, that's for sure. I've had brides try on as many as twenty and still not end up buying one." She moves next to the curtain, "Do you need some help with the zipper?" she asks.

"Yes, I cannot get this on my own," she says.

Jess pulls back the curtain and goes in. In under a minute Lizzie emerges taking tiny steps in the very tight gown.

"Yeah, I'm not sure this mermaid style is really me," she says. "I don't think I can even get myself up there," she says, eying the platform that is about eight inches high. "I'm thinking that unless I plan to spend the wedding posing by a doorway, and never moving, this isn't for me."

Gabby and Alexis each crinkle their noses and shake their heads. "Yeah, no," they say also in unison.

"Dress one?" Lizzie says. They both nod enthusiastically.

"I'll help you out of that," Jess says, smiling. "You know when you know."

"Yup, and I know. And that's my dress," Lizzie says.

"I don't think you're going to need too many alterations," Jess says and she puts a "sold" tag on Lizzie's dress, "But I'd like you to come back with the undergarments you will be wearing and the shoes, shoes are important to get the length right, and then we can make sure everything is perfect." She takes the dress and brings it up to the counter, takes the tag off and hands it to Lizzie. Gabby immediately intercepts and takes it.

"Mom, I don't expect you--"

"No, you are our only daughter, of course I am buying your dress!" Gabby says, taking out her wallet and selecting a card.

"But Mom, you really don't have to," Lizzie says, knowing full well this is a battle she will not win. When Gabby makes her mind up about something, there is no changing it.

"I know I don't have to, I *want* to. You Dad and I both want to. Really, honey, let us do this for you. We're happy and delighted to do this for you," she hands her card over to Jess.

"Oh! We didn't even discuss veil, no veil, flower crown, and all that," Alexis says, coming around the corner wearing a shoulder-length veil, stopping to pose for them.

"Oh yeah! I didn't even think of that!" Lizzie says. Maybe when I come back, sans sports bra and snow boots we could try a few looks?" She cocks her head and looks at Alexis. "Hmm, I don't know that I've ever considered myself a veil person. Did you wear one, Mom? I can't remember from the photos."

"I did not. I pretty much went non-traditional, we got married on the beach and all, I was even barefoot, much to your grandmother's dismay," Gabby says, laughing at the memory. "But I was pretty independent, I was in my third year of medical school, so she knew I would do whatever I wanted to do. Honestly, I think they were just happy to see me 'settling down,' I was so different from my cousins who married very young and were a bit more traditional than me."

"Gabby Martin, doctor, rebel, and creator of her own path," Lizzie teases.

"You are so cool, Dr. Martin," Alexis says.

"Alexis, I'm always telling you, please, call me Gabby! And you are so wrong, I am so not cool, but I appreciate the thought!"

"Oh no, you totally are...Gabby," Alexis says, stumbling a bit on her name. "Believe me, we all think so!"

Jess hands Gabby the receipt, "Listen to them, Dr. Martin, face it, you are totally cool." She turns to Lizzie. "Call me and we can make an appointment for you to come in for a fitting, make it soon, though, your wedding is coming up fast." She puts a garment bag over her dress and zips it up so it's safe and sound to be stored in the back.

Lizzie's stomach does a little flip. It *is* really soon she thinks. And then she reminds herself, it may feel soon, but it's also been years in the making. "I will, thank you for everything!"

"Are you ladies ready to scoot?" Lizzie asks. "If no one's in a hurry should we go celebrate with some cake and tea? My treat!" She looks at her mother. "I insist on treating!"

"I've got time," Gabby says.

"Me too," says Alexis.

They all bundle up as they head out into the waning sun on this cold February afternoon. It may be cold now, but Jess is right, before she knows it her wedding will be here. And with that thought, she smiles to herself. It's all working out, and it's going to be perfect. She just knows it.

CHAPTER 22

THE TRIO of wedding dress shoppers were just about finished with their celebratory feast of lavender cake, brownies, and lemon squares washed down with tea and lattes when Anika from Tall Tales came rushing in.

"Hey, all, sorry to interrupt, but do you have a minute, Lizzie?" Anika says.

"Of course," Lizzie looks at her mother and Alexis, "Is this something personal, do you want to go to another table?"

"Oh, no, not at all," she pulls up a fourth chair. "I'm so sorry to interrupt! It's about the singles night at the bookstore, the Book Lovers thing?" she says. "Apparently Leah said something to a woman who was getting coffee here, and it ended up that she's a producer with that TV show, Boston Today, and she wants to do a segment about it."

"Well that would be great publicity for the bookstore, right?" Alexis asks.

"Yes, except they wondered if we could move it up, they're doing a theme week about dating and want to include it, but our original date would be too late. It would mean doing it really soon. Do you think with social media, a story in the Gazette - thank you and please," she says with pleading eyes, "we could pull this off?"

Lizzie takes a deep breath and pauses to think. A million thoughts are running through her head. "Yeah, I mean how much else is going on around here these dark days of March? When are you thinking of doing it?"

Anika closes her eyes and scrunches up her face, "Next Thursday? Leah and Justine said they could do their live podcast then, I just need to get the word out," she says tentatively.

"Whoa, that is soon," Lizzie says. "Okay, I think we can do this, what about you two?" she says looking at Gabby and Alexis. "You game to help get the word out?"

"I've been married forever, but I am happy to spread the word," Gabby says, laughing.

"You know everyone, Dr. Martin, so that would be a huge help, thank you," says Anika.

"I can spread the word too, and I'll come, what the heck, the one interesting guy I recently met hasn't called me, so I'm in!" offers Alexis.

Just then, Sean walks in, spies them and comes over.

"Hey! Well this looks like a very serious meeting, I don't want to interrupt, but I did want to say hi," he says. "Are you four planning on taking over the town?" He teases.

"No, but we are planning a singles night at the bookstore," Anika says. "Hey, I don't suppose I could hire Ben to cater, could I? Ugh, nevermind, I shouldn't have asked, I know how busy you two are, I shouldn't have even brought it up!"

"Stop, we're not that busy actually, inn-wise, kid-wise, yeah, but we're closed for the duration while we do some construction on the place. When I get home I'll ask Ben if he'd be up for it. You're talking just some appetizers, maybe some cookies? Wine? Tea and coffee?"

"That would be perfect, right?" Anika says looking to the ad hoc committee that has seemed to have formed around this event. "Thank you, thank you! See what Ben says, and to give me a ballpark price, it's last minute, because, well, it's next Thursday, and I want you to be fair to yourselves, okay?"

"Sounds good. Well I am going to grab myself a chai and go over to see Jack at the property. He invited me to come by, so I'm using my kid-free couple of hours to do just that."

He heads to the counter to place his order, and Anika, who is looking a bit more relaxed than when she came in a few minutes ago, heaves a sigh of relief. "Oh my gosh, I feel like you have all just pulled me in from a rip tide, thank you! I was feeling so overwhelmed and now I've got publicity, a possible caterer, one participant and the one woman in town who everyone knows and listens to on my team. I don't know how to thank all of you. Thank you, thank you, you are life savers!" And with that Anika rushes out as fast as she rushed in.

Sean comes back to the table and takes Anika's seat. "So do you think the guys in this town are going to sign up for any singles event, let alone one in a bookstore?" He sees their faces fall. "Uh, not to rain on your parade and all, it's just…I don't know, I've been here for a couple of years now, and the straight guys just seem a little, kind of, sort of–"

"Stuck?" Alexis offers up.

"Yes, perfect word!" Sean says. "Maybe I'm underestimating them, it just seems that unless you sit next to them on a stool at Murphy's or their sister introduces you, they aren't doing a heck of a lot to meet women." He sits back, "But hey, I could be completely wrong, and this will be the thing that brings them out."

"Anika has her heart set on this being a success, so I think we should all do everything we can to make it so," says a very plucky Gabby.

"Agreed," Lizzie says. "I have the same fear, Sean, but maybe it's all in how we promote it? Less Jane Austin, more Stephen King," she pauses and looks at the shock on the faces of her table mates. "Okay, bad example," she says, laughing, "not Stephen King, maybe Carl Hiaasen?"

Sean laughs, "much better example. Being single on the Cape is scary enough without bringing Stephen King into it."

"Amen to that," says Alexis, finishing up her tea. "Trying to meet someone here is so hard. Mostly because the median age in Cranberry Harbor is 65, but even when you do meet someone, and you think there was maybe, just maybe a spark, and then you wait for them to call you, and they don't, so you start to think, okay, maybe there's something wrong with me, what's wrong with me? I think I'm pretty okay, no more than okay, I'm great! And what the heck is wrong with him that he can't pick up his phone and call?" She finally pauses and takes a breath, and is a little embarrassed. "Sorry, I mean, I can *imagine* that's what it's like, right?"

They all nod, unsure of what to say.

"Oh, heck, I'm not fooling anyone, I really liked Ian, and was hoping he'd call me," Alexis says.

"Ian? I feel like I missed something here, who's Ian?" Sean asks.

"Yeah, I'm out of the loop too, I don't know any Ians," Gabby says, now leaning forward on her elbows. "A tourist?"

"No, yeah, well, sort of but not really. He's living in Provincetown, or maybe Truro? His name is Ian MacFayden. He's not from here," Alexis says. "He's a filmmaker. I met him at Terra Marique when he came to check it out and maybe shoot some video."

"Oh wait, he's the guy who did that documentary about the declining number of whales off the Cape shores, right? Didn't he win an Oscar?" Sean asks.

"He did," says Lizzie. "He's a really cool guy, and we actually met his mom, Delia, a director and writer as well, in Provincetown, she's living out there now."

"Wow! I had no idea!" Gabby says. "You truly never know who you're going to meet on the Cape, we have so many fascinating people here. So we need to get him to come to the Book Lovers event, how are we going to do that?" Once Gabby sets her sights on a goal there's no deterring her. "Ideas anyone?"

"Hmmm…" Sean says, looking pensive. "I've never met the guy, but I would think if he's come here from a place with more going on he might be looking for something to do, this place isn't exactly a hotbed of activity November through April. Maybe you could invite him, Alexis?"

"No way," she says, shaking her head emphatically, "I know it's the twenty-first century, but I don't want to call and ask him, and besides, why would I invite a guy I'm interested in to an event where there's going to be lots of amazing Cape women for him to meet as well?"

"Good point," Sean gets up. "I have to run, I'm off to see Jack, but if I have any brainstorms I'll text you," he says. "I'll give Ben the info about the event and have him reach out to Anika to make a plan for food and beverages."

"Say hi to Ben, and give that baby a kiss for me, and thank you!" Lizzie says.

"Okay, so we all have our assignments for Book Lovers," Lizzie says. "Like we don't all have enough on our plates right now. But this should be fun, right?" She says, trying to convince herself.

Alexis isn't looking so convinced. "If I'm lucky maybe Billy and Bud will come, they're quite single," she teases.

Gabby and Lizzie laugh. "Oh my god, can you imagine? Though maybe if they had more going on in their lives they wouldn't spend so much time stirring up trouble for everyone else," Gabby says. "I try to never say anything bad about anyone, but so help me, those too need a hobby!"

"Amen to that," Lizzie says. "I am going to make sure to tag the local gyms, the schools–single teachers and parents," she says, shrugging her shoulders as she makes some notes. "The yoga studio, this place, lots of folks follow Sea Coast on Instagram, Sean and Ben's place, Marshview."

"Yeah, the local motels, and inns are a good bet," says Gabby. "And I'm happy to put up posters around town when Anika gets them made - places like Bradford's, the post office, library, Cranberry Harbor Hardware."

"Right, good ideas, Mom," Lizzie says, writing all that down. "And I'm sure Leah and Justine will be talking about it on their podcast, and we should also let WOMR know as well so their on-air folks can be talking about it. Maybe we could even get Anika and Jay to be guests on a show, it's last minute, but I'm betting someone could squeeze them in for 15 minutes or so." She sits back and smiles.

"What's that smile? I know that look, you had that same look after you aced your SATs," Alexis says.

Lizzie laughs, "Jeez, you really know me, don't you? No, I was just realizing that I actually think we can pull this off and make it something really fun and different for the town."

"I think so too!" Gabby says, raising her empty cardboard teacup, "Hear, hear! This would probably be more meaningful with a full cup, and hopefully I'm not jinxing things with an empty one, but I think we might just be able to pull this off."

"I never cease to be amazed what the hive mind of Cranberry

Harbor can do when we work together, am I right?" Alexis says, raising her empty cup as well. "And who knows, maybe there is actually a treasure trove of amazing single guys out there, but they commute to Boston so we just never see them!"

"Wouldn't that be funny," Lizzie muses, "if all this time there were a bunch of really nice, successful, kind, smart single guys living here, but we just don't see them?"

Alexis and Gabby look at each other skeptically.

"Yeah, I don't think so either," Lizzie says, "but it was a fun fantasy for a few seconds."

The three of them gather up their belongings, take their used dishes and utensils to the recycling counter, and get ready to leave. But before they do, Lizzie grabs two coffees for her and Jack, and meets Gabby and Alexis by the door.

"In the midst of all the excitement about Book Lovers, I kind of forgot, I bought my wedding dress today!" Lizzie says as they walk to the door.

"Indeed you did, and after this event, all we need to do is plan an entire wedding that's happening in a matter of weeks," Gabby says.

Lizzie stops in her tracks. "Whoa, yeah, well, maybe this is a good trial run of our planning skills," she says, trying to sound positive.

"I tell you, never underestimate the power of Cranberry Harbor to make things happen, my friend," Alexis says. "We've got this. The whole town is here for you."

CHAPTER 23

LIZZIE HADN'T BEEN out to the Terra Marique site in a few days, and wow, it was moving fast. Really fast.

"I hope it's okay to stop by for a quick visit," she says, walking into the trailer.

"Hi, honey," he says, moving some plans, rulers, and a T-square to make space for Lizzie to sit on a bench seat. He gestures for her to sit down. The trailer was already a mess, and Lizzie was using every amount of restraint she had in her to not get up and start straightening things out. She wasn't sure how anyone could find anything, let alone think in this place. Every possible surface had paper, tools, or clothing on it. Gloves and hats seemed to be reproducing in captivity, and there were also lots of boots, many single ones which led her to wonder where their mates were.

Jack was watching her look around. Knowing that she liked things more organized it was easy to read her face. "You want to clean this place up, don't you?" he says, smiling at her. "This is driving you crazy."

She clears her throat, and takes a sip of the coffee she brought. She shakes her head, and then unconvincingly says, "Hmm, no, I'm, I'm fine. This place just looks very…lived in. And so quickly! There's clearly a lot of people coming in and out, and I'm sure despite appearances there is a method to its madness. You could probably put your hand on just about anything you need…" She takes another sip of coffee and offers up a forced smile.

Jack laughs. "You do realize who you're talking to, right? I've known you forever, this is driving you nuts. It's probably making you break out in hives. And you're wrong, I cannot find a damn thing I need," he says, laughing. "I just spent a half hour trying to find my phone and a file I needed. It's driving me crazy, but with so many of us using this trailer as a central office, it's hard for me to crack down on the messy ones and ask them to be organized."

Lizzie stands up and starts surveying the mess. "I think a big part of the problem is you have no place to put things. You need some shelves, maybe some rolling carts to put files in, you don't want big, heavy file cabinets, but files need to go somewhere." She begins to pick up papers, put things in piles and tries to create some order.

"Honey, this isn't your mess, or your responsibility, please, I don't want you to come here and feel like you have to clean. I want you to see how much progress is already being made, it's really incredible. You want to take a walk around?" he asks, standing up.

"Yes, that would be fun," she says. Putting the papers back on the table where they were is killing her. She wants them to have an actual home, a place to go, but she walks away from the table, puts on her coat, already wearing proper work-site footwear. "Okay, show me around!"

Jack opens the door to the trailer and they step outside. Lizzie had been so focused on not spilling their coffee, and looking for where to park, she had completely missed how much things had changed in the short time since she'd been there. "Wow! Look at the community buildings, it's fantastic!"

"Yeah, remember I told you about this company we found in Oregon that is making these amazing energy-efficient, green prefab structures? Ta da! These are the ones, incredible, right?"

They walk over to where the commercial kitchen will be, where chefs will be able to use the space to create products to sell to local restaurants, farmers markets and grocery stores

"Almost all the material used to make these is either recycled or upcycled and it's much more affordable. And on top of that, they go up super fast,"

Lizzie is thrilled to see how excited Jack is. "This is amazing, sweetie, I am stunned by what's happened already!"

"We're so happy with this company, we are thinking about using them for more of the structures which will mean we could be up and running much earlier than we ever could have imagined. And with so many people unable to find places to live right now, the faster we can have people move in the better."

They keep walking around the property, and Jack is pointing out where things will go.

"Oh, did you know this spot over here," he sweeps his arms out, "this is all going to be set up for charging up to 30 electric cars. The houses will all have their own charging stations. We know not everyone will have electric cars right away, but we want to be ready for it." He's so engrossed in what he's doing, Lizzie can see his mind going a mile a minute. "Speaking of cars, we're negotiating with a manufacturer who might want to donate electric cars to people living here in exchange for being the official car of Terra Marique. We're mulling that over, we want to make sure there's no political ties or anything we might regret down the road."

Lizzie has been very quiet while they've been walking the property, deep in her own thoughts, and wanting to let Jack share all he wants to with her. Then what she's been thinking about comes out.

"Would you ever think of having our wedding here? I know we talked about the Marshview, but," she turns around taking in the beauty of the place, "but this could be perfect. And so special."

Jack is looking at her wondering if she's seeing the same muddy, messy construction site he is.

"Really? Honey, look around, this place is a mess, and it's not like it's going to be all finished and looking ready for prime time in eight weeks or so. I think we might be better off with the Marshview, don't you?"

"I don't know," she walks over to him and puts her arm around his waist, and her head on his shoulder. "It's just that this is Cranberry Harbor's future, and it seems like it might be the perfect place to start ours as well. You've worked so hard to make this happen, I can't believe what's already happening here. It's more than I ever could have imagined, and believe me, I imagined a lot."

She leaves Jack's side and walks to a spot that has a beautiful view of a marsh leading out to the bay. "You know better than me what this is going to look like in a couple months, so if you think that would be pushing it, I don't want to put any more pressure on you or the crew."

"I love the sentiment behind the thought, I really do, but I think it is being overly optimistic to think this place could be ready for a bunch of people to be here. We want people to be able to dance, and sit down, and not lose a shoe in the mud," he jokes. "We could celebrate our first anniversary here, that would be a doable goal."

"You're right, I was getting swept away by sentimentality and the beauty of the place. But I need to remember that I'm a person who always thinks a painting project that will take two days can be done in two hours. I have project optimism and amnesia," she says, laughing.

"I will make sure to remember that the first time you decide we can renovate our kitchen on Monday and have guests over for dinner on Saturday," Jack says, giving Lizzie a kiss.

"The good news is, that skill, or I guess flaw, allows me to think I can accomplish almost anything, but it does get me in hot water sometimes."

They hold hands and continue to walk, headed away from the current bustle of construction and trucks.

"Speaking of that, Sean told me that the singles night thing at the bookstore got moved up and somehow you're very involved in getting the word out and getting people there, how are you going to find time for that with the paper and planning the wedding? Not that the wedding is all yours to plan, but..."

"I know, but this is just a week, I can do it. I just have to find a way to get guys to come." She stops in her tracks and looks around. "Wait a minute, there's lots of guys working here, are they all married?"

"Nooooo.... Do not even think about asking this crew to come to Book Lovers," Jack says emphatically, "The last thing I need is a bunch of folks falling in love and being distracted,"

Lizzie laughs. "Oh, so you'd much rather be employing a bunch of men and women who are lonely and looking for love, but have no idea where to find it on this sandbar?"

"Well now I just sound like a jerk," Jack says, laughing as well. "It's not that I want this crew to be miserable, it's just--"

"You want them to just be *slightly* miserable until Terra Marique is finished and then they can go and fall in love and be all happy?" Lizzie smiles at him. She loves giving Jack a hard time. They know each other so well, it's fun to be able to tease one another because they both know how much they love one another. There's no contempt, no malice, just good old-fashioned chain yanking.

"Exactly! You read my mind," he says, putting his arm around her.

"You do know that when there is a poster ready I will be posting a few around here on the various crew buildings?" she says.

"Oh yeah, I know there's no way that's not happening," he laughs and kisses her. "I do actually hope it's a big success. We need more young people and families here. It's why I'm doing all this," he says, gesturing toward the property and buildings-in-progress. "I hope you know I'm teasing. Mostly."

"Of course I do. And besides, people who have recently fallen in love have oodles of energy!" she teases. "I'd better get back to town, I want to get going on the social media for this, and I need to check in with my dad about where this week's issue is at. Oh! And I need to write something up pretty quickly about Book Lovers for this issue, and maybe design an ad as well. Yikes! Lots to do!" She gives Jack a hug. "I am so excited for you in how this is all coming together. There's no stopping you now!"

"Shhh! Don't jinx it!" Jack says.

"You've never been very superstitious," she says. "It's all fine, it's all happening!" She exclaims as she hugs him again. "Will you be coming home for dinner?" she asks as she walks to her car.

"Can I text you a little later? I might have some Zoom meetings with investors in California and the building suppliers in Oregon. I'm not sure how late those things are going to go and don't want to hold you up. Your plate is awfully full as well, you don't need to be waiting for me."

"That's fine, shoot me a text and we will see where you're at. No pressure." She opens her car door, "Oh! By the way, I bought a wedding dress the other day, so there's no backing out now!" She smiles at him. "But like I said, no pressure." She winks at him as she gets in the car.

"I cannot wait to see you in that dress on our wedding day," he says, blowing her a kiss and heading back into the trailer office.

When Lizzie arrived back at the Gazette office she was surprised to find her dad and Stan laughing and having a wonderful time. It delighted her. Before their angel investor had come along all too often the office had the feel of a dentist's waiting room - a place filled with dread and anxiety. This was much nicer.

"What are you two so happy about?" Lizzie asks as she hangs her coat on the coat rack.

"Oh, nothing in particular honey, we're just talking about how good it feels to have the pressure off. We've had a lot of very lean years, but thanks to you and Jack, things are great."

"Well that makes me very happy," she says, sitting down at her desk. "It is a nice feeling to know we can tell the local and personal stories we want to tell without a corporation breathing down our necks telling us we're wasting ad space on stories, or worse yet, telling us what we should be covering. Toward the end at the Sentinel, it was horrible how much of what we were or more accurately, weren't covering, was coming from the top. They didn't care about the local stories, they wanted vague, non-descriptive stories that could be about anyone anywhere so they could plug them into any of the myriad of papers across the country that they owned." She sits back and takes in the room. "This is so much better, this is important. Telling the stories that matter to a community."

Lizzie is then struck, after her Sermon on the Mount moment of the importance of true journalism, that the story she needs to tell right now is about a dating event at a local bookstore. That thought takes a little bit of the wind out of her sanctimonious sails, but she chuckles to herself. These light, fun stories are important too. Okay, she thinks, not every story is going to be life-changing, though that said, if someone meets their person at Book Lovers, it could in fact be life-changing. Hmmm, she opens her laptop. Maybe that's her angle, it's not just a frivolous night out, but it's something meaningful, that's important. Okay, maybe I'm taking this a little too seriously now and taking all of the fun out of it at the same time. Something she knows she has a knack for and always has to make sure to catch.

"You look very serious over there, honey. Everything okay?" Peter asks.

"Yeah, it's this story about the singles event at Tall Tales, I want to make it sound fun, but also don't want it to come across as frivolous or silly, you know?" she says, having a little bit of a think.

She starts to type, "Hey, how does this sound: *Cranberry Harbor has lots to offer, but if you're young, or maybe not so young, and single, Cape Cod can be a lonely place.'* Does that sound like a depressing place to start from?" she asks her dad and Stan.

"How about if instead of lonely, you said, 'challenging?' That might sound less sad," Stan catches himself, "well, not *sad* exactly, but you know, less..."

"Sad," Peter says, laughing. "I agree, 'lonely' can be kind of a loaded word, I agree with Stan, 'challenging' makes it sound like an obstacle one can overcome, where 'lonely' sounds like it's a condition you have, not a circumstance, does that make sense?"

"It totally makes sense, thanks, guys. I want to be honest, but I don't want to make it sound like it's going to be a scene from some depressing movie with all these people dressed in black fighting for their last chance to find love in Cranberry Harbor!" They all start laughing.

"Yeah, *that* would not be very inspiring," Stan says. "Not that I'm not always grateful, but boy, this makes me very happy that I'm married and don't have to think about trying to meet someone special. Especially during the winter in Cranberry Harbor. I love this town, but it's not exactly a place filled with romantic opportunities, especially in February."

"After having lived in Boston for several years? I cannot say I felt a whole lot better about dating there than here. The odds were better as far as numbers go, but I didn't find anyone, that's for sure," Lizzie says.

"What's that old saying, 'the odds are good but the goods are odd?'" Peter says.

"It may well be that *I* was the odd one," Lizzie says, focusing back on her story. "Okay guys, I have to focus now and get this done because I want it in this week's paper, so pardon me while I tune you both out and write."

"We will not take it personally," Stan says, smiling at her.

Within forty-five minutes Lizzie feels like she's struck a nice balance between advancing the Book Lovers event, and touching on some emotional points about happiness and feeling fulfilled in a small town. She was especially proud of these closing sentences:

Living in Cranberry Harbor brings its own special beauty and joy, but it can be an isolated place as well, especially in the winter. Meeting someone who, as Tom Hanks says in "You've Got Mail," 'fills your heart with joy,' can feel like finding a proverbial needle in a haystack. Maybe events like Book Lovers is a way to stack the odds a bit in your favor, and if nothing else, perhaps you will leave with a greater sense of community and a new book to read.

Lizzie sits up and stretches and smiles. This is why she became a journalist, this is the joy of small town reporting, something sorely missing from the industry at large papers these days. Writing about a local singles event in a small, seacoast town may not be the stuff a Pulitzer Prize is made of, but it is the kind of story that makes people feel good, and in turn makes Lizzie feel good to share.

"You look happy, honey," Peter says, looking at his daughter. "You like your story?" Stan left while Lizzie was writing, but she was so engrossed she didn't even notice.

"Yeah, I just emailed it to you for a second read. Who says we need copy editors when we have each other, right?" she teases. "It's a quick read, after you give it a once over, I'll file it, and then I think I am done for the day." She looks around. "Jeez, I didn't even notice Stan left. I really was focused!"

Peter is done reading it in five minutes.

"Yeah, he snuck out about 20 minutes ago. This is wonderful, honey, I love the way you brought it all together at the end. I think this will definitely bring folks out for this. Heck, if I was single, I can't think of a nicer way to meet someone than over some good books. You can tell a lot about someone by the types of books they read, can't you?" He says, then he adds, "Or if they read at all, there's a red flag for you!"

"For sure, Jack and I may like different types of books, but it gives us a lot to talk about," Lizzie says. "Anything you'd change? Any typos you caught before I file it?" She asks as she herself gives it another look.

"Nope, as always your copy is perfectly clean. You certainly didn't get that from me, I've usually got errors all over the place," Peter says.

After a couple of more keystrokes, Lizzie closes her laptop, slips it into her bag and gets up. "What do you say, Dad, you ready to get out of here?"

"I'm right behind you," he says, getting up with a bit of a groan and a stretch. "I just made an old man noise, didn't I?"

Lizzie laughs. "I'm younger than you and I've been known to do it as well, occupational hazard I think." They both put their coats on and gather their things. Peter turns out the lights.

"Oh, I didn't tell you, I bought my wedding dress, well, actually you and Mom bought it," Lizzie says as they go outside. "I'm really getting married, Dad."

"Yes you are," he says beaming at her. "And you are going to be the most beautiful bride in the world." They're walking to their respective cars and he calls out to her. "Jack Chaoon is one very lucky man," he says.

"Thank you, Daddy," she opens her door, shakes her head, and laughs. "Wow, 'Daddy,' that's a blast from the past," she says to no one. What she can't see from her car is Peter tearing up as he heads home.

CHAPTER 24

WITHIN JUST A COUPLE of days the town was buzzing about Book Lovers. Gabby had put up posters everywhere, even on telephone poles all over town. It was also the hot topic on everyone's mind at Sea Coast and yoga class. Lizzie had even heard of mother's insisting their single sons and daughters who lived off-Cape come visit for the event.

"I'm getting worried we're not going to have room for everyone!" Anika says, when Lizzie stops into Tall Tales. "I'm not complaining though, it's a very good problem to have!"

"Who knew the town was so hungry for a fun singles event?" Lizzie asks, looking around the shop, wondering how many people could comfortably fit in the small store.

"Jay is thinking of moving some of the shelves over," Anika says, coming out from behind the counter and showing Lizzie their ideas. "And the community center said we could borrow some tables and chairs. Oh! Jay was thinking it might be a nice ice breaker to have some book trivia too. Or maybe some other good book games as well. Any ideas?"

Lizzie is walking around, thinking as she looks at the titles. "Yeah, I've been trying to think of ways to get people to interact, to work together on something. Maybe you could have everyone put their name in a hat when they arrive and create a few teams? Or..." Suddenly she has a flash of an idea. "What about doing something like a speed dating thing, where people can sit with someone and ask them three questions?"

Anika is curious, "Okay, and what are the three questions?"

Lizzie is a little stymied. "Okay, I am thinking we hand people a card with the questions printed on them to ask each other, and they are..." Lizzie is stuck.

Anika is waiting for something genius to be forthcoming.

"Okay, hmmm, it can't be something pedestrian like, 'what's your favorite book,' it's got to be more thoughtful, something that would create a conversation. Something more like, 'What's a book you've read more than once and why?'"

"Okay, that's pretty good. I've got an idea, as someone who sells books, and it could be a good question for this event; 'Do you judge a book by its cover?'"

"Oh, I like that!" Lizzie says. "It has so many meanings, right? Especially at an event like this. It's so easy to judge people out of hand for something as shallow as their, I don't know, shoes."

"Shoes?" Ankia laughs.

Lizzie blushes a little. "Yes, I once decided a guy was not for me when he showed up in all-white sneakers that looked like his grandfather should be wearing them." She puts her face in her hands and shakes her head. "I know that makes me sound like such a shallow jerk, but he was maybe twenty-nine, this was a few years ago, and I took one look and knew he was not the guy for me."

Anika can't stop laughing. "I will say I've noticed that Jack wears very cool shoes. "Lots of Vans, or other cool sneakers, and when he dresses up, the style is kind of vintage-y and cool." She pauses. "You're right, shoes do matter!"

"Right?!" Lizzie says, emphatically. "Okay, so is it boring to ask what book they're reading now, and what they plan to read next? Will they feel bad if they aren't currently reading a book?"

"I don't think it's bad to ask, I mean it is an event at a bookstore, you'd sort of assume they're a reader if they've come here, right?" Anika adds.

"True, what would you want to know about someone that you could learn from a book they're reading?" Lizzie asks her. "I'm sure you learn a lot about people owning this store, right?"

"Oh yeah, sometimes the special orders in particular are a bit of a surprise!" Anika says. "Jay and I often joke that we feel like there should be privacy laws covering people's book purchases. It can be so personal, especially the politics. It can be surprising to see where some people land. Shocking actually. We tell everyone who works for us that they are not to discuss customer's purchases outside the store. But boy, it's tempting to spill the beans sometimes!"

"You're so right, what we read is so personal, books help make us who we are, especially the books we read as kids, as teenagers. Maybe that's a good question, 'What was your favorite book you read as a teen, and as an addendum, is there any book you pretended to read but never have?'"

"Oh, I like that!" Anika says. She gets a legal pad from the counter and starts writing them down. "One, 'What book have you read more than once and why? Two, 'What book are you reading right now, and what do you want to read next, and for three, I don't know, but I'm kind of liking the 'What book have you never read, but have pretended you did?'"

"When I was a kid, I took *A Brief History of Time* out of the library. I think I was in fifth grade. It was thick and looked so serious and grown up that I took it out and carried it around for two weeks, and I never got past the first page," Lizzie says laughing. "And while I know Hawking was brilliant, I've still never read it. Don't tell Jack, he loves it, and I just nod a lot when he talks about it. I'm more of a fiction reader."

"The things we do to impress others, huh? Your secret is safe with me." Anika says.

"So we've got the questions, has Ben been in touch about the food and drinks?"

Just then the door opens, and it's Ben, "Hey! Fancy meeting you here," he says, giving Lizzie a big hug with baby Ollie, who is happily munching on a banana while strapped to his back.

"Hey, Ollie!" Lizzie says, rescuing a piece of banana from sliding down Ben's neck. She takes a tissue from a box on the counter and wipes her sticky, fruity fingers.

"Thank you, I knew that was probably not a good idea, but I needed something to keep him happy while I came in here," Ben says.

Lizzie takes a stuffed hedgehog out of the basket of toys in the kids play area for him to hold, and takes what's left of the banana.

"That should be a little less gooey," she says to Ben. "So, thank you for doing this! We know how busy you are."

"Are you kidding? I love town events like this. I live for all the festivals and town stuff. We're happy to help." He has a file folder in his hands, puts it on the counter and opens it up. "So since people will probably for the most part be standing and eating, and are meeting people they kind of want to impress, I was thinking nothing very messy, smelly or hard to eat standing up, and nothing with spinach for people to worry about getting in their teeth."

"Very good thoughts," Anika says. "Thank you so much for doing all this," she says, looking over his notes. "I love the baked brie, oh, and all these different cookies - macarons, madeleines, brownies, ..."

Lizzie is looking over her shoulder. "Oh yum, I love the Asian dumplings and Spanish tapas."

"My idea was, if this is okay, to have foods and wines from different regions, with books on the table, like at the tapas area, have books about or which take place in Spain, and the same with the Asian, and French foods. Is that too much? Have I over-thought this?" Ben says, suddenly worried that he went too artsy.

"Are you kidding me? I love it," Anika says. "I never would have thought of that. If this had been up to me it would have been some cheese and crackers from Bradfords and a few bottles of wine. This is amazing, Ben, thank you so much!

"Phew, I'm so glad you like it," he says. "And for the dessert table I thought we could have coffee, a nice dark roast, some decaf, and a few different kinds of tea. That sound good?"

"That's perfect," Lizzie says, as she continues to amuse Ollie in his carrier. "I'd say let him out and I will gladly play with him, but I've got the feeling you are not planning to stay for too long."

"Yeah, I have to meet Sean at Sea Coast to go over our coffee order with Leah, we get all our coffee from her now," Ben says. "She's just taken off with her roasting, she's doing so much, it is really incredible. She was telling me she might even be doing some roasting at Terra Marique? Jack is going to make sure she has a place for her roasters because the place where she's been going is hiking up her rent."

"He hadn't told me, that's wonderful!" Lizzie says. "Seriously, in a few years Leah is going to be running this town, she is a force."

Anika is looking over the menus and plans one more time. "Ben, let me pay you today, I don't want all the food purchases coming out of your pocket. Please, just let me know what I should give you. I can send it via my phone, or give you a check, whichever works best for you."

"I still need to price out the wines, but I'm giving you those at cost, so that will be easy, I can do that when I get home," Ben says. "Half of what's on page three would be great, and yeah, just send it to me through our Venmo. I think you have our Marshview account, right?"

"I do," and in a flash she has sent him the payment. "And none of this only charging us what it costs you for the wine, this is your business, you need to make a profit. So charge us what you would any person off the street."

Ben laughs, "You and Jay are hardly anyone off the street," he says. "We're all friends, and I am not taking no for an answer." It's clear from the look on his face that he is not fooling around.

"I wouldn't waste your time arguing with him, Anika. I've known him since I was in elementary school. He is firm on his moral stances. I once tried to give him a box of Girl Scout cookies that Mrs. Lanahan had paid for, then decided she didn't want them. He would not take them, he said it felt wrong, even though they were already paid for.," Lizzie says, looking at her friend.

"Oh my god, I'd forgotten all about that. I was really a bit over the top, wasn't I?" he laughs. "I would not turn those cookies down now, just so you know."

"Well, clearly your moral compass has gone awry," Lizzie teases. "I'm quite disappointed in you, Ben." Baby Ollie begins to show his boredom with his present situation by whacking Ben on the head with his hands, and starting to whine. "Okay, well, that's my signal to get out of here and continue on to meet Sean."

Lizzie gives both him and Ollie a kiss. "Thank you so much for all of this, you are the best. As are you, Ollie."

"Thanks, Ben, I'll see you the day after tomorrow," Anika says. "Thank you!"

"No problem, I'll be here with everything a little after five to set up. See you then," and with that they are out the door.

"Yikes, when you said the day after tomorrow it suddenly seemed very real," Lizzie says. "But I think we're good. Right? You think we're good?" She's starting to get a little panicky.

"Yeah, we're good, thanks to you and your mom and Alexis," Anika says. "She's coming, right? She hasn't said anything, so I wondered."

"Last I talked to her she was planning on it, but good point, I should check in with her and ask her. Or you know what, she doesn't need her friend bugging her, so I'm going to just let it be." Lizzie gets her coat from the couch, and puts it on. "Okay, I am out of here." Her phone rings. "Hey, I was just leaving Tall Tales, where are you at?" She walks to the door and waves goodbye to Anika who mouths, 'thank you,' as Lizzie goes outside.

"I just needed to hear your voice," Jack says. "It's been a long day."

Lizzie is walking down Main Street toward her car. "Yeah? What's going on?" She unlocks her car door and gets in, turns it on and starts it to warm it up.

"I'm trying to not get spooked, but Billy and Bud were out here wandering around about an hour ago. I went out and asked them what was up and if I could show them around and they just seemed weird," he says.

"What else is new, they're always weird," Lizzie says, trying to reassure him.

"Probably, but I'm just wondering if I'm going to show up here tomorrow and find them both chained to trees? Or they've destroyed something? I don't trust them."

"They may be dumb, but they're not stupid," Lizzie says. She has put him on speaker and started to drive.

Jack laughs, 'dumb but not stupid,' I like that. Okay."

"I mean they do dumb stuff, like the tree thing, but they also don't want to end up getting arrested either, you know? Dumb, not stupid."

"You're probably right, and I'm just worrying about nothing." He sighs. “So, how was your day? Everything going okay for the singles thing? Which is, wow, the day after tomorrow.”

“I know, I just had a similar epiphany, yeah, it seems to all be falling into place. I’m not sure if Alexis is coming, and I sure wish I knew if Ian MacFayden was planning to come,” Lizzie says as she drives toward her parent’s house.

“He had scheduled with me to come out here tomorrow to see what we’ve done so far, maybe I can find a way to bring it up? If he comes. He hasn’t confirmed, which is kind of odd,” Jack says.

Jack sometimes has all the subtlety of a leaf blower, so Lizzie isn’t so sure that’s the best idea. She didn’t want Alexis mad at her.

“Well, maybe if he does come and it somehow naturally comes up, don’t–”

“Be my usual self?” he says laughing. “Hey, I can be cool, I really can.”

“Okay, as long as you’re really, really cool,” Lizzie isn’t so sure how this could go, but at some point she has to let go of trying to control everything, and this seems like a good time to do just that.

CHAPTER 25

BY THURSDAY NOTHING out of the ordinary had happened at Terra Marique, despite Jack's concern, so Lizzie felt comfortable going to Tall Tales to make sure everything was set up, and check that the camera crew from Boston Today was going to be as unobtrusive as possible.

The store was abuzz with activity and looked transformed. Jay had moved several of the bookshelves to the side, Ben had the food and drinks beautifully displayed on a long table at the back of the store, and the borrowed tables and chairs looked great.

Anika, huge smile on her face, sees Lizzie and runs over to her. "Isn't this amazing?" she says, using a sweeping gesture, like she's presenting a new car you could win on *The Price is Right*.

"It is! Where did all these cool plants come from?" She sees all sorts of beautiful ferns, philodendrons trailing over shelves, and some spring bulbs in pots. "They add so much life and color to the space."

"Don't they? It was Jay's idea. We'd been wanting to get some plants, and the owners over at Plant Therapy said we could borrow these for the event, and then buy what we want to keep!" Anika says, delighted by the deal. "They'd heard about the event from customers, and apparently a couple of their employees are coming, so a total win/win!"

"I just love that, local businesses working together and helping each other out," Lizzie says.

"Oh boy, you're getting your 'Cranberry Harbor is the dreamiest place,' look on your face," Anika teases. "I know it well, I have it at least twice a day. And you're right, it's the best."

"Okay, so everything is set to go," Ben says as he walks toward them. "The regular and decaf coffee carafes are clearly marked, so people won't get mixed up and find themselves wired at 3am," he says. "So, yeah, it's all good."

"Ben, everything looks amazing, thank you," Lizzie says, walking back with him to the table full of delicious treats. She pulls out her phone and takes a few photos. "For the paper's Instagram," she says, taking a moment to post it. "If anyone is on the fence about coming this will make it impossible to not want to come."

"A part of me would love to stick around for a little bit to see how many people turn out, and how it goes, but I have to get home, Sean has a Zoom meeting with a gallery in New York who might want to rep him. I tried to tell him carrying a baby around as he shows them his work might clinch the deal, but he disagreed, so I have to run." He puts on his jacket, and pulls his hat out of his pocket and puts it on. "Let me know how it goes!"

"I will for sure," Lizzie says, giving him a hug. "Right now I have to see how Leah and Justine are doing and meet the TV person. Thank god they only sent one person and not a whole crew."

Lizzie made her way to the tall table where Leah and Justine are set up, and she's getting nervous about people feeling like they're in a fishbowl while trying to meet someone. She's worried that she's really blown it by getting too much media attention. Between podcasters and a TV camera, it's feeling a little weird, but she doesn't know how to unplug it all.

"Hi? Are you Anthony? I'm Lizzie, from the Cranberry Harbor Gazette," she says to the man with the small, hand held camera, wondering if it would be incredibly rude to ask him to leave. Yes it would, she decides.

"Hey, Lizzie, nice to meet you in person. This store is great, the whole town is amazing," he says.

"Have you been to the Cape before?" she asks, trying to get a feel for how married to this story he is.

"I have, I came here a lot when I was a kid, our cousins used to rent a place in Wellfleet, but I've never been here in the off-season. I got here earlier today, and wandered around, it's really great."

"That it is, Anthony," she's stalling and trying to think of how to make this whole situation less like a reality show. "So I had a thought--"

"Sorry to interrupt, but I did too," he says. "Would you be really disappointed if I didn't film much during this event? It's so pretty, and small, I don't want to feel like I'm a cameraman on *The Bachelor.* You know?"

Lizzie reaches over and puts her hand on his shoulder, "Oh my god, you just completely read my mind! I was starting to panic that this was going to be so cheesy and feel so wrong, thank you!"

"I shot some footage around town today, and in here before everything got set up, and a little of it looking like this now, and I thought I'd get a few seconds of people in the store, but I pitched it to my producer saying I thought a story about a Cape town in the off-season and the sense of community was a better story than a singles event."

Lizzie is so relieved, her heart has stopped racing and she feels her whole body relax. "I think that is a great story! If I can help you in any way please let me know. I can connect you with people, anything you need," she says, feeling like she just dodged a huge error that could have ruined this whole event.

By 6:45, Tall Tales is filling up, and Lizzie is happy to see, it's not just women who are arriving. Men are showing up too. As soon as she sees Alexis arrive, she makes a beeline for her.

"Hey! I wasn't sure where you'd landed on coming, I'm really glad you're here!" Lizzie says. She feels a little out of place not being single, but she's there to support the Patels, and to be able to write a follow-up story.

"Of course, what made you think I might not be coming?" Alexis asks, "I always planned on being here, we're the architects of this event!" Lizzie sees her looking around the room.

"I haven't seen him here yet," Lizzie says.

"Whoever do you mean?" Alexis says, smiling. "I've given up on him getting in touch, we had a nice couple of hours together, but clearly he's not interested. Maybe he's never dated a Black woman, there could be that."

"I'd find that really hard to believe, he strikes me as pretty worldly and not exactly sheltered. I'm betting there's a reason we just don't know," Lizzie says, keeping an eye on what's going on. She's happy to see that people are taking the cards they had printed up with the questions and seem to be finding a person to sit and have a conversation with. "Alexis, look, Ian just came in, and I think I might know why you haven't heard from him."

Alexis turns her head to see where Lizzie is looking and walks over to him as he makes his way through the crowd on crutches.

"Oh my god, what happened to you?" Alexis says, looking concerned.

He laughs, "This is my friend, Tyler," he says, "He was nice enough to offer to drive me, because, well," he looks down at his right foot that is encased in a very large, gray boot, "clearly I'm not able to drive right now."

"What happened?" Lizzie asks, also concerned and curious.

"It's such a stupid story, I'm kind of embarrassed," he says. "During the last storm I went over to help my mom dig out her car, and I fell on some ice that was hidden under the snow and I just landed the right, or wrong way, and fractured my ankle. I seriously wish I had a much more interesting story, like I was repelling down a mountain in Canada, or was saving a cat stuck in a tree, something more heroic than shoveling my mom's driveway and slipping on ice. This feels like an old man injury," he laughs.

"Would you be more comfortable sitting down?" Alexis asks.

"That would be great," Ian says. "Dragging this boot around does get pretty tiring."

"You two go sit down, I'm going to look at some books, and maybe have some coffee," Tyler, his friend/chauffeur says. He and Lizzie leave them to chat.

"When your fiance sent Ian an email about this event he told me he really wanted to come see your friend, so when he asked me to drive him, of course I had to," Tyler says.

"That's really nice of you," Lizzie says. "And I'm glad he wanted to see her. She's my best friend and is pretty amazing, so if she likes someone they must be pretty special."

Lizzie and Tyler make their way to the food and each get themselves some coffee and a cookie.

"Ian's a really good guy, I've known him since film school. We work together a lot; I'm an editor, so we team up." They find a spot to sit to have their snack. "When he told me about his ankle I decided to come out from New York for a few days to hang out. It's pretty isolating out here when you can't go anywhere."

"Are you two gearing up for any new projects? Your whale film was incredible, by the way," Lizzie says, wishing she had taken more than one cookie.

"Thanks so much," he says, "Uh, so you don't know?," he says, glancing a little uncomfortably over to Ian who's engrossed in talking with Alexis. "We got funding for a film about Terra Marique, I'm here to check a few things out before the crew arrives next week."

"No, Jack didn't tell me," Lizzie says, feeling a little weird that he didn't share something so big.

"We only just heard this week about the financing, so it wasn't certain until very recently. He'd said he didn't want to disappoint anyone again, I'm not sure what that means, but that he wasn't going to say anything to anyone until it was certain," Tyler says. "Now I feel awful that I said anything."

"No, please, don't!" Lizzie insists. "Your secret is safe with me. I know him very well, and he worries a lot about disappointing people, and himself, so I get it. This is really exciting, I can't believe you're going to be documenting this project!"

"This is the type of thing that could be a total game changer, so we really want to capture it to show people who can be real arbiters of change," Tyler says.

Around them Lizzie sees people pairing off, and Anika approaches her.

"I'm sorry to interrupt, but do you think we should do anything? Like a group game, or just let people keep talking to each other? They seem to be getting along quite well without us intruding on them," she says.

"I vote for letting them be," Lizzie says. "What do you think, Tyler? Oh, Tyler, this is Anika Patel, owner of the store with her husband, Jay."

"Nice to meet you, Anika," he says. "I'm kind of with Lizzie. Everyone seems to be having a nice time, though there is one guy all by himself over there who has looked over at me a few times. Would you be insulted if I went over and talked to him?" He stands up and pats down his shirt. "Do I look okay?" he asks, looking nervous.

"Not insulted at all, and you look fantastic, go have fun!" Lizzie says. "This is why we had this event, for people to meet each other!"

Lizzie wanders back over to the food table, she hasn't had time for dinner and is very hungry. She makes herself a plate with some of Ben's fresh baked French bread, some cheeses, and she can't resist taking another cookie. Okay, two cookies. As she turns to find a place to sit, Alexis comes over and takes her elbow, leading her to a corner.

"Hey, what's up?" Lizzie asks, taking a bite of bread and cheese. "Everything good?"

"Yes, very good. Oh my god, I flipped out over nothing. Why do I do that? I created all these scenarios in my head, completely convinced myself that the connection I thought we had was all in my head, that he just found me to be a small town, boring person, whatever…"

Alexis is very keyed up. "How much coffee have you had today?" Lizzie asks, laughing. "You are wired!"

"Believe it or not, just one, and that was first thing this morning." She takes a deep breath, and lets it out slowly. "I only have a minute, he had to take a call, but anyway, he broke his ankle the day after we met, and he said he didn't want to ask me out and have me have to come out to his house, because he couldn't go anywhere at first, he had to have it elevated all the time, and he said he wanted to do the whole thing of asking me out, come and pick me up, and since he couldn't he waited, and then he waited so long he felt self-conscious, so when he heard about this, and that I'd probably be here, he decided to come. It was all really sweet." A huge smile sweeps across her face and she looks more relaxed than she has in the entire conversation. "I really do like him, Lizzie, he's a good guy."

"I'm so glad you got an answer as to why you hadn't heard from him. It makes total sense that he got nervous after waiting so long and didn't know what to do. Isn't it nice knowing that guys don't have it anymore together when it comes to dating than we do? Whenever Jack confesses some worry or concern about something it makes me feel so much less weird, like he has the same fears and worries I do."

"Totally," Alexis says. Ian is heading toward them, looking like a pretty good expert on his crutches.

"Hey," Lizzie says. "We can go find a place to sit if you like, I'm sure it's not comfortable to stand with the boot and crutches."

"Thanks, but it's actually nice to stand for a few minutes. I've been doing a lot of sitting for the last couple of weeks. I'm not at all used to that. I run, usually every day, it's been frustrating to not be able to move."

"When do you plan on beginning shooting at Terra Marique? It could be tricky being out on a building site" Lizzie asks, wondering how he's going to navigate the uneven and rough terrain on crutches.

"Luckily, my doctor thinks I'll be able to just be in the boot, no crutches, and put weight on it next week. I'll have a chair around of course so I don't overdo it, but I'm excited to get back to some normalcy."

Tyler comes back over and joins them with Jeremy, a very nice guy who Lizzie learns has only recently moved to the Cape year-round. As she looks around she sees lots of people who seem to have paired off.

"If you'll excuse me," she says, "I'm going to go find Anika". She wants to congratulate her on a job well done. She finds her behind the counter ringing up a book order. Not only are they connecting people, they're selling books too. "Nicely done," she says. "You and Jay must be so happy!"

"This has been better than anything I could have imagined!" Anika says. "People have been so nice! I saw a few people talking to Justine and Leah, letting them record some comments, it was really nice. One guy said something about how it felt so good to connect with people in real life rather than on an app. I think we kind of forget that, you know? We're all so plugged in all the time. It's really important to have actual face-to-face interactions with people."

"It's so true. I hated using dating apps when I was in Boston, but it was so hard to meet people organically, which I know sounds weird, but even in Boston, I felt very alone sometimes," Lizzie says.

Anika looks at the clock on the wall and it's nearing 9:00, the time they'd decided to end the event. "Would it be rude of me to tell people we're going to start winding down?" she asks, a little sheepish.

"Not at all! Hey, they're all welcome to continue any conversations over at Murphy's if they want, you're a bookstore, which normally closes at 5, it's fine to give a hint," Lizzie says. "I think I'm going to head out myself, it's been a long day, need I tell you!" She goes to the back of the store where she'd left her coat and purse, then she goes to say goodnight to Alexis.

"I'm headed out, but wanted to say good night. Ian, it was so nice to see you again, I hope I will again soon. Take good care of that ankle," she says. She gives Alexis a kiss, "I'm sure I'll talk to you tomorrow, and Tyler, it was wonderful to meet you too, I'm sure I'll be seeing more of you as well over at Terra Marique."

They all send her off with a wave, and she feels so happy that Alexis is happy. When she gets outside she takes her phone out of her pocket.

"Oh no, I've missed seven calls from Jack," she says, out loud to no one, trying not to panic. She starts walking quickly to her car while calling him back.

Jack answers on the first ring. "Hey, you must have had your phone off at Tall Tales, I've been trying to reach you."

"I saw. Are you okay? You're not sick, hurt" she asks, worried.

"No, I'm fine--"

"Your parents, my dad?" She's trying not to freak out and failing miserably.

"No, yes, I mean everyone is fine, it's Terra Marique, it might all be falling apart," he says, sounding like he might cry.

"What, why, I mean, how--" she can barely get the words out.

"It's Billy Taylor and Bud Mackelroy, they've filed an injunction against the project, and are suing me for building on what they say are historic grounds. I'm completely and totally screwed."

"Okay, calm down, we can fight this, Jack, where the hell did they ever get the money or the wherewithal to do this?" She's silent for a minute. "Oh my god, I bet they've got a developer who's behind them, am I right?"

"Yup, it's that company that wanted to come in and build all those McMansions years ago, Gobel and Green, four people with axes to grind found each other and are now suing me," Jack sounds awful.

Lizzie starts her car. "Look, I'm going to come right over, okay? You're at Terra Marique, right? Or are you home?" she asks, slipping on her jacket.

"Yeah, I'm here, all the workers have left." He sighs. "This is just like last time, Lizzie, I've messed up again and the town is going to hate me."

"No one hates you, hang tight, I'll be there in five minutes." She's just about to leave, and then thinks, she should go get Ian and Tyler, this needs to get out there, how those two malcontents are trying to kill this project. She runs back into the store and finds them with Alexis.

"What's going on?" Alexis asks, she can tell Lizzie is upset. "Is Jack okay?"

"Yes, he's fine, well, not fine, but he's not sick or anything. Billy and Bud have filed an injunction against the project. They're being backed by those billionaire builders who wanted to develop the land a few years ago. Apparently they're claiming it's historic land and can't be built on, I guess if they couldn't have it they don't want anyone else to either," she says. "Jack feels like it's four years ago and that he's got another business idea collapsing in front of him, so I have to go."

"We should all go too, don't you think?" Alexis says, looking at Ian and Tyler, "I'm the community planning director, I need to be there, I understand if you don't want to."

"No, we should definitely go," Ian says. Tyler runs to grab their coats.

"Billy and Bud need to find a hobby," Lizzie says, fuming, as they head out. "Those two are the worst, they never, ever do anything positive for the town, but are always there to say no to anything progressive or positive for the town or the people, I can't stand them. I want to have a word with them."

"Don't say anything yet, we don't want to give them any ammunition to hold over Jack," Alexis says, "who knows, they could accuse you of 'slander,' sue the paper, or something stupid. Sit tight, and let's see what our lawyers will have to say."

"You're right, I'll be quiet, but boy, it's not going to be easy."

CHAPTER 26

WHEN THEY ALL arrive at Terra Marique they're stopped by two Cranberry Harbor police officers, one of whom of course, Alexis and Lizzie both know. Ian and Tyler are right behind them, having followed in Tyler's car.

"Hey Tom," Lizzie says, smiling at him. She knows he's only doing his job, and she can tell from the look on his face that he's not too happy about that job right now.

"Hey, I'm sorry, Lizzie, but I can't let you two in. Jack is collecting his things from the trailer, but after that the place is closed," he says. "I'm really sorry. This stinks."

"Tom, you can't even let us in for a few minutes to help Jack pack up?" Alexis asks, leaning out the window to talk to him.

Meanwhile, Lizze can see from her rearview mirror that Tyler and Ian have gotten out of his car, and Tyler has started filming.

"Excuse me, uh, you can't be doing that," the other officer, who Lizzie can't see well enough to identify, says. "You will have to leave sir, and please don't keep filming."

"There is nothing that says I can't film what is still apparently considered public land," they can hear Ian firmly say. "We have every right to document what is happening with shutting down this project, which by the way, is a nonprofit project that the town of Cranberry Harbor has a vested interest in. I am on the street, not on private property, and have every right to be filming from here."

"Oh boy, this is getting a little heated," Lizzie says, getting out of the car. "Hey guys," she looks at Tom. "They're friends of ours who are making a documentary about the building of the project. They're with us. They're cool."

"Well, they can't come on the property, Lizzie. No one can, so all of you just stay right here and wait for Jack, or go home," Tom says, sounding more like a police officer than friend at the moment.

Lizze takes a deep breath and wonders if this is how it's going to end, and is suddenly worried that this lawsuit is going to divide the town. Everyone had been so supportive and excited about it, but now these two naysayers were trying to ruin everything. She walks over to Ian and Tyler, Alexis is right with her.

"I'm going to find out what our rights are," Ian says, getting agitated. "I don't think they can keep us from filming, we need to show how far people will go to stop progress. I mean, this is just one project in one small town, and it seems like it's only happening because there are personal axes to grind. It just makes me think about what is happening on a global scale to stop progress on bigger green projects while the clock is ticking to save the planet."

Lizzie looks over at Alexis, who is clearly quite smitten, from the look on her face. So not the point, Lizzie reminds herself. She then hears Jack calling out to them.

"Why don't we all get out of here? It's starting to drizzle and there's no point in all of us standing out here and getting wet," he says. Lizzie can see how distraught he is. "I have to go home and have a Zoom meeting with our lawyers in California who are scrambling to get a team in Boston together to go to court."

He gives Lizzie a quick kiss and then turns to walk to his car. A familiar angst is catching in her throat. This feels like when his startup crashed, and it's scaring her.

"I'll call you later," she says as he walks up the hill. He doesn't turn around, he just keeps walking.

"I'll take you back to your car," she says to Alexis. Ian and Tyler wave to them, sensing this may not be the time to talk, and take off.

"Lizzie, don't freak out, he's got a lot on his mind. This isn't like last time, it isn't," Alexis says, putting her hand on Lizzie's shoulder as they drive away.

Trying not to cry, Lizzie nods. She hopes Alexis is right. She looks over at her and smiles. "Boy, you know me well, my friend."

"I know that look in your eyes, you are cool on the outside and freaking out on the inside," she says. "He's got a lot on his plate that he's trying to manage. The good thing is, this isn't like last time, he has people, people with means, right there with him. They're going to have the best lawyers and he's not going to be alone in fighting this, he has an amazing team."

"I know, it's just hard to not compare what happened before with what's happening now–"

Alexis turns in her seat to face her. "I've been working closely for months with Jack on this and I can tell you two things you really need to hear right now." She pauses, "One, he is madly, crazily and completely in love with you. He talks about you all the time, every story he tells features you, whenever he talks about you he beams, if I didn't love you both so much I would find it utterly sickening," she jokes. "And second? The people he has behind him on this are not only wealthy, but they are ethical, committed, and in this for all the right reasons. They aren't phonies who are trying to look good on paper, or want a loss on the books that they can use, nor are they poseurs who don't really care about the environment. They are the real deal. Believe me, I can suss out players from a mile away. They are all in. Billy, Bud and whatever self-serving, vindictive people they have gotten to help them, have no idea what they're up against."

"You really think so?" Lizzie wants so much to believe that this isn't going to fail, that Jack isn't once again going to end up in California, but she's scared. They pull up to the parking lot by Tall Tales and Lizzie puts her car in park.

"I talk with many people on the team every single day, Lizzie," Alexis says. "They are so excited about this, and always want to make sure that we have everything we need. It's true money isn't an issue for them, but it's more than that. This project, and frankly, the future of the planet means everything to them. One investor got all choked up the other day talking about his kids and how important it is to him to be able to tell them that he did everything he could to help save the planet."

"Wow, I had no idea you had gotten to know these people. I've done a few quick interviews, but you really know them, that makes me feel a lot better," Lizzie says, feeling so relieved. Her shoulders lower, and she takes a deep breath.

"Jack is one of those people who can kind of turn inward when he's upset, I've learned that working with him and I'm sure I'm not telling you anything you don't know," Alexis says. "It can't be easy for you I'm sure, but this isn't about you. He definitely knows you're there for him, it's just how he deals with stressful situations. It's not you, it's him," she says smiling, knowing Lizzie will appreciate the cliche romcom movie line.

"Very funny," she laughs.

"Well, my work here is done, I got you to laugh. I was not going to get out of this car until I'd been able to make you laugh, even if it's just a little." Alexis undoes her seatbelt. "I'm pretty wired between this and," she smiles a little, "seeing Ian again, so if you want to talk more just give me a call, okay?" She leans over and gives Lizzie a hug.

"Thank you, thank you for that, and for calming me down, I really appreciate it. I need to go home and tell my parents what's going on, I don't know if they've heard about all this yet. I'll talk to you tomorrow. Love you."

"I love you too, it's all going to work out, I know it is," Alexis says as she gets out. "Get some sleep." When she turns to get out of the car she ses Ian and Tyler have pulled up next to them, and Ian is getting out of the car, crutches and all. "Huh, I did not expect this," she says.

"You want me to stay?" Lizzie asks.

Alexis, a little confused, quickly answers, "No, it's okay, you go. We'll talk tomorrow." And with that she gets out and starts talking to Ian.

Lizzie sees she's comfortable, and laughing, so feels okay heading home.

Lizzie shouldn't have wondered if her parents had heard the news. She reminds herself that she should know that in a town the size of Cranberry Harbor something as big as the two town curmudgeons filing a lawsuit against a huge project, and another local, would not already be everywhere.

As soon as they hear her car pull into the driveway they are both at the door, on the front porch, ready with hugs, questions and cocoa.

As soon as she steps in they both envelope her in a big group hug. She does not resist in the slightest. It's good to feel safe and sound. She doesn't care that she's a grown woman, right now being hugged by her Mom and Dad feels really good.

"Oh honey, I couldn't believe it when we heard," Gabby says, arm still around her as they walk to the kitchen.

"I'm curious, how did you hear?" Lizzie asks, taking off her coat, pulling out a stool at the counter and sitting down. "Stan? Jack's parents?"

"It came up on X, believe it or not," Peter said, pulling his phone out from his pocket.

"Since when are you on X Dad?" Lizzie asks, wrinkling her brow. "I can barely get you to post on Instagram for the paper." She takes her dad's phone and looks at the post, *Cape Cod eco project sinks. Gobel and Green file suit to halt work.* She hands her dad back his phone. "Jeez, it's been retweeted close to 800 times. That's not good."

Gabby puts some cocoa in front of her, "Here, take a sip of this," she says. "How's Jack?"

"Terrible, awful, worried, angry…" Lizzie says, shaking her head, feeling worried all over again..

"That sounds about right, I have half a mind to go see those two idiots and let them have it," Peter says, pacing the floor. "But the thing is, they're just pawns in this evil corporate game Gobel and Green are playing. They found two gullible men who they could bamboozle into going along with them, to give the lawsuit some local cred, and well, here we are."

"You think this is just payback for the town not allowing them to clear cut the property and build 8000 square foot second homes?" Lizzie asks, feeling her anger rising.

"Yes I do," Peter says. "I'll never forget the last thing I heard them say at town meeting, they said, 'You haven't seen the last of us, we'll be back and we will get what we want.'"

"God, that sounds like something out of a bad gangster movie," Gabby says, putting some cookies out on the counter. Lizzie immediately takes two. "It must have been hard not to laugh."

"I did, and look where we are now," he says. "Why do the bad actors never seem to get caught or end up paying for their malfeasance? It's always the good guys, like Jack, that end up being hurt and paying the price."

"Jack isn't exactly the little guy, Dad, remember he's got a lot of very wealthy people behind him too, but they are at least rich people on the correct side of history and the planet," Lizzie says.

"Had Jack talked to the project's lawyers yet when you saw him?" Peter asks, finally sitting down after pacing back and forth in the kitchen. "I imagine all the folks he's dealing with have really good people on their side."

"He was going to be talking with them over Zoom, but he was also trying to get out of there with all his stuff because the police were there to keep everybody out." Lizzie finishes her cocoa and takes another cookie. "These are good, Mom, you did something different, these aren't your usual oatmeal cookies." It felt good to talk about something else for a minute.

Gabby shrugs, "Nothing too radical, I added some nutmeg, and cardamon, they're basically the same as always. It doesn't take much to change things up, you know? It's sometimes all in the small details. And thank you!"

Lizzie starts to think about what her mom has just said, it doesn't take much to change things, it's the little things that can make a difference. Maybe there was something from the previous lawsuit with Green and Gobel that could be the key to getting them to back off. She wasn't living on the Cape when the lawsuit with the town was happening, and hadn't really kept up, but maybe, just maybe there was something in the archives that could lead them to a solution. As she is pondering some sleuthing, her phone rings, it's Jack.

"Hey, where are you? Mom and Dad and I were just talking about you, are you okay?"

"Not really," he's being so hesitant, Lizzie is suddenly very scared.

"What happened, where are you?" Lizzie asks, standing up. Her parents are alarmed as well.

"As I was about to leave Billy showed up," he says.

"Uh oh, I don't like the sound of that," Lizzie says. "And?"

"He was right on the edge of the property and he started laughing and yelling out to me things like, 'Hey do-gooder, see you in court you treehugger!' The police were talking to him and trying to get him to leave, but he kept yelling."

"He's a jerk, don't pay any attention to him, we're going to fight this, and we will win," Lizzie says.

"He crossed a line, Lizzie, he started yelling about how we were going to be bringing the 'wrong kind of people' to Cranberry Harbor, and we all know what that's code for, and I lost it. I ran over and I knocked him down, and hit him."

Lizzie gasps, "Oh no, Jack, you didn't–"

"Believe me I know, which is why I'm calling you from the police station," he says.

"You were arrested?" She says, and both her parents stop what they're doing and stare at her, wide-eyed.

"Yes, and I need you to come bail me out." They're both silent for a moment. "I know it was stupid and I know I shouldn't have let him get to me, but he's so ignorant, and has no idea of all the good Terra Marique could do for this damn town. I wish I'd never come back here."

Lizzie doesn't know how to respond, she's absolutely crushed. "Um, I'm not sure I know what to say. If you want to go back to California, then maybe you should."

"Oh Lizzie, that's not what I meant, it's not you and me, it's me and this town, that's what seems to be the problem, every time I try to do something good here it blows up in my face. I'm not thinking straight. I'm so sorry. I love you more than anything, you have to know that."

Lizzie is at a loss for words and hurt. "This isn't the time to get into anything. I'll get the money and be down soon, how much is it?" The chill in her voice is palpable to everyone.

"It's $300. Lizzie, I didn't mean--"

"I'll be there as soon as I can," she hangs up the phone.

"Honey, why don't we go with you, you're so upset," Gabby says.

"Thanks, Mom, I'm okay," she looks around for her purse and jacket. "What is that famous quote from Maya Angelou, 'when people show you who they are, believe them?'" She quietly puts her coat on and grabs her keys.

"Lizzie, don't let this cloud what you two have been building together over the last year," Peter says. "Everyone has bad days, and everyone says things they don't mean when they're scared and angry. I know I have. Just don't add fuel to the fire tonight. Let things calm down, and see how it all shakes out."

Lizzie just shrugs her shoulders, feeling a bit numb. "I won't be long, I'll just get him and take him to his car and come home."

"You're sure you don't want some company?" Gabby asks again, wishing her daughter would let her support her.

She shakes her head, I'm good," I'll be back in a little bit. Don't feel like you have to wait up, I'm fine. I always bounce back eventually."

CHAPTER 27

Lizzie had never actually bailed anyone out, but thankfully, she knew the woman at the front window and she walked her through the whole process. She'd stopped at the ATM on her way there thinking she would have to pay in cash; who knew you could pay with a debit card? You learn something new everyday, she thinks, taking a seat while she waits for Jack to be released. Of all the things she never thought she'd be doing on this night, or any other one for that matter, it was this. Except for maybe a social justice protest perhaps, she never had envisioned a time when she'd be bailing her future husband out of jail.

In a matter of only a few minutes Jack is out, holding an envelope with his keys, wallet and phone.

"Hey," he says, looking as glum as Lizzie feels. "Thank you for coming. Let's get out of here."

They silently walk to Lizzie's car out front and get in. "Your car is still at Terra Marique?" She asks, putting the car in reverse.

"It is."

The silence weighs heavily in the car. Neither of them is sure of what to say.

"Look," Lizzie says, finally breaking the silence. "I think I should just take you to your car, and we can talk tomorrow. I don't think either of us are in the best place to have a conversation of any importance, okay?" She stops at the traffic light and puts on her left signal to head to Terra Marique.

Jack nods, he looks exhausted, Lizzie thinks, looking at him. Exhausted and defeated. She tries to ignore the knot in her stomach, and not allow herself to look backward to four years ago to the night the bottom completely fell out of his startup. Within two days he was headed to California saying he was going to see what this job offer was about, and that he'd be back within the week. He was not.

Lizzie pulls into the entrance. There are still two police officers there. Different ones, change of shift, Lizzie surmises.

Jack leans over and gives her a kiss. "I am so sorry, Lizzie. For everything."

He gets out and walks to his car, Lizzie doesn't watch him, she just backs up and leaves.

Gabby and Peter were still up when Lizzie arrived home, there was no way either one of them could have gone to sleep without having checked in with her.

"Hey," she says, not really up for talking to anyone, when she comes in the front door.

Peter and Gabby quickly get up from the couch and both hug her before she can even get her coat off.

"You get him out okay?" Peter asks.

"Yeah, it was easy, I didn't have to wait long, he was right out." She walks into the living room and sits on the couch, still in her coat. "I'm so angry at this whole stupid situation. Jack is a good guy, I have never known him to hit anyone. Those two came over for no other reason than to torment him and be jerks." She starts to cry. "I am so angry I can't even…"

Gabby comes and sits down next to her. "We're all angry, honey, this is incredibly wrong and unfair and I keep wracking my brain about what to do."

Peter joins them on the couch, and then they hear someone coming in the door, startling all of them. It's Matt, Lizzie's brother.

"Why didn't you guys call me? I just found out on the radio what had happened," he crouches down by all of them. "What can I do,

Lizzie? Besides going and beating the crap out of Billy and Bud, which I know isn't going to help anything, but it might make me feel better for a minute."

Lizzie takes his hand, "You are so sweet to come over, I feel terrible that you found out that way. I was so wrapped up in everything I forgot to call you, I'm so sorry."

"Yes, us too," Gabby says. "We figured we'd talk in the morning, and that maybe one member of the Martin family might get a good night's sleep. Our intentions were good, we thought you'd sleep right through the drama tonight."

"Don't worry about it, I'm not mad or anything, I just wish I could be of more help. This is so crazy, I can't believe that this is happening when the project is moving along so well. How's Jack?" he asks, looking at Lizzie.

She shakes her head. "Not good, as you can imagine. He said he wishes he'd never come back here." She looks down and tries to not start crying again.

"Lizzie, you know that's not about you, it's about this clustercuss of a situation. He loves you, you are getting married in a few weeks! This lawsuit doesn't have to change any of that," Matt says emphatically. "It doesn't."

"Maybe, maybe not," she says, sounding resigned. "It didn't have to change our plans last time either, but it did. So I don't know what to think. And the ironic thing is I bought my wedding dress, and was all set for this to happen." She shrugs. "Perhaps I shouldn't have pushed my luck. I should have known that something like this could happen and hedged my bets."

"Hedge your bets?" Matt says, looking incredulous. "That's not how you go into a marriage. You go into just like you and Jack have been–with your whole being, and having faith in each other and that it's all going to work out."

"Look at me, Matt," she says, getting angry. "Is this what it is all going to work out looks like? Me here in tears with all of you? Jack home, having been arrested, lawsuit pending? This is not everything working out!" She stands up. "I can't, I just..." Matt pulls her in tightly, hugging her hard.

"I'm sorry, I'm not trying to minimize how you're feeling. I just know you two are meant to be together. You are getting married. I know it," he says.

All this time Gabby and Peter have been silent, letting their kids work this out.

"I hope you're right, little brother, I sure hope you're right," Lizzie says. She sits back on the couch. "I'm sorry, Matt, I don't mean to lash out at you. It's just this is all feeling so familiar, I've been down this road before and I know how it ends."

"How it ended before, honey, is not necessarily how it ends now," her mother reminds her. "You and Jack have worked so hard to rebuild your relationship, along with rebuilding the paper and creating Terra Marique for the whole community. This is one very bad day, it is not the end of everything. It is not."

"Listen to your mother," Peter says. "She's a very wise woman," Peter sits down next to Lizzie and pulls her into a big bear hug. "Granted, this has been a *very* bad day, but are you going to let those boneheads derail everything you have worked for? I know you better than that, you don't let anyone throw you off course when you're on a mission."

"You two should hire yourselves out as motivational speakers," Lizzie jokes through her tears. "If only it were all so simple. Having a can-do spirit and a plucky attitude can't change everything, Dad. Sometimes you have to face reality and realize some things just aren't meant to be. I'm really starting to think the universe is trying to tell us something." She gets up. "If you all don't mind I am going to head to bed and try to get some sleep. It's been a really long day." As she walks out of the living room she turns to her dad. "Have you posted anything about this online for the paper Dad? We really should have something up, we can't let the fact that this lawsuit is directly impacting our family stop us from reporting on it. I'm not sure I'm up for writing anything, and probably shouldn't, but maybe you could post something brief about it, and say the story is developing and we can deal with it tomorrow."

"Will do," Peter says, "I can't believe I let that slide," he picks up his phone and gets to work.

"Dad, it's been a crazy night, you're allowed. I just don't want anyone to think we're not covering it because we're impacted by what's going on. It's not a good look," Lizzie says. "Thanks for doing that, 'night everyone."

"I'm worried," Lizzie hears her mom say as she starts up the stairs, she stops for a moment.

"Me too," says Matt. "If Jack breaks her heart again I, I don't know what I'll do."

"Let's not get ahead of ourselves," Peter says, "I'm betting cooler heads on all sides will prevail tomorrow. At least that's what I'm hoping."

Lizzie continues upstairs to her bedroom where she promptly throws herself on to her bed, grabs her ancient teddy bear, and has a good cry. You're never too old to cry into a teddy bear, and sometimes it's the only thing you can muster the strength to do.

CHAPTER 28

LIZZIE FINALLY DRIFTED off to sleep sometime after 2 am, at least that was the last time she'd looked at the clock. Daisy the wonder-mutt, came bursting through the partially open door at 6:30, followed by her extremely apologetic mother.

"I am so sorry, honey, she jumped out of my arms on our way down the hall and made a beeline for you."

Lizzie stretches, yawns and glances at the clock. "It's fine, come here girl," she says, patting the bed for Daisy to jump up. "I could use a good snuggle." Daisy jumps up and immediately begins licking Lizzie's face. "Oh, I love you, little girl," Lizzie says, pulling the small dog into her chest. "Dog snuggles are the best."

"How are you?" her mother asks, sitting down on the side of the bed. "Did you get a little bit of sleep before this one woke you up?"

"I got some, but had lots of weird dreams, nothing I can really remember, but they woke me up and then I'd fall back asleep. I do remember dreaming about Billy coming here and stealing my bike, that's strange, huh?"

"Not really. It's pretty symbolic, he's taken something very precious from you. You've put so much thought and effort into helping Jack with Terra Marique, and your wedding of course, no wonder you'd think of him stealing something from you," Gabby shakes her head. "I don't know what happened to those two. They were brats as kids. No matter how nice I was when they'd come to the office, they were always difficult. I had hoped they'd both grow out of it and become better adults, but that sure didn't happen."

Lizzie sits up and wraps her arms around her knees. "I keep going over and over in my head what Jack said about wishing he'd never come back here, and as much as I try to convince myself that he's stressed, he's scared, and angry, I can't shake thinking that's how he really feels, and that the best thing I can do is to cancel, or at least postpone the wedding. I don't ever want to feel like he was pushed into this when it wasn't what he really wanted."

Gabby is silent for a moment, collecting her thoughts. "I haven't ever known a young man more in love than Jack is with you," she says. "Sometimes I sit and watch him look at you when we're all together, and I think, I have never seen a young man look at a woman the way he looks at you."

"Mom–"

"Let me finish, honey. He loves you, I have no doubt, and I don't want to see the two of you walk away from each other again when it's so clear to everyone who knows you that you two are meant to be together."

"That may be true in theory, but the reality is, every time we get close to getting married, something major happens and it all falls apart. Maybe it's the universe telling us that we just aren't meant to be, and maybe it's time for me to pay attention to that message and stop ignoring what's right in front of my face," Lizzie says, swinging her legs off the side of the bed and standing up. "I am going to get some coffee, and then I am going to call Jack and suggest we at the very least postpone the wedding. There's no way he can be preparing for this court date–well now two court dates–and have his head in planning our wedding and feeling excited about it."

Gabby knows better than to argue with her daughter. When she makes up her mind to do something there is no dissuading her, but she can't resist. "I just think, that–"

"Mom, I need to do this to take care of myself, okay? I have to feel like I am taking control of my future, that I'm not leaving it up to Jack, to Billy, to anyone, I need to do something so I can feel like I'm in charge of my life. Can you understand that?"

Gabby nods, and then gives Lizzie a hug. "I'll be quiet now," she says. "This is your life, this is your decision, and your dad and I will support you in anything you decide to do."

"Thanks, Mom, I really appreciate that," she says. "What I'm deciding right now is that I really need some coffee, how about you?"

Two cups of coffee and a hot shower later, Lizzie is feeling a bit more human. She also knows the knot in her stomach isn't going to go anywhere until she talks to Jack and tells him how she feels.

"Your dad said to tell you that he'd hold down the fort today if you don't feel like going in," Gabby says when Lizzie comes into the kitchen, dressed for the day. "Maybe you should take the day off and just focus on you and Jack?"

"I really need to work, which is what I'm going to do after I talk to him." she says as she puts her jacket on. "I texted him and we're going to meet at the Bunny Park, I'm sure it's quiet now, and it's warm enough to sit outside this morning." She picks up her laptop bag, purse and keys, and takes a deep breath.

"I love you, Lizzie," Gabby says. "Please take good care of yourself and that beautiful heart of yours."

"That's what I'm trying to do, Mom." She turns to leave and stops, "I'll call you later, I promise."

"I'd really appreciate that, I'm going to be sitting here worrying about you!"

Lizzie nods and heads out the door to her car. It's a beautiful, bright, early spring day. A day so pretty it's hard to think that everything is anything but perfect, but it isn't.

When Jack arrives at the park, two minutes after Lizzie, he's carrying two coffees from Sea Coast. Lizzie thanks him, but doesn't think having more caffeine is a good idea–she's nervous enough already–so she politely puts it down next to her.

"Hey," Jack says, sitting down next to her. "Thanks for meeting me, I was worried you wouldn't even want to talk to me."

"Of course I'd meet you! How are you?" she asks, she can tell looking at him he's not good, but wants to know how he feels.

"Somewhere between not great, not good, and terrible, I'd say. Like how someone feels when the bottom has fallen out of absolutely everything that means anything to them," he says.

"Yeah, that pretty much sums up how I feel too." They sit side by side on this uncomfortable metal bench in silence. Then the silence is broken by them both at the same time.

"Look," they both say.

"You go first," Jack says.

Lizzie takes a deep breath. "Okay, um, boy, this is hard. But I think that at the very least we need to postpone the wedding, if not cancel it. There is so much going on, clearly you have a lot of mixed feelings about being here, in Cranberry Harbor. I think we need to reassess that this is what's best for both of us. I can't and don't want to leave here. I'm committed to running the paper with my dad, but if you don't want to be here..."

"What? What the hell are you saying? You think I am going to lose it all? Thanks for believing in me, in our team." Jack is dumbfounded.

"I didn't say that, I got the feeling last night that maybe you didn't want to fight. Well, except Billy," she knows that's a low blow, and tries to backpedal a little. "Okay, so what's your idea?" she says, trying to sound more open to hearing his thoughts than she really is.

"I was going to suggest we postpone the wedding. Just for now." He's a bit agitated. "But clearly you have other ideas. Like not getting married at all."

She honestly hadn't expected him to so readily say he wanted to postpone the wedding. "No, us not getting married is your MO, not mine," she says, knowing that's a very low blow. She takes a deep breath and regroups. "So just put everything on hold? Indefinitely?"

"Not indefinitely, but yeah, I guess, since I don't know how this is going to play out, yet, we don't even have a court date. How can we be planning a wedding when I could be in the middle of being sued?"

Lizzie shakes her head, trying her hardest to fight back any tears. "Sure," she shrugs, whatever you think is best for you and your project."

"Lizzie, that's not fair, you know I want to get married too--"

"Really? Seems like you are quite comfortable with putting it off, maybe this is a silver lining for you," she says.

"Lizzie, look, I know I'm not exactly at my best, and I was a total jackass last night talking about wishing I'd never come back here. I didn't mean that. Haven't you ever said anything in the heat of the moment that you didn't really mean? I know you have."

"Of course I have, but I also think sometimes in the heat of the moment we say the thing we don't even let ourselves know we feel deep down–"

"And you're such a mind reader that you know exactly how I really feel, deep inside? That's quite a skill you have Ms. Martin."

Lizzie doesn't say anything. She turns to look at him. "You're being mean now. You're never mean."

Jack leans forward and puts his head down. When he sits up he looks right back at her. "And telling me you can't understand why getting married when I'm going through the worst time in my life might not be a good thing?"

"Fine. I'm letting you off the hook. Let's postpone the wedding," she says, trying her best to not burst into tears.

"I don't feel like I'm on a hook, Lizzie," he says. Just then his phone rings. He takes it out of his pocket and looks at it. "It's one of the lawyers in New York, I have to take it." He gets up and begins pacing around the brick courtyard.

Throwing overly caffeinated caution to the wind Lizzie takes a large sip from the coffee Jack brought, probably not a good way to calm down, but she needs to do something.

Jack is emphatic as he talks to the lawyer. His end is filled with lots of passionate statements:"I am not giving up" "No, I'm not settling," "I am here to stay, they are not getting rid of me". Then he ends the call with a terse, "Fine, sure, right, okay. I'll talk to you later."

Hearing him talk that way to someone else makes her think maybe he does want to stay. Maybe it's just marrying her he's not so crazy about.

He breaks the silence after downing the rest of his coffee. "So the good news is they don't think that this lawsuit has legs. They think that the fact that the town didn't sell it to us, that they are letting us, a nonprofit entity use the land for the good of the community, might make their claim that the town didn't want them to have the land and then nullified their development deal, moot. Their lawsuit hinges on the claim that the town was biased against them, turned around and let us have it."

"And the bad news?" Lizzie reluctantly asks.

"It's possible the outcome could depend on what judge we get and how they interpret what the town decided to do," he says.

"But the whole town, well, most of the town, all wanted this! Doesn't that matter?"

"Yes and no. They could claim they were never given the opportunity to take their idea to the town, and one possibility is that they might ask for a town vote to decide who gets the land," he says. "And that could set us back for weeks, months, or even years while that works its way through the courts and town red tape."

"No one wanted their stupid McMansions, no one!" Lizzie says. "And the only reason Billy and Bud are with them now is because it's a way to cause trouble for you. And they are totally using Billy and Bud."

"I don't disagree." He stops talking and turns his whole body toward her. "We need to get back to the matter at hand. I'm not going anywhere, Lizzie. But maybe we should postpone, just for a little while until this is all cleared up. I love you and I want to marry you. We talked about getting married at Terra Marique, and right now we aren't even allowed to get near it. God, we're probably going to lose our whole crew, I hadn't even thought of that until this moment."

Lizzie is heartbroken, but sees that Jack is not in a place to be able to deal with her hurt, so decides to put a good face on it, to keep those tears to herself. She is going to suck it up and not tell anyone how she really feels. "Postponing doesn't mean canceling," Lizzie says, forcing a smile. "I want our wedding to be something we're both excited for, not an event to get over with before you have to meet with lawyers. I will be fine," she says, trying to convince herself as much as she is Jack.

"So you believe me that I'm not going anywhere? That I want to be here? That I want to be with you?" He takes her hand.

She nods, still pushing back the tears. "Yeah, I put myself back to four years ago, and–"

"This isn't four years ago, Lizzie, I'm not the same person, you're not the same, we've grown up, but we have to be able to talk about things and not react without talking to each other, okay?"

"You're right," she says, dying inside. "I'm sorry I overreacted. It all felt so familiar and I freaked out." At this point she wants to talk about anything other than their postponed wedding. "Did the lawyer say anything about the assault charges? I'm concerned about how that will reflect on the case, and what it means for you."

"He said that while it certainly wasn't helpful that I did something so stupid, that technically Billy was trespassing. I still had a right to be on the land cleaning out my belongings and it could be interpreted that I was defending myself against a trespasser who was harassing me, which he most certainly was. Fingers crossed that's how it goes down. I have no prior record of any kind, and Billy has one a mile long. Minor infractions, but he's been known to the community as a trouble maker, so he's hopeful that at the most I might get a little community service."

"Your whole life is serving the community," Lizzie says, trying to be positive. "The whole purpose of building Terra Marique is literally for the community."

"Good point, I don't necessarily see it that way, I'm doing it because I love it and I think it's going to be great for the town, but maybe a judge will see fit to count my work as community service. If not, I'm happy to clean up a park or volunteer somewhere."

Lizzie looks at her watch. She really wants to leave and process all that's happened, and maybe cry. "I should get to the paper and see what kind of mayhem awaits me there. Dad is probably being inundated with requests from papers in Boston and who knows where else."

"So we're good? You and me?" Jack asks.

"Yes, we're good." She then thinks about her beautiful dress, and her heart aches again. "I should tell Jess that I'm not going to need my dress hemmed right away. I don't want her to think I forgot..."

"You're sure you're okay with that? With waiting?" Jack asks, a little nervous seeing how this conversation began. "You still want to get married, right?"

"Of course!" She forces a big smile. "I think the best thing we can do is focus on getting this lawsuit to go away. We'll have our wedding when this is all behind us and you're back up and running." All she wants to do is go, before she breaks down.

"Okay," they both stand up. "It seems weird to not have an office, even if it's just a trailer to go to," Jack says. "Maybe I'll take my laptop and go to Sea Coast, or the library. I don't want to go home, that seems depressing."

Lizzie gives him a kiss. "I'd invite you to share our office, but we don't have another desk. I'll call you later. Keep me updated." She starts walking to her car. Only a few steps in the tears start to flow.

"Good talk," Jack calls after her. Lizzie doesn't turn around, she just waves.

CHAPTER 29

LIZZIE DECIDES she cannot face going directly to the paper, so she drives to the beach and hopes on this not-quite-spring morning that no one else will be there. There are only a few cars, and she finds a spot far off to the side, still facing the bay, and parks her car. Within seconds the tears start to flow. All the pent up feelings of not having any idea when or maybe even if she and Jack will be getting married come pouring out. She reaches into her back seat, fumbling around trying to find the box of tissues she keeps there. She finally feels it and pulls out several.

A part of her feels incredibly shallow and selfish as she sits there crying, considering how many people are more severely impacted by the shutdown of Terra Marique. The crew, the farmers, the business owners anxious to finally have a space to work from, and most importantly, people who need an affordable place to live.

"Pull yourself together, girl," she says firmly to herself. Then she remembers something her mother always says, *If this is the worst thing that happens to you today, you are doing very well.* On that note she dries her eyes, takes a deep breath and starts her car. She knows it's not going to be easy, but for the sake of everyone else she's not going to complain about the wedding. Like a mantra she repeats to herself as she drives to the Gazette, *If this is the worst thing...* When she arrives at the paper she promises herself to put on a good front, which won't be easy with her dad, but she's sure going to try.

After Lizzie explained the wedding postponement plan to her dad, without tears, he texted the plan to her mom, not wanting her to sit at home worrying. Lizzie is having a hard time getting work done as she tries to convince him that she is okay. He knows her, the only one who knows her better is her mom. She's going to be the hardest to convince.

Her dad now has her on speaker phone with her mom because apparently no one is going to get anything done today, especially Lizzie.

"There has to be a way you can pull a wedding together even if it isn't on the grounds at Terra Marique," Gabby says.

"Mom, we just don't have the emotional energy to devote to planning an even smallish wedding right now, and we're okay with it. It will take so much time that we don't have to plan all the details. We really need you two to be okay with it too. Jack and I are okay. Okay?" She thinks that sounds pretty convincing.

"That's a lot of okays," Peter jokes. "Gabby, dear, I think we need to let them do what they want to do and we all need to get to work. Don't you need to go pick up Sophie from preschool soon?"

"Yeah Mom, don't leave your granddaughter the last to be picked up at Kid's Cove," Lizzie says, knowing how hyper-responsible Gabby is and hoping that will end this call.

"Fine, I know when you two are giving me the brush-off," Gabby says. "As long as you're happy I'm happy."

"Thank you for caring so much, Mom, I really do appreciate it, Now I have to work." Lizzie says, glad to have to stop pretending to be happy and work.

A short time later she looks up from her laptop, "Dad, I know you're not a Twitter, I mean X person, but have you seen any of the chatter that's going on about this lawsuit?" Lizzie asks as she's intently reading her phone. "I keep trying to find something we can dig into, something about their company, their businesses, but I'm not finding anything."

"There's nothing, huh?" he says, getting up from his side of their partner's desk to look over her shoulder.

"I keep hitting dead ends, but I can't believe these guys are squeaky clean, and how did they find Billy and Bud? They're not exactly on anyone's radar."

Peter walks back to his chair. "You think we should keep exploring this and write something about it?"

"I'm thinking about it. I'm also wondering if we should hire a freelancer so it doesn't appear to be biased in any way," she says. "We're both so close to this story it might reflect badly, and I know I would have a hard time being completely unbiased."

"Yeah, me too," says Peter. "Do we even have any freelancers around anymore? It's been so long since we've hired anyone."

"I've seen a young guy hanging out at Sea Coast who I chatted with a few times, he lives here now and freelances for a few papers off-Cape, like the Sentinel. I don't know his name, but I can pop over and see if he's there. It's worth a shot." She gets up and takes her coat off the rack. "I could also use some coffee, you?" She asks, picking up her purse and heading to the door.

"No thanks, I've got enough adrenaline coursing through my body right now." He turns to his computer, "I'm going to see if I can find out anything more about these developers while you're gone. Wish me luck," he says.

"Luck!" she calls out as she leaves. The fresh air feels so good she decides to walk the couple of blocks to Sea Coast. Her mood brightens when she spots Sean, Ben and baby Ollie taking a little stroll on a chilly, but sunny Main Street. There is nothing like a baby to help you forget how crummy you feel. Especially a baby holding a daffodil he has apparently plucked from the bed outside the bank.

"Oh my gosh, has it been so long since I've seen you that Ollie has now officially become a walker?!" she says, hurrying to reach them. "Look at you!" she crouches down by the toddling baby, who immediately hides behind Ben's legs, peaking out at her before hiding again and giggling. "I have to say it, because you won't, I'm the worst godmother in the world, I am a complete stranger to him, he doesn't even know me." She stands up and hugs them both.

Ben laughs, "He's like that with just about everyone these days, don't take it personally," he says, trying to reassure her. "And the walking thing? It seems like it happened basically overnight. One moment he was crawling and then he pulled himself up and within like, three days he was walking!"

"I haven't spent a lot of time with many babies," says Sean, "but I think this proves he is the absolute smartest and most advanced baby in the world." He smiles.

"Absolutely!" Lizzie concurs. "I could have told you that months ago, it has always been evident to me!"

Ben and Sean look at each other a little nervously, "So is what we're hearing true? That Terra Marique has been shut down and Jack is being sued?" Ben asks. "If you don't want to talk about it–"

"No, it's fine," Lizzie says. "Word has definitely gotten out. Hopefully it's all going to be resolved, but it's a hot mess right now, and…," she pauses. "Did you also hear that Jack hit Billy?"

"Yeah, and let me say? Everyone we've talked to says they applaud him and think someone should have done it years ago! Not that violence is ever a good idea, but…" Ben says.

"I haven't been here very long, but even I know what a pain in the butt that guy is. He gave us a hard time about putting a sign at the end of the road directing people to the inn. I mean, it's beautiful, nothing gaudy or ugly, he just likes to hate everything," Sean says.

"He sure does," says Lizzie. "He's like the Grinch whose heart is two sizes too small," they all laugh. It's a relief to laugh. "So there's something else you might hear a rumor about," she starts to say.

"Oh no! You and Jack did not break up!" They say in unison.

"No, I came close, I have to admit, I panicked about history repeating itself, and I was scared. But we talked, and we're good. But we decided there's no way we can both find the time to focus on planning and executing even the small-ish wedding we'd envisioned right now, so we're postponing it." She grows quiet and shrugs. "It's fine, it's really fine, it will all work out. It's going to be fine."

"Okay, that's a lot of fines, which makes it really hard to believe you," Sean teases. "That stinks, we know how excited you were. You really don't think you can do it?"

Once again Lizzie smiles and brings out her plucky attitude, "Jack is going to be so wrapped up in getting this lawsuit to go away, handling the investors, the crew, and I know I'm going to be really busy managing the press and keeping the paper going… Oh! Speaking of which, do you two know the guy who I see writing at Sea Coast a lot? Mid-20s? Tall, seems really nice?" She's happy to talk about anything but the wedding.

"Yeah, he actually stayed at the inn when he first got here and couldn't find a rental," Sean says. "His name is Eric Jackson, he's from Philly, really nice guy. He was finally able to find a small apartment above the bridal shop. You know how hard it is to find rentals here."

"Yeah, it's impossible," Lizzie agrees. "Hence the need for Terra Marique. Anyway, we're looking for someone to maybe do some freelancing for us. All of us - me, my dad and Stan are too close to Jack to be able to cover this story objectively. You think he's a good writer?"

"The Times, The Guardian, Sentinel and others seem to think so," Ben says. "I've really liked his stuff, he's very thorough."

"That's what we need," Lizzie says. "I'm going to see if he's in there, and if not, can I get his number from you guys?"

"Of course," Ben says. Ollie seems to have tired of pushing his stroller back and forth around them, almost hitting a passerby, and is ready for this chat to end. "We'd better get going," he gives Lizzie a big hug. "Anything you need, just call us, and not just about Eric, okay? We're with you, one-hundred percent, okay?"

"What he said," says Sean pointing to Ben.

Lizzie gives Sean a hug. "Thanks guys, that means a lot." She bends over and gives Ollie a kiss on the head. "And you and I are going to have a playdate sometime very soon," she says.

They all wave each other off and head their separate ways. Lizzie walks into Sea Coast and scans the place for the man she now knows is Eric, but he's not there. She's disappointed but then heartened and also nervous when she sees Alexis. Talking to her will be the true litmus test of how good a liar she can be.

"Hey friend!" Alexis says, standing up and giving Lizzie a hug. "How's it going?"

"I'll tell you in a minute, let me get a tea." She takes her coat off and puts it on the back of the chair, "Can I get you anything else?"

Alexis shakes her head, "I'm good."

Lizzie is back in a minute with her tea and two scones, "I

couldn't resist, these were warm, right out of the oven, and I can't eat alone."

"You are diabolical," Alexis says, "and I'm grateful for that, thank you!" They each dive into the warm pastry. "Oh my goodness, this is perfection, orange and cranberry are a very good mix. So, enough about scones, how are you?"

"Good…good-ish," Lizzie keeps eating her scone. "I woke up planning to cancel my wedding," she says somewhat nonchalantly.

"What?!" Alexis practically chokes. "What do you mean you were 'canceling your wedding'?"

"Just what I said. I met up with Jack planning to call it off, but we decided in the end not to."

"Okay, Ms. Journalist, don't do that to me! Don't bury your lede!" Alexis takes a sip of her coffee and sits back. "So you promise me, it's all good now?"

"I'm sorry, that was mean. I should have told you that first, but it was sort of fun to see your face. Yes, it's all good. Sort of good. We're postponing it for a while. Which we both agreed to. We don't have the bandwidth to make it all happen right now, so instead of slapping something together and rushing through it we've decided to wait for a little bit," Lizzie hopes she sounds fully on-board with the plan.

"I want to throttle all those involved in this stupid lawsuit, they are screwing up the lives of so many people, and for what? It's pure spite and nothing else," Alexis says.

"Yup, there's no real merit to any of this. Hey, enough about this, let's talk about what's really important. How did things end with Ian last night after he showed up? Are you going to see each other again?"

Alexis looks down at the table and Lizzie can see a small smile. "Well, we did have a quick kiss, it was a little awkward since he had Tyler driving him, and he was on crutches, so it wasn't the perfect romantic scenario, but we did kiss, and it was nice."

"Nice? Just nice?" Lizzie asks.

"Stop it!" Alexis is looking embarrassed, and looks around to see who's nearby. "Fine! It was more than nice, but I am not going to elaborate any further, so there," she says, feigning a smug attitude.

"Fine, I will not ask anything more about your kiss," Lizzie says.

"But I'm very happy for you, I haven't seen you look like this in a long, long time."

"Look like what?" Alexis asks, curious.

"Like the girl in the romcom whose meet-cute is working out," Lizzie says.

"Ha! I've never considered myself the star of a romcom, but I have to say, I wouldn't object to a happily ever after in my life."

"You totally deserve a happily ever after…So are there plans for another date?" Lizzie asks.

"It's a little bit of a work thing, but we're getting together later to discuss the film he's doing about Terra Marique. He wants to include this twist in the story. We're meeting up at his place because of course, he can't drive," Alexis is quiet for a minute. "I'm not sure if that's really a date?"

"It's definitely a date," Lizzie says.

"He said he'd make lunch. He apparently loves to cook, so I guess it is a date. Albeit a work date."

Out of the corner of her eye, Lizzie sees Eric Jackson arrive and start setting up a table with his laptop, coffee and sandwich.

"Hold that thought, I need to talk to that guy over there," Lizzie says getting up.

"Eric?" Alexis says.

"Yeah, you know him?"

"He comes in all the time, he's a really nice guy. You looking to hire another writer?? Alexis asks.

"Not full time, but to freelance for us about Terra Marique," Lizzie says.

Alexis gets up, "Come on, I'll introduce you," she says leading the way.

"Hey Eric, I wanted to introduce you to one of my best friends. Lizzie Martin, this is Eric Jackson.

Eric stands up, "Hi Lizzie, it's really nice to meet you, finally!" he says, shaking her hand.

"Finally, huh?" Lizzie laughs. "It's nice to meet you too. I've seen you here writing, and I should have introduced myself, I'm sorry for that."

"Please, sit down," he says, gesturing to the two empty seats at his table. He closes his laptop. "No apology needed," he says. "I've been aware of who you and your dad are for a while and have been meaning to come by and introduce myself. It's always nice to meet other working journalists. We're such a shrinking population."

Lizzie sighs, "Sadly, that is way too true." She's never hired a freelance writer before and is a little nervous. She can't help but think their little weekly paper is not in the same caliber of the national and international publications he writes for.

Alexis knows her so well she can see what's going on and jumps in. "Not sure if you saw anything today about the injunction that's been filed against Jack Cahoon and Terra Marique?" she asks.

"Yeah, I did. Wow, I'm so sorry about that, Lizzie. It seems to have come completely out of left field. I've followed the project since it was first brought to the town, partly because I was on my own desperate search for a place to live, and have been so fascinated by the whole project. This totally stinks."

"It does stink, Eric," Lizzie says. "Look, I know we're just a small town weekly, and you write for all these much bigger papers and magazines, but I need someone who isn't personally connected to the project, like my dad and I are, to write something for us about this lawsuit. I know we're not–"

"I'd love to," he says without hesitating. "I was considering pitching something to the Sentinel or the Times, about this, but it would be great to investigate this for the community that it's actually impacting."

"Are you kidding? You'd really do something for the Gazette?" Lizzie is stunned, she didn't expect him to say yes, at least not right away. "I can't even…"

"Stop, you have created something amazing–well, recreated–your father is a legend in my book for starting a newspaper, and for keeping it going on his own for so long while everyone else was getting swallowed up by corporations," Eric says. "Your commitment to an independent and local voice is so admirable. I'd be honored to write for you."

"They are the greatest people around," Alexis says. "You will love working with them."

"I'm sure I will," Eric says. "So what are you thinking?"

"The main thing I'm thinking is 'thank you'!" Lizzie says. "Okay, so this company has been around for a long time, and in the little bit of digging I've done, I just can't help but feel there's something off. They have had a lot, or it seems like a lot, of bankruptcies and yet they're still getting financing? It doesn't make sense."

"It doesn't," Eric says. "I've done some other finance stories and their names come up here and there, and not in a great way. I have several contacts, and I'm betting since this is a green nonprofit they're trying to kill, there are people who would like to talk."

"That would be great," Lizzie says. "I'm not sure what your usual rate is, but please know we do have amazing investors who are one-hundred percent behind us, so please don't feel you can't ask for what you need. We will cover any travel you have to do, like if it means going to New York or anywhere else."

"Thank you, I appreciate that. I will be very fair, I promise you," he says. "Do you have a deadline in mind?"

Lizzie looks at Alexis, "Yesterday?" she says, and laughs. "As soon as you can get us something, it could be a series, we could run stories as you have them ready to go."

Eric nods, "Okay, I'm almost done with the story I'm working on now, and the next one can be pushed, it's an evergreen, so by tonight I'll start making some calls and see where that leads. Sound good?"

"It sounds great, thank you so much, Eric, this is such a relief," she and Alexis stand up. "Alexis, do you have his contact info?" Alexis nods.

"No worries, I'll send you an email with my phone number and we'll be in touch, " he says, as Lizzie shakes his hand,

"Thanks again, I've got a really good feeling about this." Before she leaves she asks him a question that has been eating at her. "You are so good, it seems lots of papers would want to have you on staff. I'm curious why you choose the freelance life?"

He smiles at her, "You are not the first person to ask that. I'm still young, and I want to pick and choose what I want to work on. If I was on staff at a major paper I couldn't be saying yes to this story, I'd be writing what they want me to write. That's why."

"Got it, I can certainly understand that," Lizzie says. "Thanks for doing this for us, I'm looking forward to seeing what you come up with."

Eric nods, "Me too. Alexis, thanks so much for the introduction!"

"Always happy to network in our little community," she says.

Lizzie takes her coat off the back of the chair and puts it on. "I can't wait to go tell my dad that we've got someone. Someone amazing. Thank you so much for helping facilitate that, friend." She gives Alexis a hug. "And don't forget, I want to hear all about this lunch Ian is making for you."

"Oh, I will let you know! And for the record? You were right." Alexis says.

"About what? I'm right about so many things," she jokes.

"I do really like him, I hope he's everything I think he is, Lizzie."

"So far the Magic 8 Ball looks like it's pointing to a big yes, but the good news is, no matter what, you know you're awesome and you are fine."

"You're so right, friend. We are always good, guy or no guy," Alexis says.

"And don't forget– he's the lucky one here," Lizzie says.

"So is Jack."

"Heck yes, those are two lucky men," Lizzie says, feeling her heart sink a little. "We are total catches. Love you, talk later," she says as she heads to the door.

"Love you too!" Alexis says to Lizzie, who just missed seeing the look on Alexis's face. The 'she's hatching a plan' look. Lizzie also doesn't see Alexis pick up her phone and make a call as soon as she's out the door. Nope, she doesn't see any of that.

CHAPTER 30

LIZZIE PRACTICALLY SPRINTED BACK to the paper, she couldn't wait to tell her dad all about hiring Eric. She's got a good feeling about this. like she's hired her own Bob Woodward or Carl Bernstein.

"Dad?" she says when she walks in not seeing Peter at his desk.

Peter comes walking out of the bathroom dabbing his shirt with some wet paper towels, "I had a run in with a breakfast burrito and I'm afraid the burrito won," he says, laughing as he tries to get the salsa off his shirt.

She walks over to her side of their desk and opens the drawer. "Here, try this," she says, tossing him a stain stick. "Clumsiness must run in the family, so I keep one of these handy at all times."

He goes back into the bathroom and is talking to her while working on his shirt. "I dropped my burrito while I was reading a little bit about those sleazy developer guys," he says. He emerges stain free, albeit a little wet. "They sure seem like real shady characters, there's got to be some way to expose them."

"Well, interesting that you should say that, because I met Eric Jackson, the freelancer I told you about. And he's going to start working on the story later today. I hired him," she says happily. "We're going to nail these guys, Dad, I have a really good feeling about this."

"You do know that these corporate criminals almost never get what they deserve, right? I don't want you setting your hopes too high," her dad says, like the very experienced journalist he is.

"I know. I'm sure I'm being very naive, it would be nice though, if for once people that go around hurting others had to pay for it, you know?" She sighs. "Anyway, I really liked Eric. Alexis knows him a bit and he even stayed at the Marshview for a while, so Ben and Sean also know him, so he's thoroughly vetted by our friends who say he's really good."

Peter is on his computer, "I'm doing some internet sleuthing on him, and you're right, he has written some very high profile stories. I wonder why he's not on staff anywhere?"

"Oh, I asked him about that, he said he likes to be able to write about what he wants to write, not just the stories assigned to him. Like having the freedom to work with us, he likes that," she says. "He's really young, and I think he sees this as the time to be able to live his life how he wants, and besides, this isn't too bad a place to work from."

"Have you talked to Jack since you saw him earlier?" Peter asks. "I wonder if he's been able to find out anything more, if he's heard about a court date or anything."

"No, I'm kind of giving him some space, I'll reach out a little later, maybe see if he wants to come have dinner with us," trying hard to keep up her act. She takes out her laptop. "Have you talked to Mom? Is she still upset about us postponing the wedding?"

"She texted a bit ago, she's not upset about anything other than you being disappointed. That's all she cares about. As long as she knows you're okay she'll be fine. You know your mom, it's always all about you kids," he says.

"I know, but I'm not a kid and I'm okay," Lizzie says mostly convincingly.

"If you choose to have kids you will see honey, that no matter how old they are they are still your babies, even if they are over 30, engaged, and successful in their career," Peter says, looking over at her.

"But you treat me like an equal! You entrusted me with your other baby, this newspaper, you see me as an adult," Lizzie says.

"I do see you as an adult, but the second I think anyone is messing with your happiness or hurting you, you're my little girl, and all common sense and professionalism go out the window. But I can catch myself and keep my mouth shut," he laughs. "Hence I've never stepped on your toes, I don't think."

"You have not," she grows pensive for a moment, "I really do appreciate how much you and Mom love Matt and me, and Jack, Shannon and Sophie. I know how incredibly rare that is and how lucky I am to have that when so many don't, so scratch my complaining about it, okay?" she says, choking up a little as she looks at her dad and trying hard to not let her emotions get away from her.

"We try *very* hard to not overstep and let you be the adults you are, and run your own lives, and most of the time I think we succeed pretty well, but boy, there are times it's not easy!' he says.

"I will try to remember that the next time I feel like you're thinking I'm seven. I love you, Dad, and I'm so grateful I get to sit here and be your colleague every day," she says, choking up again. "Okay, so let's get to work here, enough sentimentality for one day, huh?"

"The older you get the more you will realize that there's never too much sentimentality," he says. "But you're right, we've got a paper to put out!"

By the end of the day, deadlines met, they are both ready to get out of that office.

"Oh, I did hear from Jack, he's going to come over for dinner," Lizzie says, hoping she can keep her feelings under wraps.

"Great," he says, looking at his phone, "Your mom just texted that Matt and family are coming over too. I think it's a great idea to be together and change the channel for a little bit."

They both get up and put their coats on. Lizzie hesitates before she packs up her laptop thinking it might be good to leave it there and forget about work for the night, but with everything going on she decides she should have it, just in case. She slips the strap over her shoulder as they walk out, Peter hitting the lights as they open the door.

He puts his arm around her, "Another good day, partner," he says.

"Yes, it feels good to feel good about what we're doing at the end of a workday, unlike my past job." They each go to their respective cars."See you at home!" she calls out, getting in, ready to go home and relax.

Sophie is waiting by the door when they arrive within seconds of each other. "Auntie Wiz!" she yells, throwing her little arms around Lizzie's legs.

"Hey, Sophie-cat," Lizzie says, scooping her up after putting her things on the floor. "I am so excited to see you!" Lizzie says, twirling around with her favorite–well, only niece. This is the absolute best medicine in the world. "Where is everyone?"

Sophie points to the kitchen. "Hi Grandpa!" she says, acknowledging Peter whose entrance was ignored during the twirling.

"Hi, my girl," he says, giving Sophie a kiss.

They all head into the kitchen, where Gabby has put together an amazing spread. There is a huge casserole with homemade mac and cheese, which Lizzie immediately knows is vegan, salad, fruit, whole grain bread, it looks delicious and much needed on this cold night.

"Mom, thank you so much," Lizzie says, walking casually over to Jack, who's also just arrived. She gives him a quick kiss. "You doing alright?"

He nods,and Lizzie notes how tired he looks. "I'm okay, talked with the lawyers a few times." Everyone except Sophie has stopped talking. Her brother and sister-in-law have paused in the middle of filling their plates.

"How's it looking, bro?" Matt asks, looking worried.

Jack shrugs. "It's hard to say, these guys come lawyered up, and since they don't always play by the rules, it's hard to know what they might try to do, but I feel good about the team we have. They're all really good, really experienced, as one might expect from the caliber of investors we have. So for the moment I'm going to try to forget about it, and enjoy this wonderful meal and being with all of you. We have three weeks until the first court date, so we shall see."

Lizzie knows him well enough to know he can't forget about it, but she's going to do her best to make sure they both relax and have some fun tonight, despite how she feels.

"Okay, everybody take a bit of everything and enjoy!" Gabby commands.

"Thank you, Gabby, this is incredible as usual, every working mom should have someone like you in their life," Shannon says, giving her a squeeze.

"I'm very happy to be retired and have the time to do it, it makes me so happy to have all of you here," Gabby says.

There's a fire crackling in the living room and they decide to be very casual, skip the table and all sit on the floor, pillows and couch in the living room by the fire.

Sophie, done eating in quick order, is entertaining them all with a dance she created that afternoon when Shannon had let her play with her phone while she was wrapping up her work day. She settled on the song *Shining Star* by Earth, Wind and Fire, and has created quite the dance number full of kicks and twirls. It is just the distraction and fun they all need right about now.

When she's done, she's celebrated with applause from everyone, and dessert–ice cream sundaes. Made of course with frozen almond milk.

While they're finishing up their dessert, Lizzie's phone rings. She kicks herself for not having turned it off, but when she sees it's Eric she immediately answers it.

"Hey, Eric, what's up?" she asks, curious.

"I'm sorry to bother you at night, but I wanted to tell you I'm getting a flight to Florida in the morning. I have a source there who's willing to talk to me, but only in person," he says.

"Wow, you sure work fast," Lizzie says, motioning to her dad to follow her to the kitchen. "We will reimburse you all your costs, I can Venmo you some cash now for any expenses, we're happy to do that." Peter looks confused. "It's Eric, Dad, he's going to Florida to meet with a source. Sorry, Eric, I was getting my dad and co-editor up to speed."

"Got it, I'm fine, I already got the ticket, and will text you if I end up needing anything, thanks. I've got a good feeling about this, I think it's worth the trouble of going down there. This could really be something," he says.

Lizzie nods, "Okay, well, we trust you, keep us in the loop, and safe travels," Lizzie says.

"Will do. I'll be in touch," he says.

Lizzie puts her phone back in her pocket. "He seems to think this source is worth going to Florida for, and that this could be big."

"Let's hope he's right," says Peter. "For Jack's sake, and for Cranberry Harbor."

CHAPTER 31

"ARE YOU SURE YOU'RE OKAY?" Shannon asks Lizzie, as they are cleaning up the kitchen together. "It's just, well, Matt told me about the wedding being postponed and I wanted to check. It would be natural to be upset, sad, mad…all of the feelings." She sighs. "Can you tell I spend most of my life around little kids?" She laughs and shakes her head. "I sound like an idiot!"

Jack left right after dessert, having calls to make, and Lizzie and Shannon would not allow anyone else to help.

"You do not sound like an idiot, you sound like a very caring person," Lizzie says, scraping plates into the compost. "It is really hard, but I don't want to make anything worse than it already is, you know? There's so much happening. Still, when Jack said he wanted to postpone the wedding, it hurt, but I thought I should go along with it and not say anything." She stacks the scraped plates by the sink and begins to rinse them.

"Not telling him how you feel while in the short term might be good, but probably isn't a great way to start a life together," Shannon offers quietly, not wanting to rock the boat any more than it had been over the last few days.

Lizzie sits down at the counter and sighs. "I know, and I'm usually a regular Brené' Brown, talking about how I feel, but right now how I feel doesn't seem like the most important thing happening here. I mean, Jack could lose everything he's been working for, and heaven forbid, go to jail for smacking Billy, but I am hurt that he so quickly thought not getting married was a swell idea."

"Most men are not great multi-taskers, you know that," Shannon says. "They aren't like us, we can do the whole 'bring home the bacon, fry it up in a pan' thing, guys are better uni-taskers." She sits down next to Lizzie, "I so understand how you feel, but you and Jack *are* getting married."

"Please don't tell Matt about this, okay? I don't want anyone worrying or getting upset about all of this. I'll be fine, really, I will."

Shannon stands up and gives her a hug. "I know you will be, you're going to have the wedding you want, and it's going to be amazing." She steps back to the sink to keep cleaning.

"You and Matt need to get Sophie home, I'll finish this up. Thank you for all your help," Lizzie says.

"We should get her to bed. Sure you don't mind?" Shannon asks.

"No, absolutely not, we're almost done anyway.Go home and get some rest," Lizzie says.

Shannon puts on her coat and picks up Sophie's and Matt's from the bench. "I hope this writer you hired can dig up some dirt on these guys."

Lizzie looks surprised, "Please don't say anything to anyone about that, okay?" she says as she and Shannon walk into the living room. "Really, no one can know we're investigating Gobel and Green."

"I understand," Shannon says. She hands the coats to Matt, who bundles up a very sleepy Sophie.

After they leave, and Gabby goes upstairs to bed, Peter and Lizzie are alone sitting by the dwindling fire.

"I'm scared, Dad. I've been a journalist for a while, but this could be big and it's scary. All eyes will be on us. We need to get this right, whatever this is."

"We'll do all the right things, and we'll make sure every T is crossed and I dotted," he reassures her. "We'll see what he comes up with, and make sure everything is substantiated. I've had 40 years in this business, and if I don't have an answer I know people who do. He'll be fine."

"That's very reassuring, thank you, Dad." She stands up and stretches. "I'm exhausted, it's been a long couple of days. Want me to spread out the embers here?" she asks, picking up the small shovel by the fireplace. Peter gets up and takes it from her.

"I've got this, honey, you get to bed," he says.

"Thanks," she says, handing him the shovel. Walking toward the hall, she stops and turns around. "Thanks for everything, Dad, mostly for being my dad. I love you"

"It's the best job I've ever had," he says. "I love you too."

Lizzie tossed and turned through much of the night, and finally gave up around 5:45, and got out of bed.

"Wow, you're sure up early," Gabby says, coming down into the kitchen to the smell of coffee already having been made. "Thank you," she says, pouring herself a cup and taking it to the table. "Trouble sleeping?"

"Yeah, I kept thinking about this whole thing, wondering how the community could rally and what the heck happened to Billy and Bud that they would cozy up with bad guys against the town," Lizzie says, joining her mom at the table with her coffee.

"Who knows what they promised them? They are not the most worldly of fellows and have no idea who they've gotten involved with. They are naive on their best day, and easily manipulated. One need only look at the political signs in their yards to see how gullible they are," Gabby says.

"You're so much kinder than me, I want to call them all sorts of names and make them move away," Lizzie says.

"I believe everyone is redeemable, well, most everyone," Gabby says smiling. "I've known a few people in my life who I don't hold out much hope for, but you never know, maybe they can be brought around."

"I'm not holding my breath," Lizzie says.

"I'll keep the faith for both of us," Gabby says.

"I can always count on you to be my positive force, Mom. I get awfully discouraged."

"Other than that, are you okay?" Gabby asks, sensing her stress isn't just about Terra Marique.

Lizzie gets up and starts busying herself cleaning up the coffee making items. "Yeah, I'm fine."

"Okay, I sort of believe you," she gets up and leans against the counter with her coffee. "You don't have to be chipper or hide how you're feeling from me, honey. I'm always behind you."

"I know," Lizzie puts down the sponge she's using to clean the counter. "I need to be okay. I don't know if that makes sense? I have to keep myself together. Me being upset doesn't serve anyone or anything."

"Neither does not talking about how you feel," her mother counters.

"I know you love me and only want the best for me, but my wedding isn't happening when I hoped it would and there's nothing I can do about that.o I'm going to do my work, I'm going to support Jack, and I'm going to put my sadness and disappointment on the back burner. And as I say this, I'm well aware that I'm really fortunate, so I don't want to sound like some spoiled brat. I know this isn't the end of the world, but it still kind of stinks. Please keep this between us, okay? As far as Dad and everyone else knows, I'm completely cool with it."

"Mum's the word," Gabby says, miming zipping her lips. "I will not say a word, I promise. And you are far from spoiled, it's completely understandable for you to feel angry, sad, all the feelings. Is there anything I can do to help you?"

Lizzie shakes her head. "Other than making this stupid injunction go away and getting the charges against Jack dropped, I don't think so. Oh, maybe you could call Jess for me and tell her that the wedding is postponed indefinitely but that I still want the dress and will be in to get it hemmed soon? It's a phone call I really don't want to make. It makes it real."

"Consider it done," Gabby says. She walks over to Lizzie and pulls her in for a big hug, and it takes every bit of willpower for Lizzie to not just sink into her embrace and cry.

"Thanks, Mom," she wipes a couple of tears away. "I'm going to hop in the shower and get to work early. I want to make sure other stories don't fall through the cracks just because we're dealing with this whole thing." She stops before she goes upstairs and turns to her mom. "Thank you, I really needed that. I love you."

"I love you too, sweetie, and I know it's hard to believe, but it's all going to be okay," Gabby says.

Lizzie nods and walks upstairs, hoping as she usually is, her mom is right.

By the time Lizzie has showered, dressed and is ready to go to the office her dad is in the kitchen having his coffee and a bran muffin, a basket of which seems to have miraculously appeared on the counter. "Where did these come from, Mom? I wasn't gone that long!" She puts on her coat and gathers her things.

"I had the batter all set to go in the fridge, I was planning ahead," Gabby says.

"Well I am taking one for the road," Lizzie says, picking one up, then a second one, wrapping them in a cloth napkin and putting them in her bag. "I'll see you later at the office, Dad," she says as she walks to the door. "Thanks, Mom!" she yells as she closes the door.

When Lizzie arrives at the office and gets settled after eating her muffins, she sees that Eric has sent her an email with all his travel information. He's one organized guy. He also sent her the name of the woman he's meeting with, and the time and the place. It becomes clear to her that he's protecting himself, in case something goes wrong and she gets a chill. Her usual stories at the Cranberry Harbor Gazette don't require a reporter to be backing up their whereabouts. Such information isn't needed when covering a local bake sale or the cost of lobster that week. Suddenly she's very concerned for Eric's safety and wondering if this was a good idea. She wants to help Jack, but not to the point of someone risking their life. Just then her dad comes in.

"Dad, should we be worried about Eric? Come over here," she gestures to him to come look at her screen. "He's detailed who he's meeting, where and when. I'm worried, is he going to be okay?"

"That's pretty standard, honey. He's just covering all his bases. From all the research I did on him he's an experienced and savvy guy. He's spent time in Ukraine, Afghanistan…I'm confident he knows what he's doing."

"Okay, I'll try not to worry," Lizzie says, knowing that's impossible. There's way too much at stake, Eric's safety being number one, along with the future of Terra Marique, and running a close third, Cranberry Harbor.

CHAPTER 32

PETER AND LIZZIE had made a deal not to tell anyone about Eric's trip to Florida. It was hard to not tell Jack or her mom, but they needed the element of surprise both so no one close to Gobel and Green and their legal team could be alerted, and for the surprise element for the media.

By mid-afternoon Lizzie is feeling antsy. She's completed her deadlines, worked on the paper's social media and even prepped some stories for next week's issue.

"I need a break Dad, how about you?" she says, standing up and stretching. It was always amazing to her how easily they worked across from each other, neither one bothered by the other's presence. Part of it was all the years they each had working in newsrooms, but it was also from their total comfort with each other. Lizzie had never felt so good, even in a stressful time, in a workplace.

Peter stretches as well. "Your mom texted a while ago, encouraging me to get out, we're going to meet at the Bunny Park and have some lunch in about a half hour. You're welcome to join us."

"Thanks, but you two need some alone time. You're always surrounded by kids, in-laws, and Sophie who–no matter how delightful she is–doesn't allow much space for you two to just be together." She stands up and puts her coat on and her bag over her shoulder. "I'm going to walk down to Sea Coast and maybe have some soup and a coffee. I'll see you in a bit!"

The Cape is not known for its spectacular spring weather, so when there's a day in March that is full of sun and little wind, it's practically cause for a parade. As soon as the fresh air and sun hit Lizzie she feels her whole body relax. She closes her eyes for a moment and takes a deep breath. This is exactly what she needed. Despite everything going on she finds herself actually smiling at the sight of daffodils and crocuses, and is thrilled to see the cherry trees that line Main Street are probably just a couple of weeks from blooming, turning the street into a sea of pink.

Within a few minutes she's walking into Sea Coast where she is very surprised to see her mom, Shannon and Alexis all deep in conversation around a small table.

"Lizzie!" Shannon calls out. Alexis closes her laptop and her mom turns to greet her. "Hey, honey, this is a nice surprise. Look who I ran into! This almost never happens!"

Lizzie can't figure out what's going on, but her mother is a terrible actress. She decides whatever it is they do not want her in on it, so she points to the counter, "I'm going to get some soup, any of you want anything?" They all shake their heads.

By the time she gets back with her bowl of vegan lentil soup and a piece of warm French bread, her mom is getting up to leave. "Here, take my seat, honey, I'm meeting your dad. I came in to get us some lunch and ran into these two, and we had fun catching up."

"If you're sure," Lizzie says, taking her mom's seat. "Thanks, have a good lunch with Dad." She's still confused about what's going on. Are they worried about her and were meeting in private to discuss her mental health or something? Is she presenting like she's having a hard time? She thought she was doing pretty well. She picks up her spoon and tells herself to calm the heck down, all while smiling at Shannon and Alexis. Great, now they'll really think I'm not doing well. Stop! She yells in her head.

"Bye, Gabby, talk to you soon," Shannon says as Gabby leaves. "So, how's your day going?" she asks Lizzie, trying to look casual.

Lizzie nods, "Fine, everything's fine." Stop saying 'fine', she tells herself. "What's up with you two?" Wondering if either of them will spill the beans.

"I'm good," Alexis says, "but I have to get going, I'm supposed to Zoom with some of the team, we're assessing what to do with the crew etcetera."

"Me too, I hate to leave you to eat alone, but I have to get back to the library for afternoon story hour," Shannon says.

"Okay, I feel like I scared everyone off," Lizzie says. "Are you upset with me?"

"Oh my gosh, no!" Alexis says, looking concerned. "We'd all been here for a while before you came in. It's timing, that's all." She stands up and gathers the empty cups and takes them to the recycling bin. "I'll call you later, okay?"

Lizzie nods, "Sure."

Shannon leans over and gives her a hug, "You doing okay today?" she whispers.

Lizzie nods again, "Yup, I'm hunky dorey," she says trying to convince herself as well. "We'll talk later, okay?" Shannon says.

"Sure," Lizzie says, still feeling a little bit like a party ruiner.

She's not alone for long. Jack walks in and while she's happy to see him, it's not without some angst.

"Hey, I was hoping I might find you here," he says, giving her a kiss.

"Perfect timing, I seem to have just scared away my family and friends. I would love the company, it's no fun to eat alone."

"That soup looks good, let me get some and I'll be right back," he says.

While she's waiting for him her phone rings. It's Eric. "I'll be right back, I have to take this," she says to him as he's walking back to the table and she steps outside.

"Sure," he says, sitting down.

"Hey, Eric," she says, her heart racing. "You okay?"

"Yes, I'm fine. So I'm headed to the airport, I'm coming back. I don't want to linger around here too long."

"Wow, that was fast. So this source ended up having something for you to use?"

"Yes, and then some," he says. "I don't want to talk about this on the phone. My flight, if I make it on time, is leaving in an hour. I'll call you from Boston and let you know when I'll be on the Cape and we can meet in person. I'll just say, hold on to your hat."

"Should I be happy or worried?" she asks, her pulse quickening.

"Mostly happy, but there are a lot of people who aren't going to be, so there's always room for a little worry," Eric says. "I'm going to run so I can focus on catching my flight. Talk to you soon."

"Okay, travel safe, and I'll talk to you later," She puts her phone down, and stands outside for a moment gathering her thoughts, knowing she can't share any of this with Jack. She does her best to shake it off, and then goes back into Sea Coast where Jack has finished his soup and is on to a cookie, there's another one sitting on a napkin for her. She smiles and thanks him for the cookie, and takes a bite, even though she hasn't finished her soup, which has now gone cold anyway.

"Everything okay?" he asks, taking a bite of his salted chocolate chip.

"Yeah," she nods, "Everything's fine." She smiles, and tries to be present, even though her mind is a million miles away. "How are you doing? Anything new I need to be caught up on?" She breaks a piece of the cookie off and pops it in her mouth. She really doesn't want a cookie right now, but it's a distraction and something to do with her hands.

Jack takes a big sip of his coffee, "Yeah, there's a lot. The legal team is gathering in New York and then will head here at some point in the next couple of days to prepare for court. I talked to them about my assault case, which is sounding much less scary. I forgot that we have security cameras set up on the periphery of the land, and they found footage of Billy and Bud skulking around and even taking some building supplies, and attempting to sabotage some of the equipment."

"Wow, really? I find that shocking! Even though I've known those two my whole life, that seems low even for them," Lizzie says. It's so hard to not tell Jack that some even bigger news could be coming on a flight from Orlando in a few hours, but she doesn't want to risk jeopardizing anything. This is bigger than something you want to share with your fiance, this sounds like it could be criminal, so she bites her tongue.

"I know, right? I mean, I know they didn't want Terra Marique to happen, but committing a felony is a whole other level of misbehavior. I always thought they were malcontents who didn't have anything better to do. But, by sabotaging heavy equipment they could have caused an accident that could injure someone. But enough about all this stuff, how are you doing? You okay?"

Lizzie shrugs, and eats some more of her cookie. She doesn't know what else to do, she can't tell him about Eric's story, and she doesn't want to tell him how she's really feeling about postponing the wedding, so there's not too much to talk about otherwise, so once again she puts on a smile and acts like everything is okay. "I'm fine. Boy, this cookie is so good!" she offers up, lacking anything more that she feels comfortable sharing.

"I know, when I got to the counter Hope was taking them right from the cookie sheet to the display case. Can't get much fresher than that. You want another one? I think I'm going to have one more," he says, getting up.

She shakes her head, her mouth full of the last piece of hers, "I'm good," she manages to get out despite the cookie. While he's gone she takes the opportunity to check Twitter, she's been following Gobel and Green and keeps waiting for them to post something about having filed this injunction, but there's nothing, which after a couple of days surprises her. Usually the modus operandi of these types of companies is to build buzz and sympathy for their misdeeds. There's not usually a shortage of a certain type of media outlet that loves to slam people who are working hard to stem the tide of climate change and make them look like the bad guys, not the corporations who are pillaging the planet.

When Jack comes back he not only has more cookies, but he also has two lattes. Lizzie accepts hers, but is worried about how she will ever get to sleep tonight with more caffeine in the afternoon.

"It's decaf," he says, "I know you, you've reached your cutoff time," he says, smiling at her.

She leans over and gives him a kiss. "You're the best, which is why I know you'll understand that I have to get back to the paper and see how my dad is doing, and check on a few things. Don't hate me for leaving you here all alone, okay?" She says, getting up and putting on her coat. "Thanks for this," she says, raising the decaf latte. "It was very thoughtful of you. Things seem not terrible," she says. "And not terrible right now is a very good thing."

"Yes, right now not terrible is about the best bar I can hope to reach." He's quiet for a moment. "We were really moving along, Lizzie, you know? We were looking to be able to have this place habitable well before our original date. I'm so angry at these people, but I can't let that get in the way of doing all I have to do. The lawyers say to keep doing everything I've been doing that isn't related to the site–all the future planning, reaching out to possible residents and all the rest. They said to keep going as if nothing is wrong, so that's what I'm trying to do. It's hard though, my mind keeps going right back to crisis mode."

"They wouldn't tell you that if they weren't confident about winning this case. Jack, this isn't a bunch of fresh-out-of-school lawyers who don't know what they're doing, so listen to them," Lizzie says. "It is going to work out." She hugs him. "Call me later, okay?"

"I will,' he says. "And thanks for the pep talk, I needed it."

"Anytime," she says. As she walks back to the paper she's trying to give herself a pep talk, quietly, under her breath, "It's all going to work out, this is just a speed bump, this will all get fixed and everything will be okay for everyone." The closer she gets to the paper the less sure she is, but she's trying to have faith.That's all she can do.

CHAPTER 33

As soon as she's in the office, before she can even take her coat off, she starts telling her dad about the conversation with Eric. She's glad Stan isn't there; this can't get leaked anywhere, and she needs to talk.

"Slow down, honey," Peter says, putting up his hand. "I'm having a hard time keeping up with you."

She sits down and tries to compose herself. "Sorry, I know I'm babbling. Okay, Eric called," she looks at her watch. "He should be getting on a plane right now, if he made it on time. He said the source he talked to gave him lots of information, and that it's more than he thought it would be. But he didn't want to talk about it on the phone."

"Wow, that is big," he says. "I wonder what it could be? Money laundering? Bankruptcies?"

Lizzie shrugs her shoulders, "I have no idea. I mean we had a feeling that Gobel and Green had some shady deals, that's been their reputation, but he made this sound like it was more." She opens up her computer, trying to create some semblance of a normal work day, but it's hard to think of focusing on anything but this. "Okay, so this issue is all set to print tomorrow. How are you looking for next week?" she asks, truly not the least bit interested but hoping she will be.

"Well, there's the hockey team finals, the elementary school is hosting a plant sale to encourage everyone to start an organic garden, and I got a memo from the fire department that they're starting fire hydrant flushing next week," Peter says, looking at the list on his desk. "It's not exactly a hard-hitting list."

They both laugh. "Ah, March in a seasonal community, I have to admit with everything else going on I am longing for the days when these *were* the biggest stories of the week," Lizzie says. "We should get some photos of the plant sale for print and for the online edition and social media. Those will be sweet and hopefully encourage people to go organic. Stan might like to cover the hockey team, yeah?"

"Definitely," Peter says. "I'll text him to get in touch with the coaches and preview the big match up." They both sigh at exactly the same time. "This is hard," he says.

"Like trying to forget about the elephant that is clearly sitting in our office that we're trying not to look at?" Lizze offers.

"Yes," he looks at his watch. "When is Eric landing?"

She in turn looks at her watch. He called me around 1? Said the plane was in an hour, if it's direct that will get him to Logan at around 5? Then he's got the drive back to the Cape–"

"During rush hour no less," Peter says.

"Yup, and if we're lucky he will be on Cape maybe by 8 or a little before?" Lizzie says.

"Why don't you tell him to come to the house straight from the airport rather than here, if this is as big a story as he's making it sound, I don't know, maybe we're better off not meeting here, in case anyone is on to him or the source he met with."

"I'll text him," she says, picking up her phone. "I really do feel like we're in the middle of Watergate or some other big scandal. It's nerve wracking!" Text sent, she's not sure what else to do.

"I know, I feel the same way. I'd say let's go home and call it a day, but what are we going to do there? Sit around there and be nervous and drive your mom crazy?" Peter says.

"Why don't we each do as much of our to-do list as we can tolerate, and then go home?"

"Sounds like a plan," Peter says.

They manage to quietly work across from each other for a

couple of hours, each jumping a bit when their phones ding with text messages, none of which are consequential.

At 4:45 Lizzie closes her laptop. "Okay, I'm done pretending to be at all interested in anything I've been doing," Lizzie says, as she gets up. "I'm going to get out of here and go pace at home."

"Sounds good to me, let's get the heck out of here," Peter agrees.

"Eric should be landing soon and we will hopefully have some answers in just a few hours," Lizzie zips her computer bag closed and puts on her coat.

She holds the door for Peter as they walk out. "You know Mom has a sixth sense about everything," she says as they walk to their cars. "What are we going to say about Eric, if he comes over?"

"She's been married to a newspaper guy for 35 years. She understands, honey, she knows when and when not to ask questions. See you at home," he says. "What about Jack? He can't know anything about this, not yet."

"I know. I'm thinking of telling him I'm tired and turning in early, I don't want him there if Eric does in fact come over tonight. I hate lying, but it's for his own good. And the good of Terra Marique and Cranberry Harbor."

"Absolutely," Peter says. "Okay, so I'll see you in a minute."

They each get in their cars. Lizzie looks over at her dad and is so grateful that she has him to go through all this with. She gives him a little wave, and he gestures for her to back out first. She does and as she drives home can't help but feel a little bit excited about nailing these bad guys.

"You two never arrive home at the same time," Gabby says as they come through the door together. "Is it a national holiday I don't know about?" she jokes.

Peter gives her a kiss, "Yes, it's national 'Let's leave work at a reasonable time' day," he jokes. "We both finished our work and decided to get out of there." He looks over at Lizzie who is picking at a salad in progress on the counter.

"Can I do anything to help?" Lizzie asks, popping another piece of cucumber into her mouth.

"Nope, it's all done. I just didn't think you'd be here this soon.

You could put the salad on the table," Gabby says. "And I will toss the pasta with the sauce I made. Oh, there's some parmesan and the grater on the counter, could you grab that too?"

In under five minutes they're all sitting at the table enjoying Gabby's delicious tomato and fresh basil sauce. Lizzie is finally relaxing a bit and her phone rings. She looks down and sees it's Eric.

"Excuse me, I have to take this," she gives her dad a little nod and gets up from the table, walking into the living room.

"Hey Eric, you get to Boston okay?" she asks. She's extremely concerned for his safety.

"Yeah, I'm on 93 South and headed to the Cape. I should be in Cranberry Harbor around 7:30. Should we meet?"

Lizzie has never had stealthy meetings before and isn't sure if she should be speaking in code or what. "Can you come to us?" she asks. "We aren't at the office, do you know where we live?" She doesn't want to give the address over the phone, she's hoping it's a small enough town that he's talked to someone who's told him where their house is.

"I'm pretty sure I do. If I have any problems I'll reach out. I should go, traffic is picking up a bit," he says.

"Okay, drive safe," she says. "We'll see you soon." She walks back into the kitchen and sits down at the table.

"Everything okay?" Gabby asks, twirling some spaghetti around her fork.

"Yes, it was a freelancer Dad and I hired to write a story. He's coming over in a little bit to go over some notes with us. Hope that's okay? We won't be too late I'm sure."

"Wow, I didn't know you'd hired someone new. That's great!" Gabby says.

"Yes, he's been living in town for a while and writing for publications all over the country, so we thought we'd give him some stories to do," Peter says.

Gabby, being the savvy woman she is, starts to read between the lines. "I'm sure he's going to be a big help to you both," she pushes her chair out from the table and stands up. "I'm going to get some more water. You two need anything?" she says.

"No thanks," Lizzie and Peter both say.

"He'll be here in about an hour, Dad," Lizzie says, pushing her salad around her plate, a bit too nervous to eat. Peter nods.

After Lizzie puts the final plate in the dishwasher, she takes her phone out of her pocket to call Jack, hopefully intercepting him calling later while they're meeting with Eric.

"Hey, I was about to call you," he says. "How's it going?"

"Good!" she says a little too enthusiastically. Calm down, she thinks to herself. "I mean, I'm tired, but everything's okay. How about you?"

"I'm okay," he says, sounding discouraged. "I lost two crew members today who even though we're still paying them, decided they were going to move on to other jobs off-Cape. It's making me worry about how many other people are going to feel like they don't want to spin their wheels sitting here waiting."

"The court date isn't too far away, it's only a couple of weeks," Lizzie says, trying to buck up his spirits. "Maybe there's something everyone could be working on together off-site? Some project? I think everyone feels better when they're being productive."

"Hmm...that's a really good idea. I know at the last selectboard meeting they were talking about working on the town square, repairing the gazebo, putting in new benches and plantings...that's a great idea, sweetie."

"It's also a way to keep the town on your team. Not to sound manipulative, but it will help reinforce that you and this project are here to help make Cranberry Harbor better in lots of ways," Lizzie says. "The weather's improving, and it's kind of the perfect time to do it, before traffic picks up and the snowbird folks start to return."

"Yeah, yeah," Lizzie can tell Jack's wheels are turning. "Thank you! I'm going to make some calls and see what I can get going." He's quiet for a moment, "Maybe we can even get some local artists who would like to be a part of this with some sculptures. I needed something positive to focus on. This is great. Thank you, thank you!"

Lizzie loves hearing him sound excited and happy. "I will let you go, and you're welcome. We're a team, babe, I've always got your back."

"Right back at you," he says. "Love you, I'll talk to you tomorrow."

"Love you too," she says.

She looks at her text messages to make sure she didn't miss a message from Eric while she was on the phone. Nothing. She fills the electric kettle with water, turns it on and walks to the living room where her parents are cozying up on the couch in front of the fire.

"I was going to make some tea, you two want some?" Lizzie asks.

"That would be great, honey," Gabby says.

"Me too, please," Peter says.

"I will be right back with it."

Before she even has a chance to put the hot water into the waiting mugs, the doorbell rings.

"I've got it," she calls, hurrying to the door. "Hey, please, come in," she says, welcoming Eric in. "You made great time, I didn't expect you quite yet."

"There was surprisingly little traffic," he says, slipping his backpack off his shoulder and taking off his coat.

"Here, let me take that," she says, reaching for his coat and hanging it on one of the hooks in the hall near the kitchen, "Come and meet my parents," she says, gesturing to him to come into the living room.

Gabby and Peter stand up, "Eric Jackson, this is my dad, Peter Martin, founder and editor of the Cranberry Harbor Gazette," Lizzie says.

"Co-editor" Peter says, smiling at Lizzie. "It's very nice to meet you, Eric," he says, shaking his hand.

"And this is my mom, Dr. Gabby Martin."

"Welcome to our home," Gabby says, shaking his hand as well. "Are you hungry?" she asks. "We have plenty of leftovers, I'd be happy to get you a plate."

" Thank you, Dr. Martin, but I've eaten. Some water would be great though, if it's not too much trouble, " he says.

"Please call me Gabby," she says, "I'll be right back with some water."

Gabby is back in a flash with the water, which she hands to Eric.

"I am going to leave you all to your work and go upstairs and read. So nice to meet you, Eric, we will have to have you over for a proper dinner very soon."

"Thank you, Dr., I mean, Gabby, I'd love that. Thank you for letting me intrude on your evening," He takes a big sip of his water, then opens his backpack and takes out an overstuffed file folder. "I think you're going to be as surprised by this as I was," he says.

They all sit down. Lizzie and Peter each take a deep breath and begin reading.

CHAPTER 34

For a half hour the three of them are silent, except for the occasional, "Oh my God," no one is saying anything as they read document after document.

Finally Peter stands up. "Anyone else feel like a glass of wine?" he says. "I need a little break." Eric and Lizzie nod, and he is back in a minute with a bottle of Cabernet, and three glasses.

"How did you get all this?" Lizzie asks, a pile of papers in her lap.

"I'd had some experience with Gobel and Green years ago while I was working on another story for a paper in London, and when we met I reached out to a few people I knew, and that led me to this source, Gloria," he pauses, taking a sip of wine. "A guy I know had heard about this incident at a nuclear power plant in Florida, and put me in touch with her."

"How did she ever get all these documents?" Peter asks, "Do we know they're legit?"

"She worked at Dunhill Energy, the nuclear power plant, for 23 years," Eric says. "There were always protests within the community, people concerned over safety…"

"With due cause it sounds like," Lizzie says.

"Yes, things seemed to have never been run well. Gloria was a shift supervisor and throughout her time there was often filing reports over shortcuts being taken, protocols not followed, etcetera, so she was relieved when it was decided to close the plant down and decommission it."

"So how did Gobel and Green get involved?" Peter asks.

"They have never been short on bravado, and decided to throw their hat into the ring, with no experience, mind you, to decommission the plant," Eric says. "From the get-go there were problems. They hired inexperienced people who cut corners and ignored NRC protocols and rules."

"Wow, what could possibly go wrong? An inexperienced team of people with no regard for the law," Lizzie asks, rolling her eyes "Where did all these documents come from? Gloria took them?"

"She did. She became very concerned when they began laying off more and more people, and she could see they were ignoring safety protocols when dealing with radioactive materials, acting like they were nothing. When she started to hear rumblings of what they planned to do with the stored water, dumping it into the Gulf of Mexico, she decided to risk everything and take action. She would go to work and when she was alone she made copies of everything she could get her hands on, a few pages at a time and snuck them out under her clothes. It was incredibly brave of her. I cannot imagine the courage that took. And now, to give me copies, it's unbelievable," he says.

"I'm curious, why you? Why now?" Peter asks.

"We have a mutual friend who vouched for me. She felt like she could trust me, and when she heard that they had shut down this project, something that was poised to help the community and the planet, she decided now was the time. It hasn't been that long, this has all been going on very recently, and she's been staying on the down-low for her own safety. She didn't think they'd actually begun dumping the water, but all of a sudden dead sea fowl and fish have been washing ashore across the west coast of Florida, so she thinks they did it." Eric says.

"Oh my God, this is just so abhorrent," Lizzie says, trying to wrap her brain around such disregard for the life and safety of others. "Okay, so what comes first, the story or the lawsuit? Do we owe it to Jack and the Terra Marique team to let them know, or do we go full Watergate and print the story and let the cards fall where they may? I'm trying hard to be objective, which is impossible since it's my fiance."

"Peter, you've been a journalist a lot longer than me, what do you think? I have my thoughts, but I want to know what you think is the right thing to do," Eric asks, looking a bit worried.

Peter sits back and looks at them both. Lizzie has never seen her dad look so serious. He then leans forward, elbow on knees. "I think we print the story and deal with the fallout from there. Gobel and Green will go after us of course. They'll say we're lying, then they'll try to shut us down." He's quiet, and turns to Eric. "You are 100-percent sure everything she is saying is true?"

"Yes, sir, I am," Eric replies. 'I have seen the reports of the damage to the ecosystem, of people in the fishing industry reporting illnesses. It happened. And right before they did it they let everyone who had worked at Dunhill Energy go. They thought they covered all their tracks."

"Okay, write your story, and we'll back you," he says. "You agree, partner?" he says, looking at Lizzie.

"Yes," Lizzie says, "I back you too, Eric, one-hundred percent. It's going to be hard to not tell Jack, but we have to do it. What about Gloria? Is she safe? Do we need to see if we can get her protection? These kinds of people will stop at nothing, I don't want anything to happen to her."

"My original sources are looking out for her. She's been moved to a secure location with round-the-clock protection," Eric says, finishing his glass of wine. When Peter offers him more he shakes his head. "Thanks, but after almost no sleep, the travel and stress I don't dare have more than one and drive home."

"Okay," Peter says, and then asks the question Lizzie is wondering too. "How about your safety? Are you feeling okay going home, or would you feel better staying here?"

"Yeah, you're welcome to stay with us. All we have for protection is a scrappy rescue dog, but you wouldn't be alone," Lizzie says. She's grown quite fond of Eric and doesn't want him to be alone in his apartment. "We have a guest room, WiFi, food in the fridge, anything you need."

Eric, who Lizzie estimates can't be any older than 25, looks touched by their offer. "I'd hate to put you out in any way, are you sure? I am feeling pretty spent and wouldn't mind not being alone and wondering about every noise I hear."

Lizzie can see her father getting his emphatic dad face on, "Look, we think it would be a good idea for you to stay here with us and we would both sleep better knowing you're not all alone."

Eric actually looks a bit relieved, "If you're sure," he says.

"We're sure," Lizzie and Peter say in unison.

"I kind of wouldn't mind the company," he says. "I'll be honest, the whole way back I was looking over my shoulder–at the airports, the parking lot. Heck, driving here I kept looking in my rear-view mirror to check if I was being followed."

Peter stands up, "Then it's settled, you can stay here tonight and for as long as you like. Are you sure we can't give you anything to eat? I feel like a terrible host."

"No, really, I'm good, all I need is a hot shower and some sleep, it's been a long couple of days," he says.

"Do you have a bag you need to get from your car?" Lizzie asks.

"Nope, I travel light, everything is in my backpack here," he says, pulling it onto his lap. "Would you be insulted if I crashed? I suddenly feel completely exhausted."

"Not at all," Lizzie says. "I'll take you upstairs."

Lizzie is back in a few minutes having gotten Eric settled, gotten him some towels and even an old pair of Matt's sweatpants and a T-shirt that were laundered and in the bureau.

"I told Mom that he's staying over so she wouldn't be surprised to run into him in the hall," Lizzie says, plopping herself down on the couch. "So how do we handle this? Do we put out a special issue? This weeks' edition has already gone to the printer, and I don't think we should hold on to this for a week. What do you think?"

"The only time I ever put out a special issue was right after 9/11 back in 2001. This does seem to warrant moving fast, though. I say let's do it," Peter says.

"Okay, so as soon as he gets the story to us, we will run a short issue with some context pieces from us to get people up to speed with what has transpired, the town's history with Green and Gobel, and then the rest will be Eric's story," Lizzie says. "I sure hope Jack won't feel like I was holding out on him. It feels weird to not share this with him, but we have to be so careful."

"You're doing exactly what you're supposed to do, honey. You're being a professional. There's no other option. He'll know soon enough, and so will his lawyers," he says.

""I know you're right, it's just so counterintuitive to how we are with each other, you know? We share everything." Then she thinks about how she's not being honest about the wedding, and feels like a liar. "Most everything."

"I think we need to get to bed too. It's been a long day today, and I have a feeling the next few are going to be as well," Peter says, getting up off the couch. He spreads out the ashes on the dwindling fire and closes the glass doors.

"I'll be right up," she says, "I promise." Peter kisses her on the head, and he goes upstairs.

After he's gone, Lizzie sits alone on the couch still trying to take in all that Eric shared with them, and wondering what the fallout will be for Jack, and also for them as a newspaper. She doubts that these people who are treacherous enough to spill toxic waste into the ocean care much for their fellow humans and shudders to think what they might do to retaliate. Also, for the first time she thinks about Billy and Bud, assuming they have no clue about the kind of people they have hitched their wagon of resentments to. "This is going to be a mess," she says out loud. With what feels like the weight of the world on her, she pulls herself off the couch, turns out the lights and heads to bed. As she crawls under the covers she thinks about Jack and hopes he's able to sleep, and can't wait for them to finally begin their life together. Whenever that may be.

CHAPTER 35

When Lizzie woke up, and glanced at the clock on the nightstand she was shocked to see it was almost 8. She never sleeps that late. Granted it was after 2 by the time she fell asleep. She kept thinking she heard noises, first outside and then downstairs. She had the storylines of multiple movies running through her head, and kept expecting something nefarious, straight out of Hollywood to happen in her beloved Cranberry Harbor home. First it was the FBI she was thinking about, maybe they'd show up to arrest Eric, and then it was bad guys, sent by bad guys to kidnap him and take him…someplace. Someplace not good.

She throws the covers off, treads into the bathroom, and comes out a few minutes later, teeth brushed, hair in a messy bun, and now wearing the yoga pants and sweatshirt she had hanging on the back of the door. She feels okay seeing a relative stranger at the breakfast table in this outfit, it's not exactly glamorous, but a bit more presentable than her Hello Kitty pajamas.

"Good morning," everyone else says to her as she enters the kitchen. Eric is on his laptop, typing away with headphones, while Gabby and Peter are having breakfast. She pours herself some coffee and joins them.

Eric removes his earbuds, "Morning, I hope I didn't wake you up, I slept for a few hours and then couldn't stop thinking so I decided to come down here and write."

Ah, so that was the noise she heard, she was not crazy. "Not a problem, how's it going?"

"I'm close to a decent first draft. When that's done I'll send it to you two for notes, if that's okay?" he asks.

"Of course," Peter says. "We should get to work on our part of this, Lizzie. How do you want to split it?"

Lizzie is still barely awake, and is trying to get up to speed. "Um, how about I write the present day stuff? What Terra Marique is, how it got approved, who it's going to serve, the lawsuit, and you can write about the history with Gobel and Green and the town? That sound okay?"

"I was thinking the same thing," he says. "Great minds." He finishes his oatmeal and gets up to take his bowl to the sink. "I'm going to shower and get to the office. Eric, why don't you keep working here? If that's okay? This probably isn't something to work on with public WiFi at Sea Coast."

"You've already been so generous, are you sure?" Eric asks.

"Yes, we're sure," Gabby says, getting up from the table too. She has no idea what Eric is working on, and as the long-time wife of a journalist knows better than to ask. "You're welcome here for as long as you like," Gabby says. "Just let me know if you need anything. If you have any laundry I can point you to the laundry room. Just let us know what you need, and help yourself to anything,"

"Thank you so much," he says, looking a little embarrassed.

When Gabby and Peter are gone and it's just Eric and Lizzie, he stops typing for a moment.

"Your parents are so nice, this almost doesn't seem real. I think I've spent too much time lately around people doing bad things, you sort of forget what it's like to be around people who are genuinely kind," he says.

"That they are, and it is genuine." She gets up to start getting ready for work. "I can't not ask, how's it going? Do you think you have everything you need?"

He nods. "Yeah, and then some. There's no way given what they've done that they should be allowed to do business anywhere. They should all be in jail."

Lizzie feels a bit of a chill hearing that, it's exciting and scary, and she hopes they don't end up falling on their faces with all of them losing everything.

Before going upstairs to get dressed she turns around. "You're completely sure Gloria is legit? Sorry, it's not that I don't trust you, it's just I worry we're being duped and she's a plant from them to keep us off their scent."

"No apology needed, I can understand that this all feels awfully surreal, I thought so at first too, but the more digging I do, it all adds up. And I've been able to corroborate her claims with scientists in the area who have been, on their own, testing the water due to the devastation they're seeing."

Lizzie nods, still unable to believe that people, for money and power can be so selfish and cause such damage to the world around them. "What makes people do things like this?" she asks, not really to Eric, but to the universe really.

Eric shakes his head. "I wish I knew. I do a lot of stories about financial impropriety, shady real estate deals and things like that. But it's the ones that actually harm people, wildlife, the environment that leave me the most stymied. I don't know how people sleep at night." He shrugs his shoulders. "But sometimes, justice does prevail and they pay for what they've done, and I really hope this is one of those times."

"From your lips, Eric," Lizzie says. "Okay, I'm going to let you work. Thank you for all you're doing."

"Thank me when they're led off in handcuffs," he says, getting back to work.

On her way to the paper Lizzie stops at Sea Coast to see if Alexis might be there working remotely. She needs to see a friend and think about something happy, like how her lunch with Ian went. She's thrilled when she sees Alexis standing in line, waiting to be served.

"Hey friend," she says, tapping Alexis on the shoulder. "I was hoping to run into you."

"You were? What are the odds you'd find me here?" Alexis says, laughing. "Are you in a hurry?"

"I can't stay too long, but I can definitely have a quick cup of coffee and hear all about your lunch!" Lizzie says.

They each get their coffee and find an empty table.

"You've been a bit MIA for the last couple of days, everything okay at the Gazette?" Alexis asks.

Lizzie, not a natural liar, does her best to wave her off, "Oh yeah, everything is fine," she says, waving her off. "Just busy, and trying to be supportive of Jack...So enough about me, how'd it go with Ian? Was it a date date or a business meeting?" She smiles, and drinks some of her coffee.

Alexis looks down and when she looks up she's beaming. "Yeah, it was a date date, not a business meeting. Though we did discuss the film, Terra Marique, and the lawsuit."

"But you like him," Lizzie is so happy for her friend. "He seems so great, this is the best news I've heard in a long while."

"Given how things are going in your life I'd say that bar is pretty low," she jokes.

Lizzie laughs. "Good point! I haven't had a lot of good news of late, but things will get better. Anyway, so how long is he going to be laid up with that cast?"

"Three more weeks, hopefully. He won't be going running with me anytime soon, but he will be able to drive, which he's very excited about," Alexis says. "So, where are you at with your wedding at this point? Are you still making plans? Choosing flowers? What kind of flowers were you thinking? Food? Were you thinking of a buffet? Sit-down dinner? Did you and Jack already get your wedding rings? What about a cake? Have you already picked flavors? I know you mentioned once having the ice cream truck come and how fun that would be, but maybe you don't want to do that anymore, but it could be really cool... "

"Whoa, that's a whole lot of questions, my friend!' Lizzie laughs, but is a little confused. "Are you taking a survey? Getting ideas for your own wedding?"

Alexis puts her hands over her face, "Argh, I'm so sorry, too much coffee, I think. I've been thinking about your wedding, and all the things we were planning to do together, and it all just came out in one flood of questions!' She pushes her coffee away, "I am officially cut off from any more caffeine today."

Lizzie sighs, "I was so looking forward to all those things, and wow, I'd forgotten about the ice cream truck, that is a pretty cool idea!" She keeps thinking. "And I love peonies, they are totally my favorite flower. And Jack had mentioned a grilled cheese bar…We hadn't gotten to pick out the wedding rings yet. I was planning on doing that in a week or two, before this stupid lawsuit happened. Those jerks ruined everything, Alexis."

"What were you thinking of for food, you know, other than grilled cheese, which by the way is a great idea." Alexis says. "You know, just wondering."

Lizzie shrugs, "We hadn't decided the time of day yet, so we hadn't narrowed down a menu.You're awfully curious about all of this, how come?"

"Can't a girl be interested in her friend's wedding?"

"Yes, of course, I'm sorry," she shakes her head. "You're a really sweet friend, but a part of me still wonders if this is ever going to happen. I know Jack says he wants it to happen, but I'm still not quite convinced it will. Sorry to be such a Debbie Downer, it's hard to feel too hopeful right now."

Alexis reaches across the table and takes Lizzie's hand. "This IS going to happen, Lizzie, I know it is. Jack loves you and he wants to marry you. This is a speed bump, a glitch, you're going to get past this and have your happily ever after. You've got this, it's all going to work out."

Lizzie nods and smiles, "I would settle for 'happy for a while' at this point. But thank you for that,"

"For what?"

"For still believing in…hope? I guess. I haven't been feeling too hopeful lately and that was a very good pep talk," Lizzie says.

"So I'm a good pep talker, huh?"

"Oh, I'd say world class pep talker. If there was an Olympics for pep talking you'd win a gold medal," Lizzie says. She looks at the clock on the wall. "I really should get to the office, I don't want to leave my dad to handle everything." She stands up and puts on her coat. "Thanks for all of this, for reminding me there is a life beyond this crisis. It's easy to forget that." She hugs Alexis. "I will be better about staying in touch, and please don't hesitate to call or text. Actually, please do, okay?"

"I will," Alexis says. "I promise. We'll talk later."

"Later, gator," Lizzie says and with that she's out the door.

CHAPTER 36

As she's driving to the paper she stops dead in her tracks. Thank goodness no one was behind her. There are many people bustling about the town green carrying plants, shovels, and there's a big truck full of…she's not sure what. Fencing? A new gazebo? Then she spots Jack in the middle of the action, papers in hand, talking to someone. She pulls over, after someone who has come up from behind her beeps, and parks. Jack sees her walking towards him and runs over.

"Hey!" he says, looking a little overwhelmed but excited.

"Hey, yourself, what's going on?" She's taking in the flurry of activity, trying to figure it out for herself.

They start walking toward the middle of the square. "Well, remember that idea you had about fixing up the town square, utilizing the crew I have sitting idle?"

"Yeah, that was like…last night! How the heck–"

"It was incredible, Lizzie, I made one phone call to the chair of the selectboard, and within an hour I had permission, I sent them some plans I'd roughly drawn after we talked, and by this morning the crew had everything organized, had gone to pick up materials, and were here by 8:30, it's crazy!"

"Wow, from now on I'm going to have to be careful what I tell you to do!" Lizzie says, still incredulous at what's happening all around her.

"Justine and Leah put the word out on their Instagram and apparently they've been organizing volunteers to come help later as well. I'm really overwhelmed." He pauses and looks around. "I really thought everyone in town would be so mad at me, that they'd blame me for the lawsuit, that I was the bad guy," he says.

"Jack, no one thinks that!" Lizzie is shocked he'd think that. "They're all on your side, on the side of Terra Marique. Almost every person in this town voted for it, they're not going to suddenly turn on you."

He shakes his head, "I've let people down before, I didn't know what they'd think."

Those words are no sooner out of his mouth when several cars pull up, people get out, dressed in work clothes and approach him.

"We heard you need help," says one young guy, "Just tell us what to do."

Lizzie is near tears, she can't believe how people have turned out. "I'm going to leave you to do what you need to do, though I am going to take a few pictures to put up on the Gazette's social media." She gives him a kiss. "I'll talk to you later. I'm so happy for you!"

After grabbing a few quick shots Lizzie gets back in her car and drives to the paper.

"Dad, you're not going to believe what's going on," she says to her father who's focused on his screen. "Jack has everyone fixing up the town green, it's incredible. There's a bunch of his crew and more people from the town showed up to help as I was leaving. It's amazing. Just when I think I couldn't love this town more, it does something even more extraordinary and tops itself."

"It is a one in a million place to live," Peter says, not even looking at her.

Lizzie sits down, "What's up? You seem very distracted. Did something else happen?"

"No, just more of the same. Eric sent me a first draft, not even a whole first draft, to give us an idea of where he's going with this. It's shocking, and damning, that's for sure," he says.

"There's more than what he told us?" Lizzie asks, feeling concerned.

"Yes, it's incredible how high up this goes, his source claims that many people at the top levels of government knew this had happened, but since Gobel and Green are huge donors they didn't say a word, lest that well dried up. I truly have no words."

"Wow, that's unbelievable," she opens her computer, "Did he send it to me too?"

"Yes, prepare yourself to feel very angry," he says.

They both sit and read in silence.

"There truly are no words, Dad," Lizzie says, getting up from her desk and pacing after reading the article. "I'm angry, furious, and I can't deny, a little scared about all the attention that is going to come at us. Are we sure we want to be the ones to break this story? Not have Eric pitch it to a big, national paper?"

"I understand your trepidation, but I think this has to come from a local paper. And we've done due diligence hiring an outside journalist, a very well-respected one. It's not like it's an inside hit job on someone hurting our family. This is completely legitimate and well sourced. We're good." He walks over to his very nervous daughter and puts his hands on her shoulders. "I know it's scary, I'm a bit nervous too, but we have facts on our side, and thanks to our investors, good lawyers who will support us." He stops for a moment and a smile comes across his face. "And damn it, it's a testament to the importance of good, thorough, local journalism and the value of independent newspapers. We're still important."

"You're right, I was having cold feet and letting fear of these terrible people take over. But that's what they count on, that they're too big, and people like us are too small," she feels riled up now. "But we're not too small, this country needs little guys to push back against greed like this, and we're going to win."

"That's the spirit!" Peter says, high fiving her.

They both laugh. "I don't think we've ever high-fived before," Lizzie laughs.

"Yeah it's a little awkward, but well-deserved." He goes back to his side of the desk and sits down. "Now we have to strategize. When are we going to drop this bombshell?"

"As soon as possible," Lizzie says. "As soon as possible."

"Okay, so we both need to get to work right now putting our pieces together to run with this. And also introducing Eric to our readers so they know we trust him and they should too," Peter says. "Why don't you write a short piece about Eric, his background, and how well-respected he is? Sound good? And I'll work on the background piece, making sure everyone is up to speed with the history of the project Gobel and Green wanted to build, the town's rejection of it, the vote for Terra Marique and the purpose of this particular project, how the town will benefit etc."

"Sounds like I'm getting off easy. I can contribute to that piece, Dad, gather the stats from Town Meeting?"

"Thank you, that would be great, and I'm going to need your excellent editorial eye as well to make sure I don't drift into opinion here, which would be very easy to do," Peter says.

"Yeah, it's going to be really important we don't give these people any ability to say we're being prejudicial in any way," Lizzie agrees.

And with that, they both grow silent and get to work. Lizzie's piece about Eric is done in about an hour. "I sent you my piece," she says, stretching. "I'm going to run out and get a sandwich before I get to helping you, you want me to get you something?" she offers as she stands up.

"Anything healthy that your mom would approve of," he says, still typing. "Basically nothing fun," he smiles.

"Got it, nothing fried, or that had a face," she says. "I'll be back in a few minutes."

As she steps outside she's surprised to see Eric pulling into the parking lot, she stops and waits for him to get out of his car.

"Hey, I didn't expect to see you here," Lizzie says. "How's it going?"

"Good, I think I've got the whole first draft done for part one," he says.

"Wow, you're fast," Lizzie says, impressed by all he's done.

"Yeah, I got a call while I was at your house, and there's more. Apparently they've been dumping toxic waste all over the country, a factory in New Jersey, one in Pennsylvania, and another in Oregon," he says.

"Whoa, but this was the only radioactive one, right? The others were just, you know, normal poison?" Lizzie asks, shaking her head that this is even something she's asking.

"Yes, these others were just run of the mill poisons they dumped into various waterways. I can't believe they got away with this for so long with no one looking into it," Eric says.

They're both leaning against his car. "How could they do that?" Lizzie asks, feeling a little naive.

"I was surprised, though I shouldn't have been, that they have ties all the way up to the EPA in the past administration," Eric says. "I guess I'm glad that I'm still shocked at how corrupt things can be. I haven't totally lost my belief in goodness and doing right."

"Seriously, how do you keep believing in anything, Eric? You do lots of stories uncovering the terrible things people can do, I couldn't do it."

"It's not always easy, but I take solace in knowing I'm doing some good in uncovering the bad things, and holding people responsible," he says. "That helps keep me going. That and doing some feel-good stories too."

"You're very brave, Eric," Lizzie says. "And I hope that if you're up for it that maybe you'll want to do more stories for us, I can promise you we have lots of feel-good stories here."

"I'd really love that." He moves from leaning on the car. "But for now, I have this not-so feel-good story to finish."

"I was running out to get us some sandwiches, what can I get you?" she asks him.

"Wow, um, anything really, I'm easy, thank you." He reached into his pocket.

Lizzie shakes her head, "No way, this is on us, I'll be back soon," Lizzie says, opening her car door and getting in.

After lunch, they move at breakneck speed pulling the special edition together. Lizzie has teased that a special issue is coming on their Facebook and Instagram pages, and comments have been adding up. The people of Cranberry Harbor are well aware that the Gazette hasn't put out a special issue since 9/11, so there is tension building.

Peter has been with the same printing company for so long, they have told him they will print the issue whenever it gets to them, and by 4:50 pm, holding his breath, Peter hits send.

All three of them exhale loudly at the exact same time.

"Dad, when do we put it up online?" Lizzie asks. "I'm sure most people will read it that way, not the hard copy. That seems like more of a formality than how we're going to get the story out there."

"You're right," Peter says. "I'd say as soon as we know they got it, and it's going to print, we post it online. You agree, Eric?"

He nods. "Yeah, and I'd make sure to tag all the people you want to make sure to see it. The Selectboard, the Sentinel, Washington Post, New York Times, the Terra Marique team, our backers, anyone you think is going to do something with the story."

Lizzie is on her computer working away. "Okay, I've got this ready to go when you give me the word, Dad." She sits back and rubs her hands on her knees. "Wow, I'm really nervous."

"Me too," say both Eric and Peter.

"But I'm also excited, is that weird?" Lizzie says.

Eric laughs, "No, I'd say that sounds about right, I feel that way every time I file a story that calls people out."

"Okay, I just heard from the printer, they're going," Peter says.

"Here goes nothing," Lizzie hits publish, and then the posts she has ready to go on social media. "It's out there."

"Now we just wait for all hell to break loose," Peter says.

Lizzie picks up her phone and calls Jack. As soon as he answers she stands up. "Hey, go to our website and read the special edition we just put up. It's big, Really big. After you read it, call me back. I love you."

CHAPTER 37

WHILE SHE WAITS for Jack to call her back Lizzie paces the office, straightens her desk and sits down and stands up at least a half-dozen times.

"Honey, it's going to be okay," her dad says, trying to reassure her. "Try to relax"

"I can't," she says, sorting her paperclips by size.

"I know how you feel, Lizzie," Eric says, standing up himself. "I put it on my Twitter feed about five minutes ago, I'm second guessing my headline, you think it's okay?"

"*Gobel and Green Dump 1000s of Gallons of Radioactive Waste in Florida: Insider Reveals New York Company Guilty of Massive Cover-ups Across the Country* has a really good ring to me," Lizzie says. "I think it might get people's attention, just maybe." She laughs, a little nervously, but it feels good to laugh nonetheless. Her phone rings, "Okay, it's Jack. 'Hey'," she says, sitting down and looking at Eric and Peter. "So?"

"How long have you known about this?" He asks, "And how did you keep so cool? This is, I can't even… I'm still absorbing it. It's crazy–"

"I know, I know, it's a lot to absorb, we couldn't believe it all either," she says. "I hope you understand that I couldn't say anything, I hated keeping it from you–"

"Oh my god, yes, I totally understand, you had to be completely professional about this. Where did you find this writer? Wow, he's good!" Jack says.

"He's a freelancer who's living in Cranberry Harbor. Alexis knows him. I knew neither of us could write the story and have any credibility," Lizzie says. "He really did his homework, Jack. Dad and I believe in him and what he wrote completely. We wouldn't have published it if we didn't."

"Oh, it's clear it's well sourced, and he backed every accusation up. I sent it to our lawyers, I expect I'll be hearing from them… okay, they're calling me right now, I'll call you back."

"Jack's lawyers just called him," she says, still holding on to her phone. "I wonder when ours are going to call us, or at the very least we'll start hearing from people in town."

"What the heck?!" Gabby comes running into the office,waving her phone. "So this is what you've all been working on? I can't believe it! Eric, you are a fantastic writer, thank you for all your hard work. This could literally save our town."

"You are being way too generous, Dr, Martin–"

"Eric, it's Gabby," she says.

He smiles, "Gabby, thank you. We'll have to wait and see what the state of Florida and several other states have to say. If they decide to press charges or pursue other legal avenues. They have many high-up friends who've allowed them to get away with all these crimes for a long time."

"It just makes my blood boil," Gabby says. "The idea that these people have been polluting the planet for lord knows how long, killing wildlife, and threatening human health. They all need to end up in jail."

"From your lips, Mom," Lizzie says. "And you're right, Eric did an amazing job. We're very lucky to have found him, and that he had all these incredible connections. I hope we can take these guys down so they can't hurt anyone else."

"You and me both," Peter says. "Gabby, how about we go get some dinner for all of us?"

"I'll go, Dad. I'd love to get out. I'm feeling so antsy I need a project, and getting dinner for everyone sounds like a good one," Lizzie says.

"Why don't we go together?" Gabby says, picking up her coat.

"I'd love the company," Lizzie says,

When they get to Bradford's, Lizzie and Gabby make a beeline for the freshly made vegetarian entrees in the organic section of the store.

"Darn, I should have asked Eric if he's okay with something like vegetarian lasagna or if he's a carnivore who'd prefer something with meat, that wasn't very thoughtful of me," Lizzie says.

"You've got a few things on your mind," Gabby says, choosing a few different things. "He's a young guy who is probably thrilled that someone is providing food for him," Gabby teases. "In my experience, unless it's something like aspic, he will be happy with anything."

Lizzie laughs. "I'm sure you're right," as she picks up a couple of salads.

"We can grab some dessert in case this feels too healthy," Gabby smiles at her. "Ice cream sandwiches? Cookies?"

"I vote for both," Lizzie says, heading toward the ice cream aisle. And then she sees him. Billy Taylor. Gabby wonders why Lizzie has stopped in her tracks and then sees him too.

"You have a lot of nerve," Gabby says to him.

"Hello to you too, Doc Martin," he says.

"Mom, it's not worth it," Lizzie says, putting her hand on her mom's shoulder. "Let's go."

But Gabby, like a mother lion won't be deterred. "Have you seen the special edition of the Gazette, Billy? Do you see who you've sided with against the people here who you've known all your life?"

He shrugs, and looks down at the floor. "Yeah, I saw it."

"And what do you think?" Gabby says, stepping closer to him.

"I think, I think you're son-in-law-to-be punched me, and that he..." he trails off.

"And you did nothing to deserve that? You weren't taunting him? You weren't trying to ruin the project he and the whole town want?" Lizzie is impressed, her mother the doctor is sounding more like a lawyer. Lizzie, arm through her hand-held grocery basket, folds her arms across her chest, enjoying the show.

"Okay, so I told him he was a tree-hugging loser who was going to ruin the town and bring in a bad element with his," and then he uses air quotes, "'green community.'"

Gabby tilts her head and furrows her brow. "By 'bad element' do you mean farmers, craftspeople, people who work…here," she says, gesturing to the young staff in the store. People who aren't millionaires, or who didn't, like you, inherit a family home, who just want to live and work here? Those 'bad' people?"

Lizzie is enjoying this. It seems, she thinks, that Billy is actually getting smaller as her mom talks and she's loving it.

"Places like that attract elites," he counters. "Snobby folks who think they're better than us."

Gabby shakes her head. "Did you not listen to anything at Town Meeting? Or read one piece in the Gazette, Billy? These are locals, local chefs, artisans, tech people, people who want to live in Cranberry Harbor and make it better. You think Gobel and Green really want the best for Cranberry Harbor? For the Cape? They're criminals."

For once in his life, Billy has nothing to say. Lizzie is speechless herself. Her mom, one of the kindest people in the world, can also be formidable. Especially to a guy who grew up with her as his doctor.

"Doc, I didn't know," he finally says, actually looking remorseful.

"You can do the right thing, Billy," Gabby says.

Lizzie's mesmerized by her mother's power of persuasion. She's purposely staying silent so as to not break the spell. She glances down at the ice cream sandwiches in her basket, and thinks, after this is done she's going to exchange them for another box.

"You mean like drop the charges against Jack?" he says.

Gabby nods. "You could be the hero here, Billy instead of the villain."

Lizzie sees his face visibly brighten, "Hero?"

"Yup," Gabby says.

"We'd even want to do a story," Lizzie says.

"You think everyone would stop being mad at me? That I could go back to Sea Coast? I miss Miss Hope's cookies," he says.

"I will personally make sure that you can go back to Sea Coast, Billy," Lizzie says. "If you drop the charges that is."

"You're getting married soon, right?" he asks.

"We were, but all of this forced us to postpone our plans," Lizzie says.

He looks down at his feet. "Fine, I'll do it, but you two better be right about me being a hero and everything." He's quiet, they can tell there's something more, finally he clears his throat. "I'm, I'm... sorry."

"Thank you, Billy," Gabby says. "Shall we give you a ride to the police station?"

"No, I've got my car, ma'am, I mean Dr.Martin, thank you," and without another word he walks to the exit and leaves.

"Mom! You missed your calling! You should have been a hostage negotiator! I have never witnessed anything like that!"

Gabby lets out a deep sigh. "I have no idea where that came from, but I saw him and, I don't know, it just came out."

"Well, I always want you on my side no matter what the situation is! You were amazing, Mom! Thank you!" Lizzie puts down the basket and gives her mom a big hug."Until we know for sure, let's not say anything, okay?"

"Deal!" Gabby looks at their basket. "I don't think we can put these ice cream sandwiches back, but we should get another package, don't you think?"

Lizzie nods and gets another quart of ice cream, and they walk to the check-out. After they pay, and are walking out Lizzie stops her mom and begins singing to her, *"Did you ever know that you're my hero and everything I would like to be? I can fly higher than an eagle. For you are the wind beneath my wings,"* They are both laughing so hard people are looking at them. They manage to get to Gabby's car and get in. "Boy, it feels good to laugh," Lizzie says.

"It sure does," Gabby agrees, fastening her seatbelt. "Let's go back to the paper and wait for the good news."

CHAPTER 38

THEY DIDN'T HAVE to wait long, within ten minutes of their return Jack called Lizzie and told her the Cranberry Harbor police had called him and said Billy had dropped the charges. Lizzie literally jumped up and down.

"I will give you all the details tonight of how that came to be," she says to him."I'm sure you've got a million things to do. Love you!"

She turns her attention to her parents and Eric.

"Dad, Eric, you should have seen Mom in action, she confronted Billy, and it was amazing," Lizzie says, taking the cover off her lasagna, warmed from the office microwave. "I have never seen her be so stone cold tough and unwavering. It was amazing to behold!"

"I would not want to mess with your mom when she has being right on her side," Peter says. "She is formidable."

"Billy's face was like, like, I don't know, a cross between a deer caught in headlights and a kid who got caught cheating on a test. I was glad I wasn't him," Lizzie says.

Eric is quiet as he eats his food, though he keeps checking his phone.

"You okay?" Lizzie asks.

"Yeah, I guess I'm waiting for the other shoe to drop, I keep checking Twitter to see if anything has shown up from the major newspapers, but there's nothing so far," he says.

No sooner are those words out of his mouth, then his phone rings. He answers and abruptly gets up from the table.

"Yes, this is he, who is this again?" He asks, "From the Washington Post?" he turns to look at the three Martins looking right back at him. "Yes, I'd be happy to answer your questions. Shoot."

For twenty minutes he paces back and forth across the office, Lizzie half expects to see a worn path in the rug. Gabby, Peter and Lizzie are trying their best to not eavesdrop, and talk amongst themselves, but it's pretty difficult in their small-ish office. Lizzie's stomach drops every time she hears him emphasize these are vetted documents, yes, they have documentation for his source's employment at the facility…she knows the reporter on the other end is just doing due diligence, but she can't help herself from worrying that no one is going to believe them. That Gobel and Green will find a way to weasel out of this, like every rich corporation and billionaire seems to do. She finds herself pleading and bargaining with the universe to not let these folks off the hook yet again.

"Okay, phew, that woman was grilling me," Eric says, taking a seat and looking drained.

"Everything seems okay?" Peter asks.

"Yeah, at first I was worried that she was doubting me, doubting us and Gloria, but as we kept talking I could see that she was making sure she had all the facts and I could tell that she was shocked as much as we were by all that we uncovered," Eric says.

"The story *you* uncovered," Lizzie corrects him. "We may have run the story, but it was all you. Thank you, not just for our paper, but for our community, and at the risk of sounding like a movie or something, thank you for saving the country from them doing any more harm."

"Well, let's see if anything happens to them, we all know how slippery these kinds of criminals can be. They have the best lawyers and no end of money so they are seldom the ones who go to jail or are punished in any real way. Let's hope these accusations are egregious enough that justice finally wins out," Eric says.

Gabby begins to gather the discards from their meal. Thankfully she'd had the presence of mind to put the ice cream in the freezer of their small fridge when they'd arrived, so they do not have a puddle of it on the table.

"I'm going to head home, Peter. Lizzie, please keep me posted, okay?" Gabby says, picking up her purse and jacket.

As she gets ready to leave they hear some noise out on the street, Lizzie looks out the window, "Oh my gosh, there's a whole bunch of people outside–they've even got signs!"

The others come over to look, there are about 30 people outside, many with signs with messages like, "Thank you!" and "Terra Marique Forever!" "Cranberry Harbor Wins!"

"Would you look at that," Peter says. "We have fans!"

"We should probably go down and say something, don't you think?" Lizzie asks her dad.

"Yes, we should," he says.

They all put on their coats and go outside, and when the crowd sees them they erupt into applause and cheers.

They all stand there for a moment, unsure what to do. Peter starts saying, "Thank you, thank you," trying to get them to stop; he's embarrassed, he's never done what he does for the accolades.

"You are all so kind to come here, we can't believe it," he says. "Thank you for your support and for believing in us, and for reading! And thank you to this wonderful young man who found out all the wrongdoing that's been going on, Eric Jackson," he says, gesturing to an embarrassed Eric. The crowd cheers.

Lizzie can see he's feeling very emotional, so she steps up, putting her hand on her dad's shoulder. "Yes, thank you! We did this to tell the truth, and to save Terra Marique, and for this town, and all of you who make this the most incredible place to live. Thank you so much for your support. We love you all. Now, if you'll excuse us, we have more work to do!"

A few people come forward to shake their hands and thank them again, but then all three of their cell phones start ringing and they have to go. As they walk back into the building, each having conversations with either a government official or reporter, it's clear, this story isn't going anywhere any time soon. Gobel and Green are going down.

CHAPTER 39

TO SAY the following weeks were crazy would be an incredible understatement. Gobel and Green had withdrawn their lawsuit, now very busy with many others across the country. They were being served, literally.

The Cranberry Harbor Gazette made it onto CNN, MSNBC, CBS, NBC, ABC, and every major newspaper in the country. Lizzie was especially excited that even Seth Meyers, Jimmy Fallon, Jon Stewart, and Stephen Colbert talked about them. She was a serious journalist of course, but there was something about making into a monologue of a late night TV host that seemed to signal a certain arrival of sorts.

Jack was seeming more like himself and it felt like life was slowly returning to normal. If normal included a documentary film crew and reporters from around the world watching you work. Terra Marique was progressing well, and was actually ahead of schedule. They hadn't discussed their wedding, and Lizzie felt reluctant to bring it up because...well, she just was. As their intended wedding day approached she could feel a sadness coming over her, but tried to push beyond it, and focus on enjoying the Gazette's 15-minutes of fame.

She was sitting alone at a table outside Sea Coast, contemplating her future as a forever-engaged and never-to-be-married woman, when Ben walked by, saving her from herself.

"Ben!" she calls out to him.

"Hey! Fancy meeting you here, I figured by now you'd be on a plane to Los Angeles for your appearance on Jimmy Kimmel," he says, sitting down across from her.

"Yeah, he wanted me to come, but I said no, I have to work on my screenplay," she says, laughing.

"Wait, are you actually working on a screenplay?" Ben asks.

She laughs, "No, but isn't that what everyone does when they have a brush with fame? Seems like the thing to do next, now that running a small town newspaper seems so...small."

"Oh, you're way too big for that, you definitely have to write a movie and we need to think of who will play you!" Ben teases.

Lizzie laughs. "So back in the real world...How are Sean and Ollie?"

"They're great, Ollie is walking everywhere, on the verge of running, so life as we know it is about to end. We will not be sitting down for the next few years, I suspect. But it's great. I love it, Lizzie. Being a dad is more than I ever could have imagined."

"I'm so happy for you, for all of you," she says, tearing up. "Ugh, sorry, I do this at least twice a day lately, I think it's all the overwhelm, and, well, wondering if I'll ever have what you and Sean have. Ugh, sorry!"

Ben takes her hand, "Of course you will!" He keeps holding her hand, "Speaking of the future, what's your favorite kind of cake?"

Lizzie shakes her head, "Um, okay, that's one way to change the subject!" She laughs.

Ben laughs too, "Sorry, I've been baking all day and have cake on the brain," he says.

"I'd say chocolate with chocolate frosting and raspberries on the side," she says. "Or vanilla with vanilla icing and sprinkles. I love sprinkles."

"Duly noted, loves sprinkles," he pretends to write. He smiles at her. "It really is all going to be alright, Lizzie."

"Promise?" she asks.

"Yes, I promise." He stands up, "I hate to, but I have a small window before Ollie wakes up and Sean has a meeting with the gallery in P-town. I love you, friend."

She smiles at him. "I love you too, my dear, dear friend." Ben leans over and gives her a kiss on the cheek. "See you soon, I hope! Give Ollie and Sean a kiss for me."

"Will do,"

On that May morning that Lizzie had been dreading, she woke up planning to ignore the date when her wedding was supposed to happen at all costs. It had been six weeks since the news hit the stands. Legal wheels were turning and it looked like that evil duo, Gobel and Green were finally going to pay for their crimes. Everything was falling into place, except her wedding. She got out of bed and headed down to the kitchen for some coffee, hoping one of her parents had already made some.

The scent of coffee hit as she descended the stairs. "Yay! Whoever made coffee, thank you, thank you," she says out loud to… no one. "Hello? Where is everyone?" she calls. Daisy, her parent's loveable mutt, who comes skating around the corner. "Hey girl, unless you developed some new skills I'm thinking you did not make this coffee," she says, patting her on the head.

"No, that would be me," Peter says, walking in from the living room in sweatpants and t-shirt. "You mom ran out to do an errand, she'll be right back."

"It's a little after 8, where the heck would she be going this early?" Lizzie asks, pouring herself some coffee.

Peter shrugs, and picks up a muffin on the counter and puts it on a napkin. Mouth full of blueberry bran muffin he shakes his head and sputters out, "Don't know, she didn't say anything."

"Very mysterious," Lizzie says, picking up a muffin for herself, walking to the table and sitting down.

Peter joins her, "You mom is a mysterious woman, my dear."

No sooner has he said those words when Gabby comes bustling through the door, garment bag in hand.

"Good morning, sleepy head!" she says, kissing Lizze on the forehead.

"What you got there, Mom?" Lizzie says, popping the rest of her muffin in her mouth."Going somewhere?"

"Yes, as a matter of fact we all are," Gabby looks over at Peter. "Should I tell her or do you want to?"

Lizzie's phone rings, it's Jack. "Hold that thought," she says, holding up a finger. "Morning! How are you this morning? Okay, I'll put you on speaker," she says, a little perplexed.

"Morning, Jack," Gabby and Peter say in unison.

"Okay," Jack begins. "We have a bit of a surprise for you, and I hope it's a good one," Jack says. "Gabby?"

She unzips the garment bag and takes out Lizzie's wedding dress.

Lizzie's confused. "What the heck?"

"I took a dress of yours to Jess and she hemmed it using that as a template. Other than that it fit perfectly, so it's good to go," Gabby says.

Lizzie is still confused. "Okay, so...?"

"Today was supposed to be our wedding day," Jack says, "and thanks to your parents, Ben, Sean, Alexis, Hope, and well, half the town, we're still going to get married today."

Lizzie sits down. "What? When? Where? I mean how?" She's stunned. "Dear lord, I'm a mess!"

"You're not, but I knew you'd feel that way, so Hilary is coming in an hour to do your hair, nails, makeup, whatever you want," Gabby says.

"So this is really happening?" Lizzie says, looking at her dress, her parents, and feeling stunned.

"I hope you're not mad at me," Jack says. "I wanted us to have our wedding, and since it was my project that almost ruined it, I wanted to fix it."

"He's been incredible, honey," Peter says. "He's gotten the whole town on board, I actually can't believe that Cranberry Harbor kept this secret. You really had no idea?"

She shakes her head. "No, I mean I thought it was weird when Alexis asked me about flowers, and then Ben asked me what my favorite cake is, but I didn't think about it, honestly. But now, it all makes sense." She pauses. "Wait, is this why the town square is all fixed up, and yesterday I noticed the gazebo was decorated. Are we getting married in the town square?"

Gabby and Peter smile and nod, "Yes you are," Gabby says.

"I hope that's okay," Jack says. "Once everyone wanted to help it seemed like it had to be there."

Lizzie takes a deep breath. "Okay, so what time is this happening?" she asks, glancing at the clock on the wall.

"Two o'clock," all three of them say.

Lizzie sits back in her chair and starts to cry.

"Oh my gosh, I hope those are happy tears," Gabby says, putting her arms around her.

"Lizzie? Oh no, I'm sorry, I thought this would make you happy," Jack says, freaking out a bit.

"No. no, I'm happy," she says. "I wanted this to be our wedding day so badly, and now it's happening. I can't believe it. Thank you, really, thank you to all of you for doing all this for me."

"You're sure? It's all good?" Jack asks, still sounding worried.

"Yes, it's more than good, it's perfect," Lizzie says, reaching for the tissues her mother has gotten for her. "I will see you at two o'clock, Mr. Cahoon. You better not be late."

Jack, sounding choked up himself says, "No way will I be late. I love you Lizzie and I cannot wait to marry you."

"Right back at you," she says. "Now I have to go and make myself presentable! Love you."

Lizzie stands up and hugs her parents. "I can't believe you all did this for me," she says, hugging them. "This is going to be the best wedding ever. And I say that having no idea what we will be eating, drinking, dancing to, if there is dancing, or who will be there. It's kind of crazy but I love it!"

Four hours later, after Hilary has come and gone, Lizzie descends the staircase where her parents both gasp and begin to cry a little.

"Oh my, you look amazing!" Gabby says, hugging her a little awkwardly so as to not muss her look in any way.

"Yeah? You both like it?" she says, trying not to cry and ruin her makeup, turning and twirling a little.

"You are the most beautiful bride I've ever seen," Peter says. "Next to your mom, of course." He smiles and hugs Gabby.

"Alright, enough of all these tears, let's get a move on," Gabby says, trying to pull herself together.

When they arrive at the town square Lizzie is speechless. There are flowers everywhere, and it looks like the whole town has turned out. "Oh my word," she says, barely able to believe it.

They get out of the car and she sees Jack waiting at the gazebo, Reverend Thomas is waiting too. She sees her brother Matt, Shannon and Sophie, who comes running up to her.

"You are the most beautifulist girl in the world, Aunt Wiz," she says. "And I'm a flower girl!"

"Yay! I'm so glad! You know what to do?" Lizzie asks, leaning down.

"Yup, Mommy told me, you ready?" Sophie already has the basket of flower petals on her arm, ready to throw. Just then, Alexis emerges with a beautiful bouquet of pink peonies.

Lizzie smiles at her niece's can-do attitude and confidence.

"Congratulations, friend, here you go," Alexis says, kissing her on the cheek.

"These are gorgeous, thank you, thank you for everything, I love you, friend," Lizzie says.

The music starts and she takes her dad's arm.

"You ready, Sunshine?" he says.

"I've never been more ready, Dad. I love you,"

"Love you too," he says.

When Lizzie reaches the gazebo, and climbs the three steps, Jack looks at her just how she'd always imagined. Like so many brides, she hears *most* of what the minister is saying, but is struck by all the people she loves standing there with them at this moment. She swears she even sees Billy and Bud standing off to the side. When it comes time for them to say their vows, Lizzie realizes she's going to have to wing it, not having written hers.

"Jack, this has been a long time coming, and I'm so happy to be here now, so in love with you, and excited for our life together to start right now. Thank you for loving me, and for being who you are, the kind of man who in the midst of a massive lawsuit would stop and plan a wedding," she laughs, and the crowd does as well. "May our lives always be filled with surprises and love. Happy surprises," she says, smiling.

Then it's Jack's turn.

"First, thank you for not being angry at me for doing this, not everyone would be so amenable about a surprise wedding," he jokes, and everyone laughs again. "I'm so grateful to have a partner like you who is so kind, smart, and obviously, up for anything," he laughs. "And I too hope our lives are filled with surprises, love and of course, fun."

"Alright then, by the powers bestowed upon me by the state of Massachusetts, I now pronounce you husband and wife," Rev. Thomas says.

Lizzie and Jack kiss, and the whole town square erupts.

"This is truly the best wedding ever," Lizzie says, kissing Jack. "I wouldn't change a thing."

"Good, because neither would I," he says. "Are you ready to celebrate?"

"With you? Always," she says, as they walk out of the gazebo and into the arms of everyone they love.

The End

ACKNOWLEDGMENTS

I'm so grateful to have found my ideal publishing home with Sea Crow Press. It's the perfect home for my books, and I'm so grateful to the entire team, especially my publisher, Mary Petiet, and my wonderful editor, Anastasia Drost. I'm also incredibly grateful to Maggie Marr for her career guidance and expertise!

I'm so grateful to have the best first/beta reader in the world, my friend Sarah Shemkus. Your notes, bulleted no less, help me take a messy first draft, and turn it into an actual book. I can't imagine doing this without you. Thank you, thank you.

To all my local Cape Cod bookstores, especially the ones right in my neighborhood, Sea Howl Bookshop and Brewster Bookstore, thank you for all the support!

And lastly, the publication of Christmas in Cranberry Harbor showed me how even though I created Cranberry Harbor on the page, I actually kind of already live there. I am so fortunate to live in an incredibly creative, supportive, and beautiful town that has shown me so much love and kindness, it's been quite humbling. I want to keep paying it forward and help our little town to continue to be the absolute best place to live

ABOUT THE AUTHOR

Candace Hammond grew up and still lives on Cape Cod, but will forever be considered a washashore for not having been born there. She is a journalist, playwright, and novelist, who also hosts an arts podcast/radio show on WOMR out of Provincetown, because people in the arts have the best stories. She is the mother of three adult children who are scattered around the globe, and grandmother to one amazing little girl. She lives with her musician partner and their very large cat on the Lower Cape.

ABOUT THE PRESS

Sea Crow Press is an award-winning woman-run independent book publisher based on Cape Cod in Massachusetts committed to amplifying voices that might otherwise go unheard. We publish creative nonfiction, literary fiction, and poetry. Our books celebrate our connection to each other and to the natural world with a focus on positive change and great storytelling.